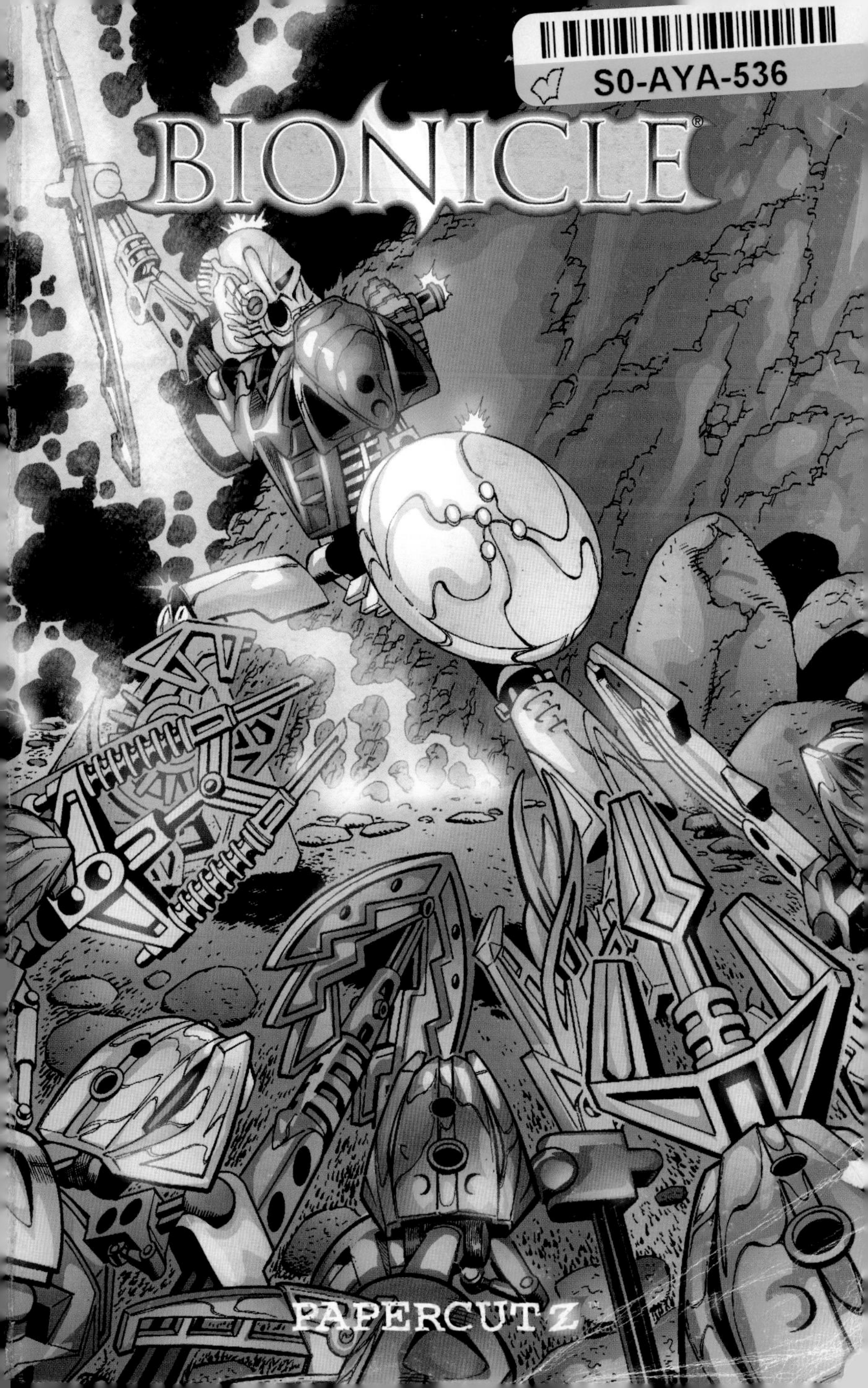
BIONICLE®
PAPERCUTZ™

BIONICLE® GRAPHIC NOVELS AVAILABLE FROM PAPERCUTZ

Graphic Novel #1
"The Rise of the Toa Nuva"

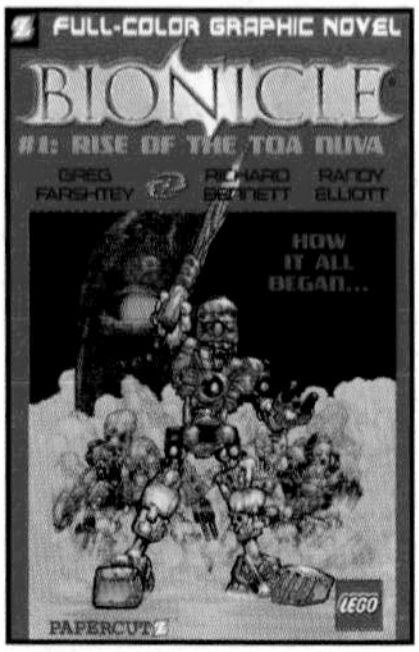
FULL-COLOR GRAPHIC NOVEL
BIONICLE
#1: RISE OF THE TOA NUVA
GREG FARSHTEY
RICHARD BENNETT
RANDY ELLIOTT
HOW IT ALL BEGAN...
PAPERCUTZ
LEGO

Graphic Novel #2
"Challenge of the Rahkshi"

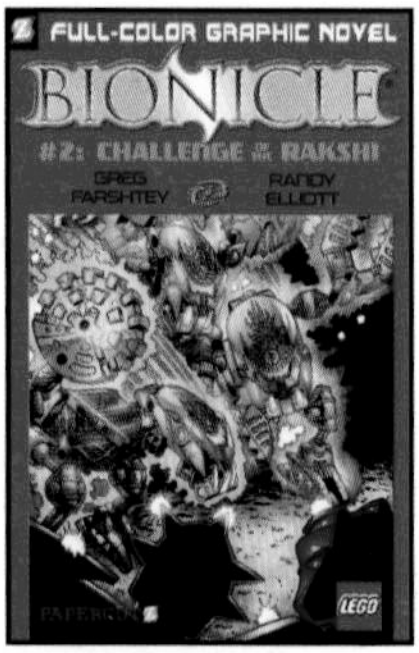
FULL-COLOR GRAPHIC NOVEL
BIONICLE
#2: CHALLENGE OF THE RAKSHI
GREG FARSHTEY
RANDY ELLIOTT
LEGO

Coming in November: Graphic Novel #3
"City of Legends"

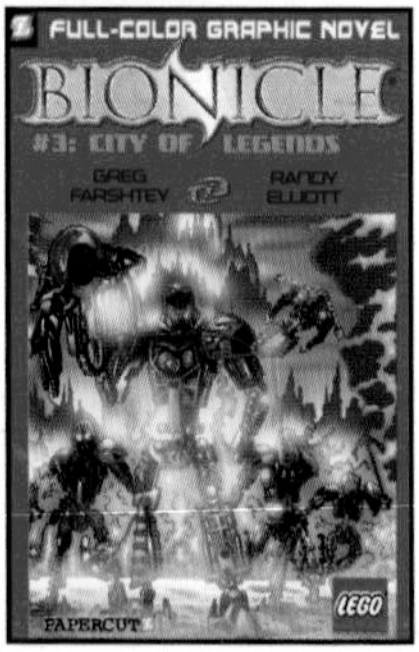
FULL-COLOR GRAPHIC NOVEL
BIONICLE
#3: CITY OF LEGENDS
GREG FARSHTEY
RANDY ELLIOTT
PAPERCUT
LEGO

$7.95 each paperback, $12.95 each in hardcover. Please add $4.00 for postage and handling for the first book, add $1.00 for each additional book. Please make check payable to NBM Publishing. Send to: Papercutz, 40 Exchange Place, Suite 1308, New York, NY 10005 • 1-800-886-1223 • www.papercutz.com

#2 Challenge of the Rahkshi

GREG FARSHTEY
Writer
RANDY ELLIOTT
Artist

PAPERCUT Z™
NEW YORK

Challenge of the Rahkshi

GREG FARSHTEY – Writer
RANDY ELLIOTT, CARLOS D'ANDA, RAY KRYSSING – Artists
TOBY DUTKIEWICZ – Comics Layout and Design
PETER PANTAZIS – Colorist
KEN LOPEZ – Letterer
JAYE GARDNER – Original Editor
JOHN McCARTHY – Production
JIM SALICRUP
Editor-in-Chief

ISBN 10: 1-59707-111-0 paperback edition
ISBN 13: 978-1-59707-111-6 paperback edition
ISBN 10: 1-59707-112-9 hardcover edition
ISBN 13: 978-1-59707-112-3 hardcover edition

Originally published as comicbooks by DC Comics as BIONICLE #9 - 15.

Printed in China.
Distributed by Macmillan.
10 9 8 7 6 5 4 3 2 1

PROLOGUE

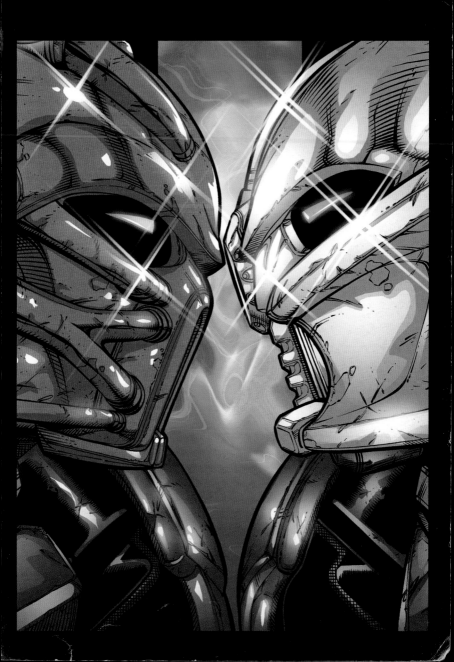

DIVIDED WE FALL

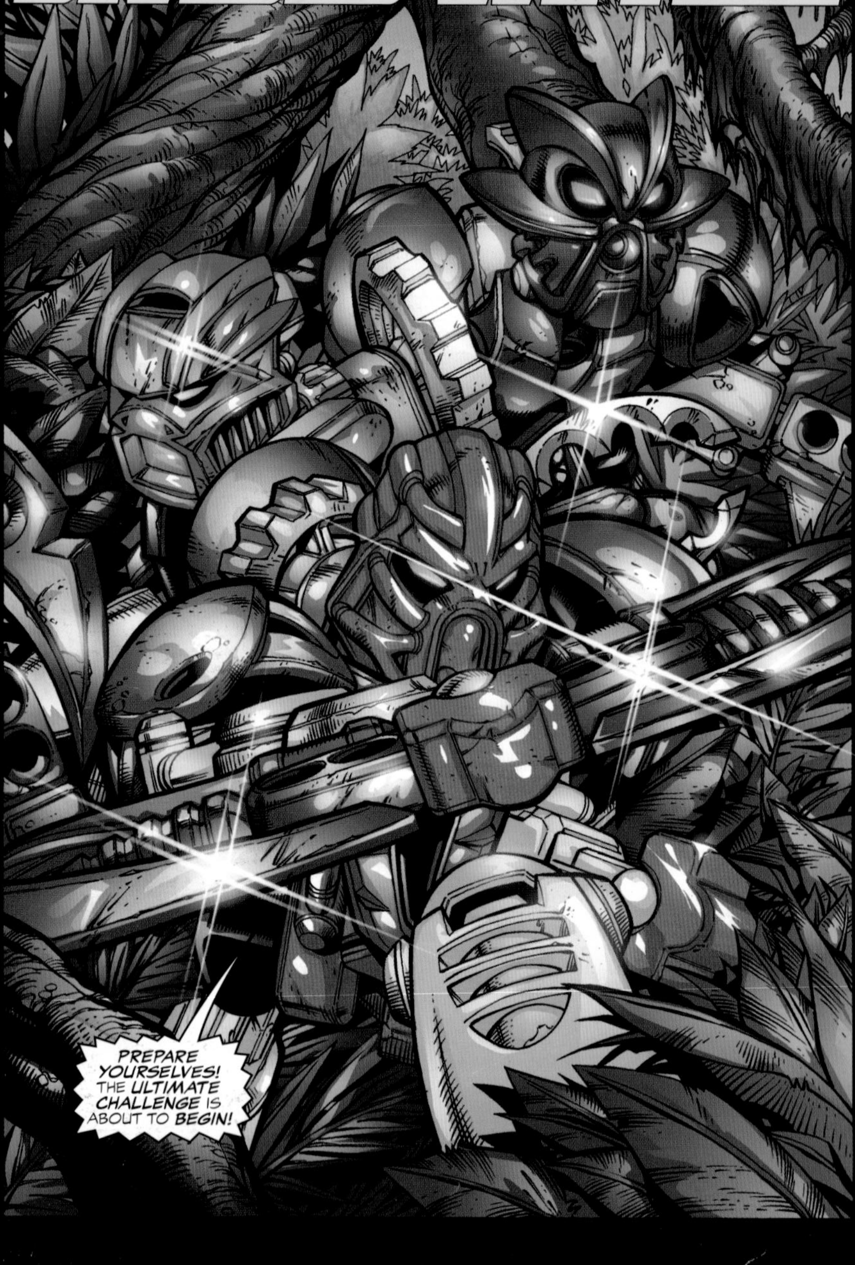
PREPARE YOURSELVES! THE ULTIMATE CHALLENGE IS ABOUT TO BEGIN!

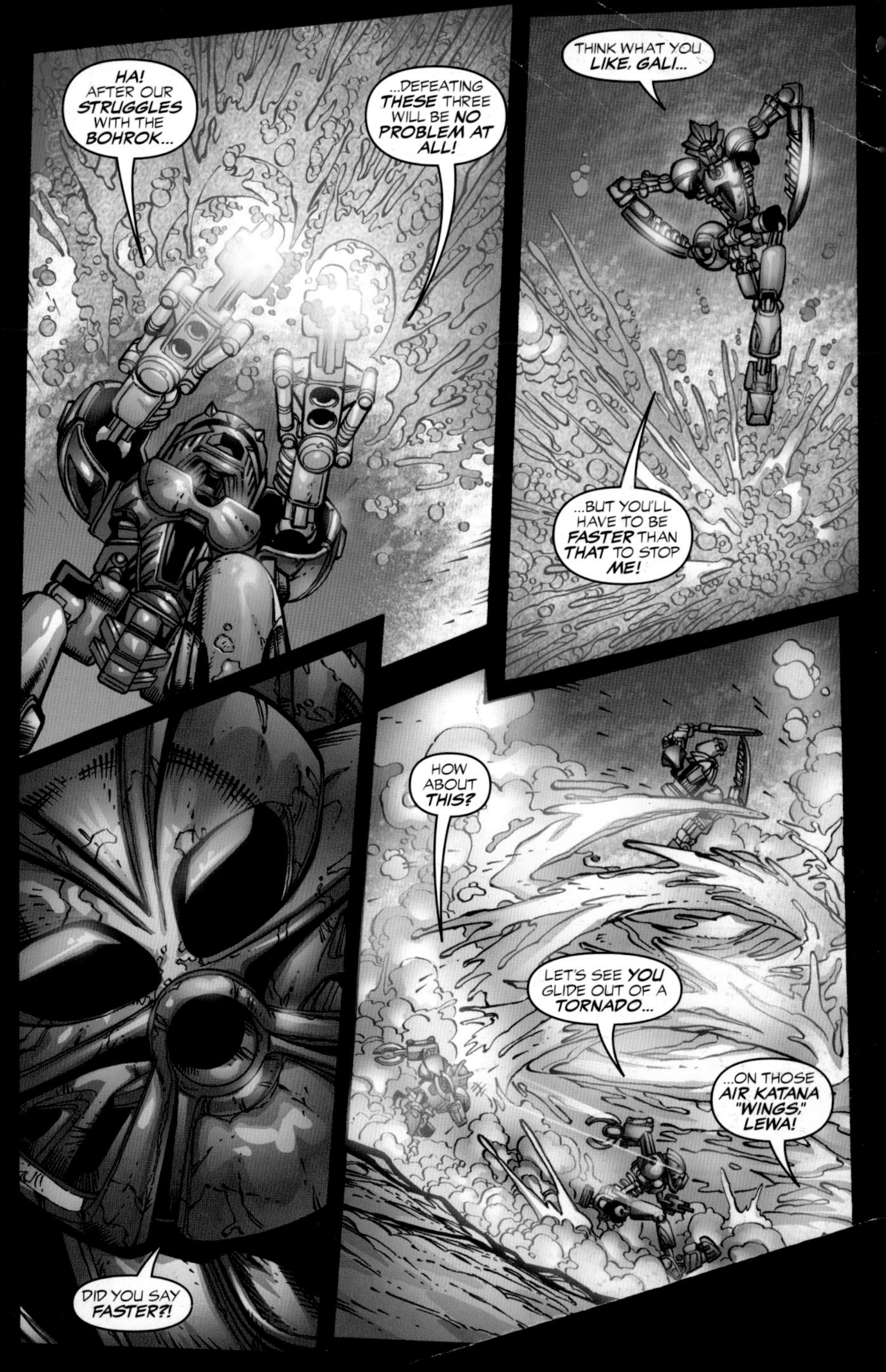
HA! AFTER OUR STRUGGLES WITH THE BOHROK...
...DEFEATING THESE THREE WILL BE NO PROBLEM AT ALL!
THINK WHAT YOU LIKE, GALI...
...BUT YOU'LL HAVE TO BE FASTER THAN THAT TO STOP ME!
DID YOU SAY FASTER?!
HOW ABOUT THIS?
LET'S SEE YOU GLIDE OUT OF A TORNADO...
...ON THOSE AIR KATANA "WINGS," LEWA!

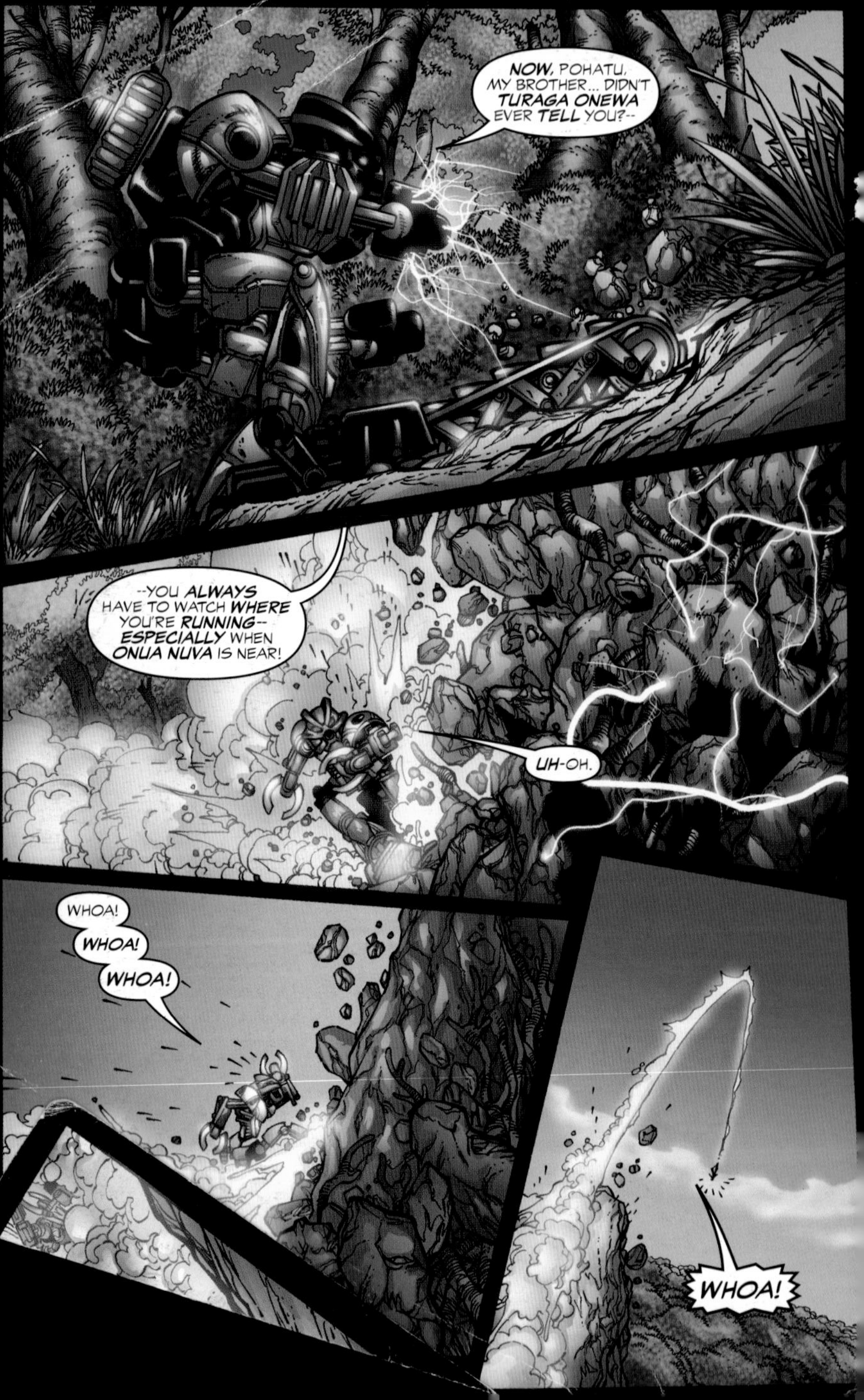
NOW, POHATU, MY BROTHER... DIDN'T TURAGA ONEWA EVER TELL YOU?--
--YOU ALWAYS HAVE TO WATCH WHERE YOU'RE RUNNING-- ESPECIALLY WHEN ONUA NUVA IS NEAR!
UH-OH.
WHOA!
WHOA!
WHOA!
WHOA!

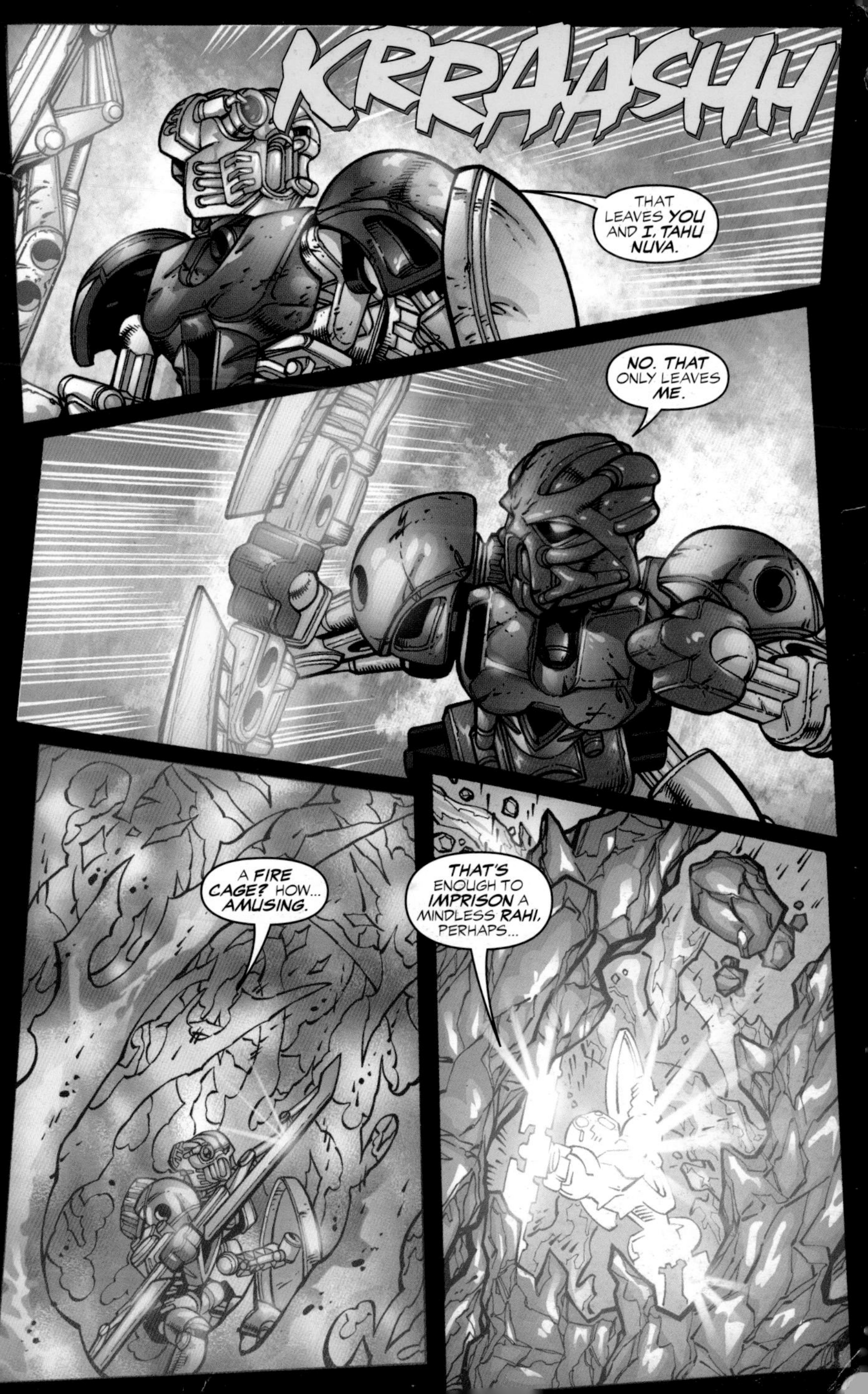
KRRAASHH
THAT LEAVES YOU AND I, TAHU NUVA.
NO. THAT ONLY LEAVES ME.
A FIRE CAGE? HOW... AMUSING.
THAT'S ENOUGH TO IMPRISON A MINDLESS RAHI, PERHAPS...

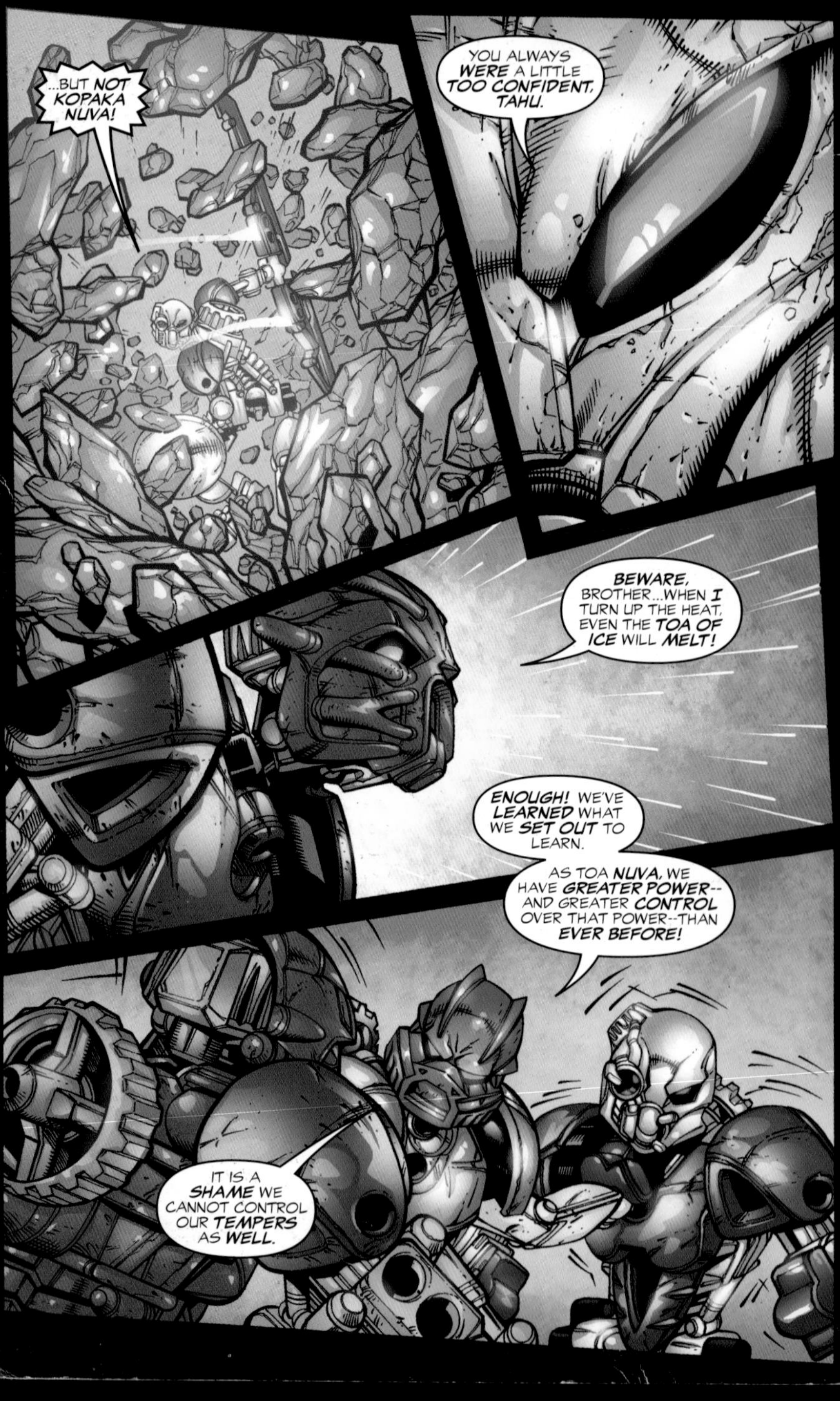
...BUT NOT KOPAKA NUVA!
YOU ALWAYS WERE A LITTLE TOO CONFIDENT, TAHU.
BEWARE, BROTHER...WHEN I TURN UP THE HEAT, EVEN THE TOA OF ICE WILL MELT!
ENOUGH! WE'VE LEARNED WHAT WE SET OUT TO LEARN.
AS TOA NUVA, WE HAVE GREATER POWER--AND GREATER CONTROL OVER THAT POWER--THAN EVER BEFORE!
IT IS A SHAME WE CANNOT CONTROL OUR TEMPERS AS WELL.

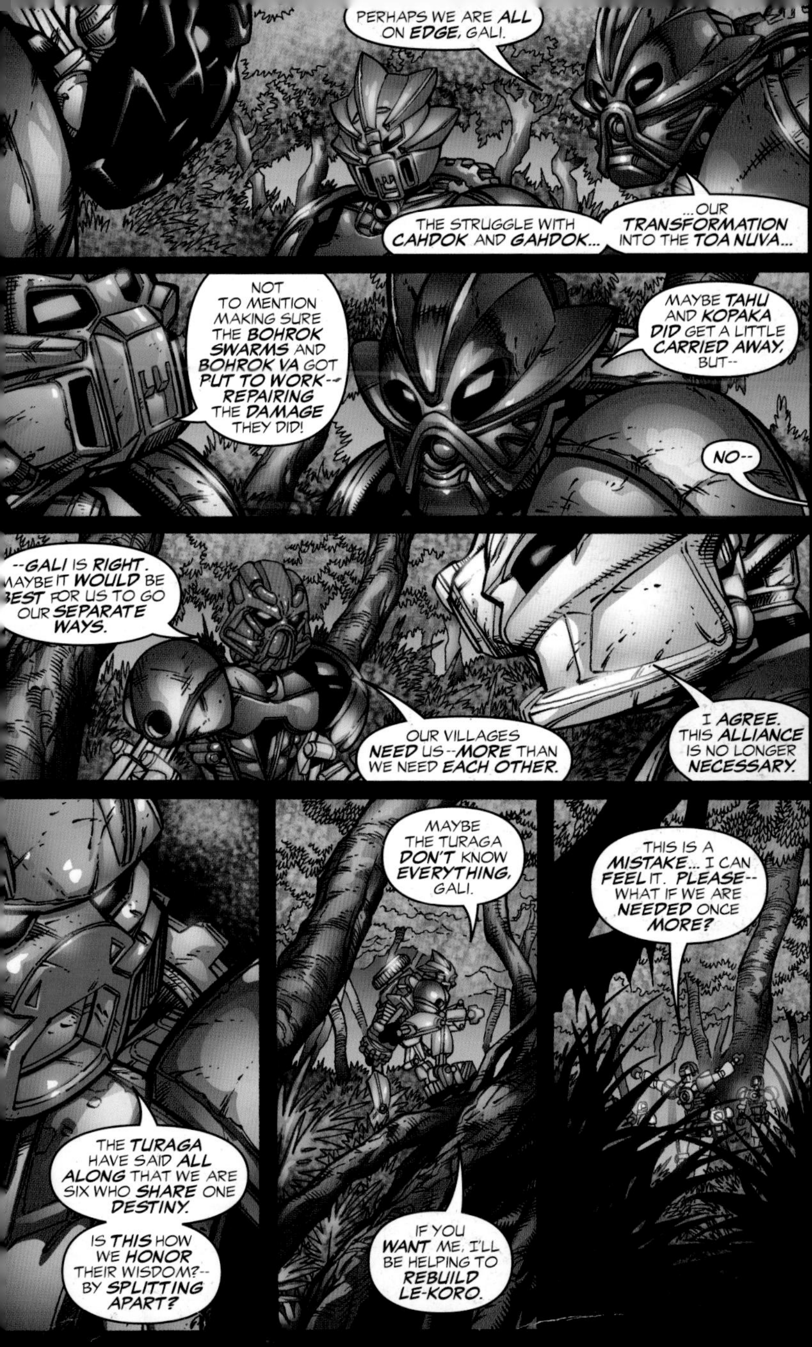
PERHAPS WE ARE ALL ON EDGE, GALI.
THE STRUGGLE WITH CAHDOK AND GAHDOK...
...OUR TRANSFORMATION INTO THE TOA NUVA...
NOT TO MENTION MAKING SURE THE BOHROK SWARMS AND BOHROK VA GOT PUT TO WORK-- REPAIRING THE DAMAGE THEY DID!
MAYBE TAHU AND KOPAKA DID GET A LITTLE CARRIED AWAY, BUT--
NO--
--GALI IS RIGHT. MAYBE IT WOULD BE BEST FOR US TO GO OUR SEPARATE WAYS.
OUR VILLAGES NEED US--MORE THAN WE NEED EACH OTHER.
I AGREE. THIS ALLIANCE IS NO LONGER NECESSARY.
THE TURAGA HAVE SAID ALL ALONG THAT WE ARE SIX WHO SHARE ONE DESTINY.
IS THIS HOW WE HONOR THEIR WISDOM?-- BY SPLITTING APART?
MAYBE THE TURAGA DON'T KNOW EVERYTHING, GALI.
IF YOU WANT ME, I'LL BE HELPING TO REBUILD LE-KORO.
THIS IS A MISTAKE... I CAN FEEL IT. PLEASE-- WHAT IF WE ARE NEEDED ONCE MORE?

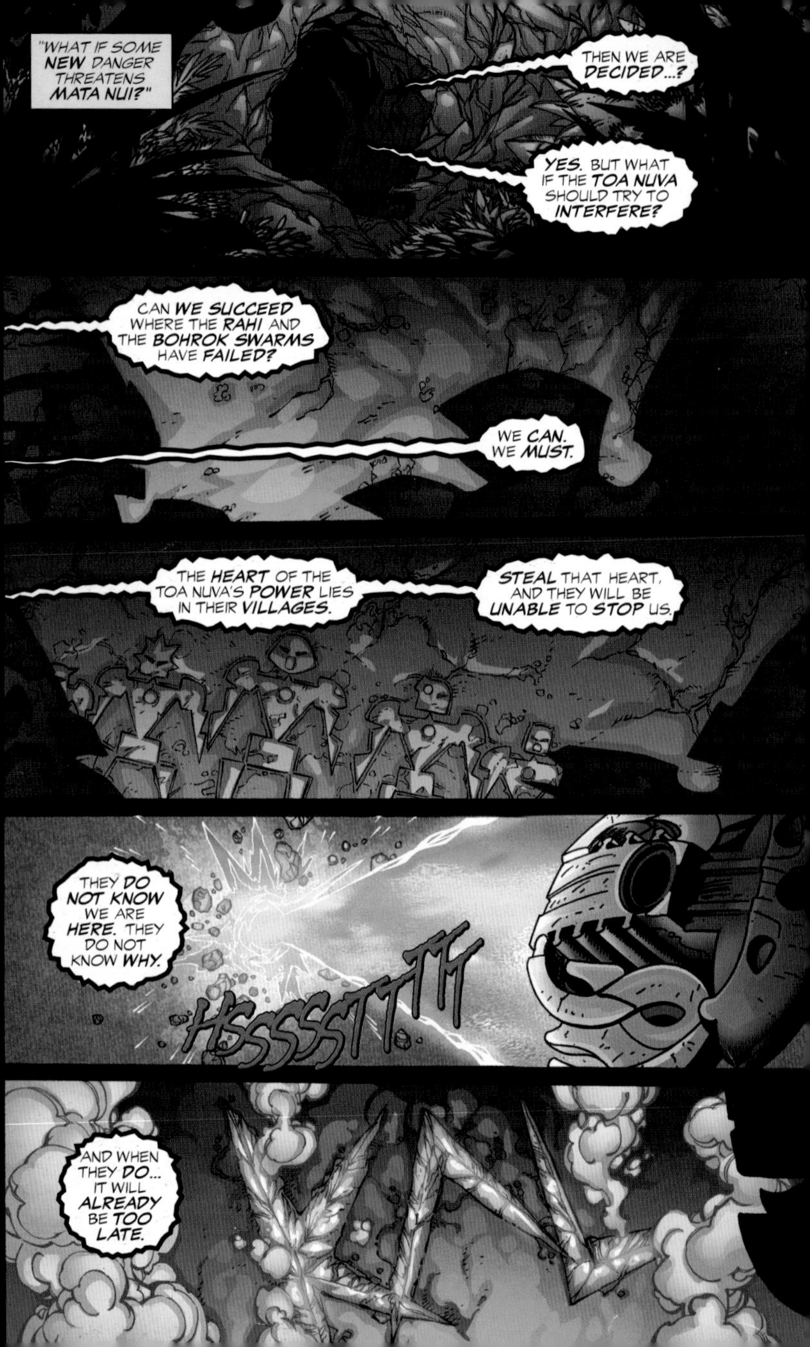
"WHAT IF SOME NEW DANGER THREATENS MATA NUI?"
THEN WE ARE DECIDED...?
YES. BUT WHAT IF THE TOA NUVA SHOULD TRY TO INTERFERE?
CAN WE SUCCEED WHERE THE RAHI AND THE BOHROK SWARMS HAVE FAILED?
WE CAN. WE MUST.
THE HEART OF THE TOA NUVA'S POWER LIES IN THEIR VILLAGES.
STEAL THAT HEART, AND THEY WILL BE UNABLE TO STOP US.
THEY DO NOT KNOW WE ARE HERE. THEY DO NOT KNOW WHY.
HSSSSSTTTTH
AND WHEN THEY DO... IT WILL ALREADY BE TOO LATE.

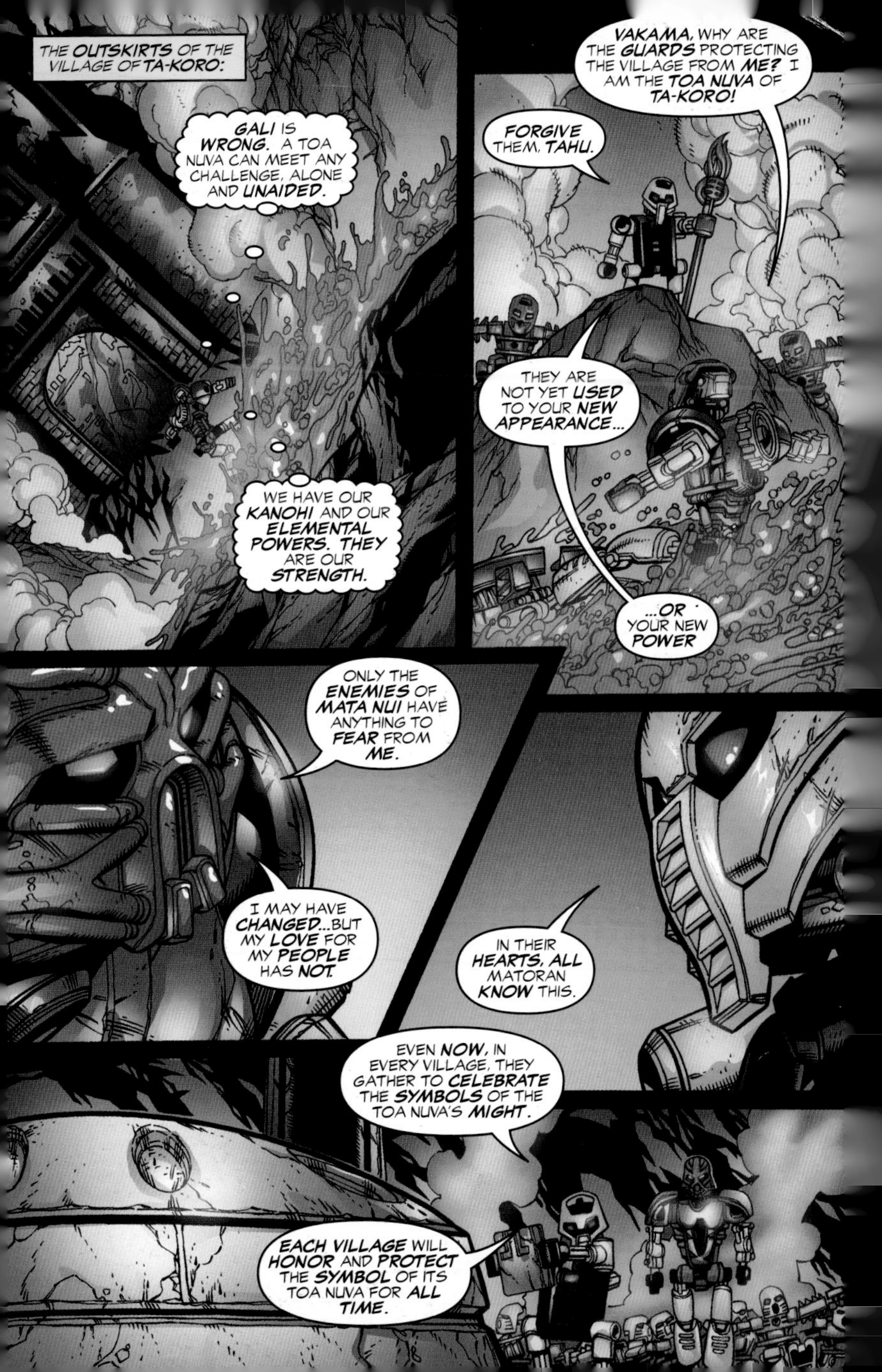
THE OUTSKIRTS OF THE VILLAGE OF TA-KORO:
GALI IS WRONG. A TOA NUVA CAN MEET ANY CHALLENGE, ALONE AND UNAIDED.
WE HAVE OUR KANOHI AND OUR ELEMENTAL POWERS. THEY ARE OUR STRENGTH.
VAKAMA, WHY ARE THE GUARDS PROTECTING THE VILLAGE FROM ME? I AM THE TOA NUVA OF TA-KORO!
FORGIVE THEM, TAHU.
THEY ARE NOT YET USED TO YOUR NEW APPEARANCE...
...OR YOUR NEW POWER
ONLY THE ENEMIES OF MATA NUI HAVE ANYTHING TO FEAR FROM ME.
I MAY HAVE CHANGED...BUT MY LOVE FOR MY PEOPLE HAS NOT.
IN THEIR HEARTS, ALL MATORAN KNOW THIS.
EVEN NOW, IN EVERY VILLAGE, THEY GATHER TO CELEBRATE THE SYMBOLS OF THE TOA NUVA'S MIGHT.
EACH VILLAGE WILL HONOR AND PROTECT THE SYMBOL OF ITS TOA NUVA FOR ALL TIME.

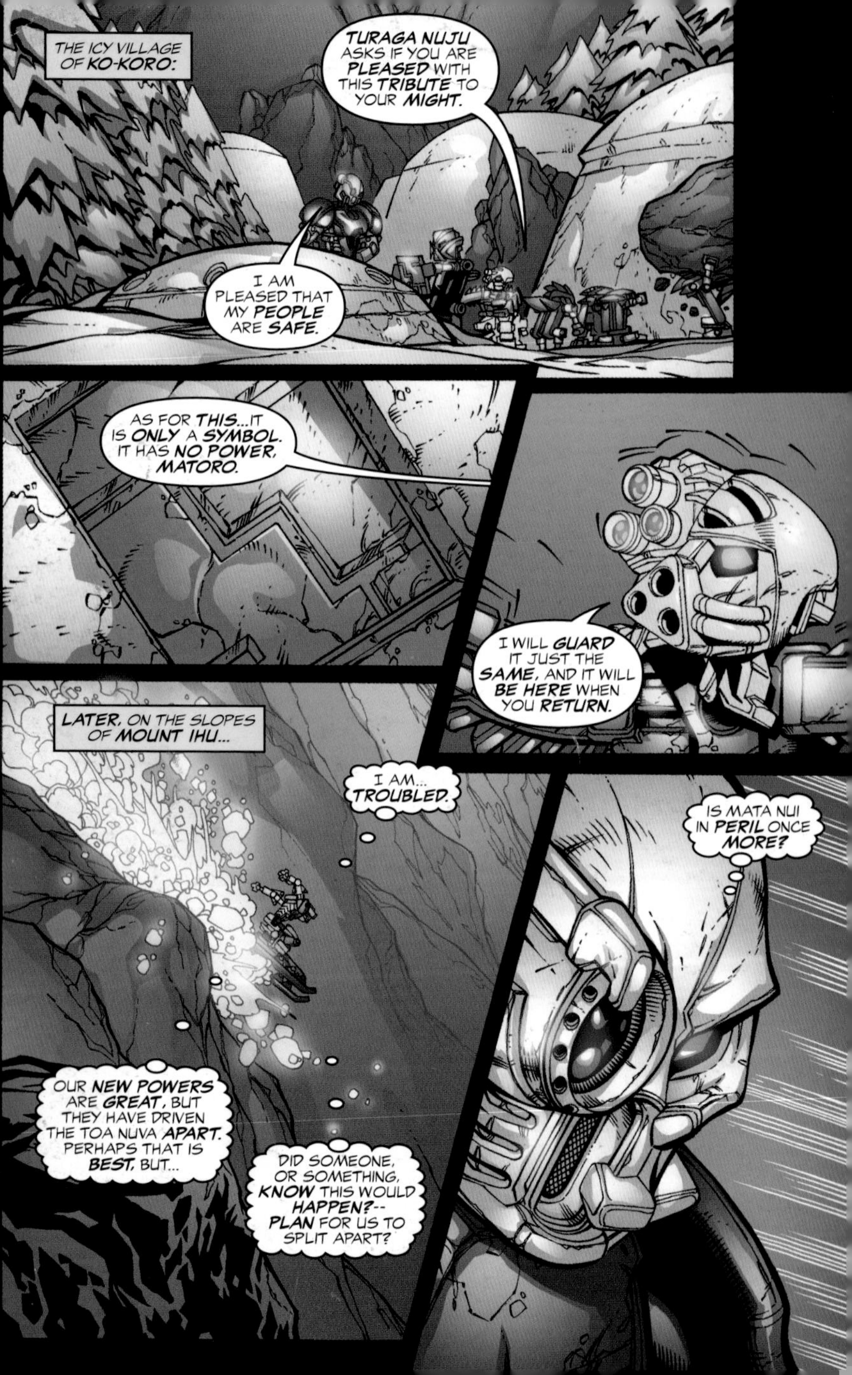
THE ICY VILLAGE OF KO-KORO:
TURAGA NUJU ASKS IF YOU ARE PLEASED WITH THIS TRIBUTE TO YOUR MIGHT.
I AM PLEASED THAT MY PEOPLE ARE SAFE.
AS FOR THIS...IT IS ONLY A SYMBOL. IT HAS NO POWER, MATORO.
I WILL GUARD IT JUST THE SAME, AND IT WILL BE HERE WHEN YOU RETURN.
LATER, ON THE SLOPES OF MOUNT IHU...
I AM... TROUBLED.
IS MATA NUI IN PERIL ONCE MORE?
OUR NEW POWERS ARE GREAT, BUT THEY HAVE DRIVEN THE TOA NUVA APART. PERHAPS THAT IS BEST, BUT...
DID SOMEONE, OR SOMETHING, KNOW THIS WOULD HAPPEN?-- PLAN FOR US TO SPLIT APART?

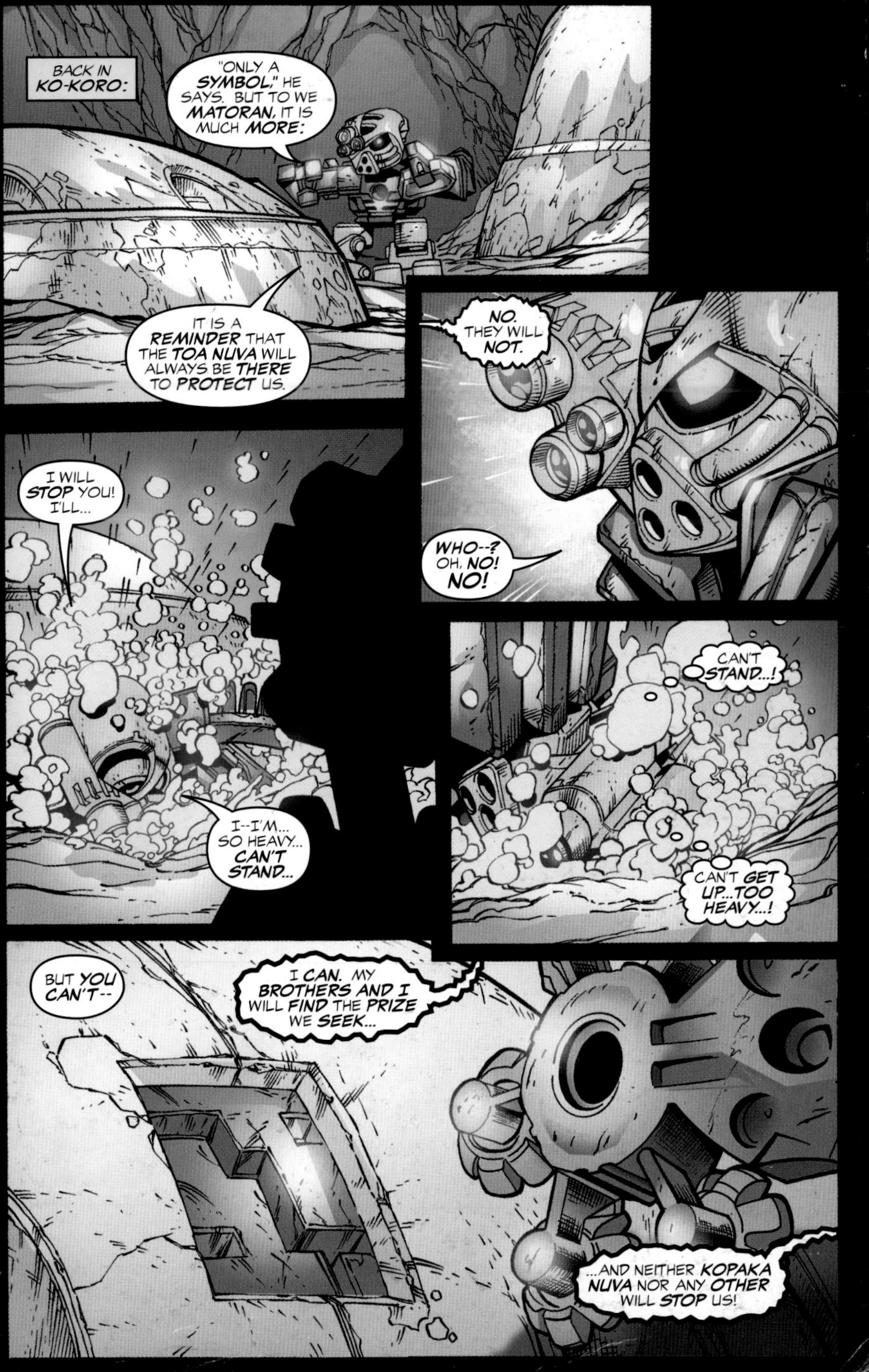
BACK IN KO-KORO:
"ONLY A SYMBOL," HE SAYS. BUT TO WE MATORAN, IT IS MUCH MORE:
IT IS A REMINDER THAT THE TOA NUVA WILL ALWAYS BE THERE TO PROTECT US.
NO. THEY WILL NOT.
WHO--? OH, NO! NO!
I WILL STOP YOU! I'LL...
I--I'M... SO HEAVY... CAN'T STAND...
CAN'T STAND...!
CAN'T GET UP...TOO HEAVY...!
BUT YOU CAN'T--
I CAN. MY BROTHERS AND I WILL FIND THE PRIZE WE SEEK...
...AND NEITHER KOPAKA NUVA NOR ANY OTHER WILL STOP US!

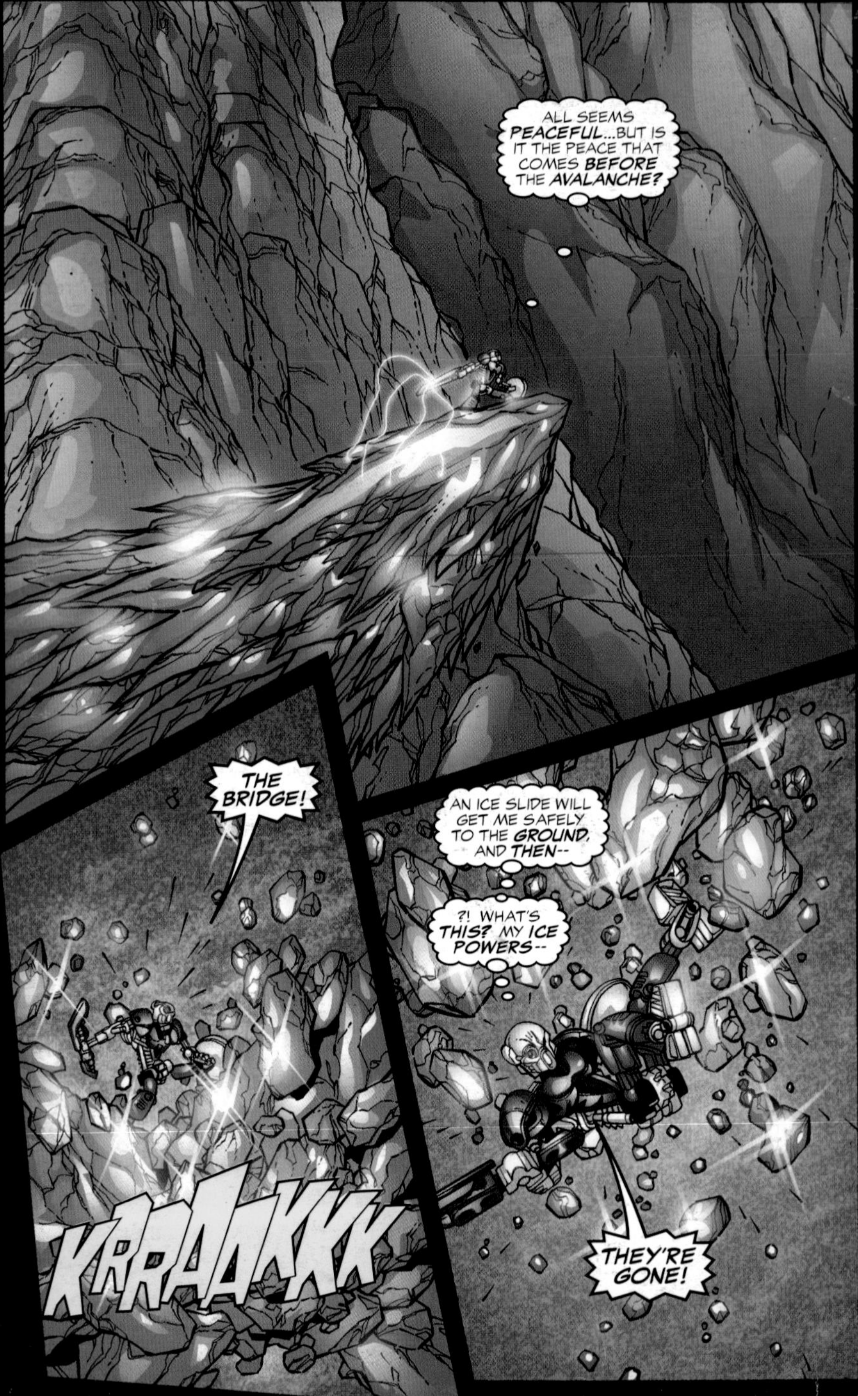
ALL SEEMS PEACEFUL...BUT IS IT THE PEACE THAT COMES BEFORE THE AVALANCHE?
THE BRIDGE!
KRRAAKKK
AN ICE SLIDE WILL GET ME SAFELY TO THE GROUND, AND THEN--
?! WHAT'S THIS? MY ICE POWERS--
THEY'RE GONE!

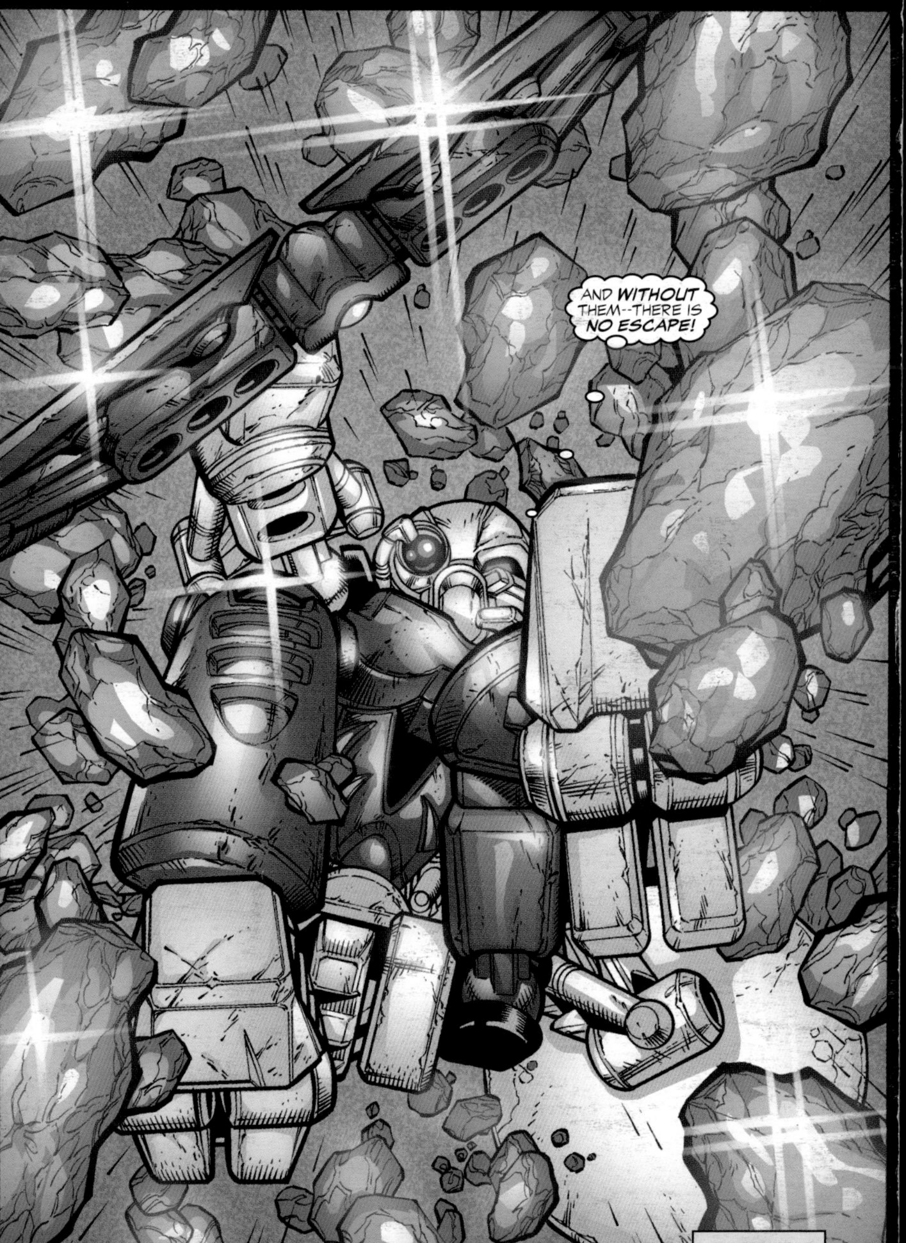
AND WITHOUT THEM--THERE IS NO ESCAPE!
END PROLOGUE

CHALLENGE OF THE RAHKSHI
CHAPTER ONE

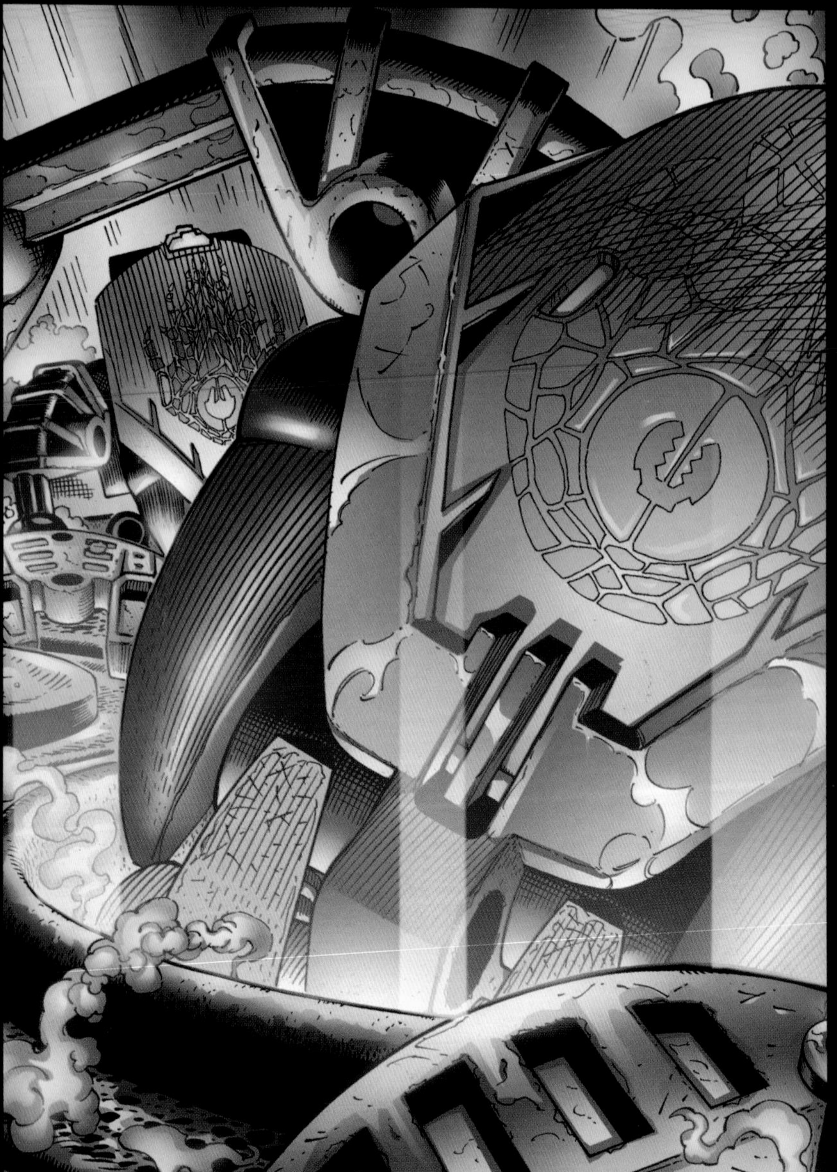

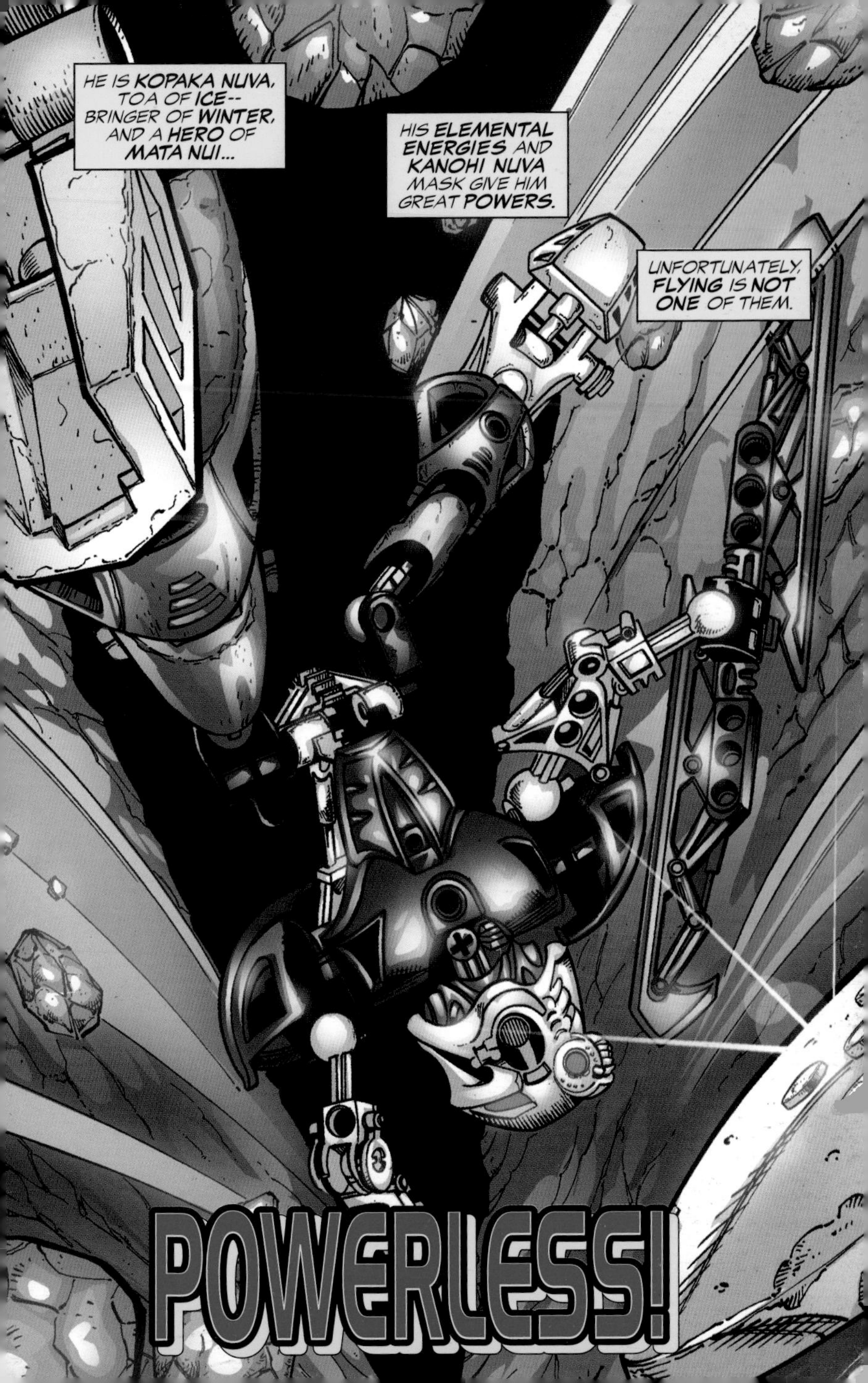
HE IS KOPAKA NUVA, TOA OF ICE-- BRINGER OF WINTER, AND A HERO OF MATA NUI...
HIS ELEMENTAL ENERGIES AND KANOHI NUVA MASK GIVE HIM GREAT POWERS.
UNFORTUNATELY, FLYING IS NOT ONE OF THEM.
POWERLESS!

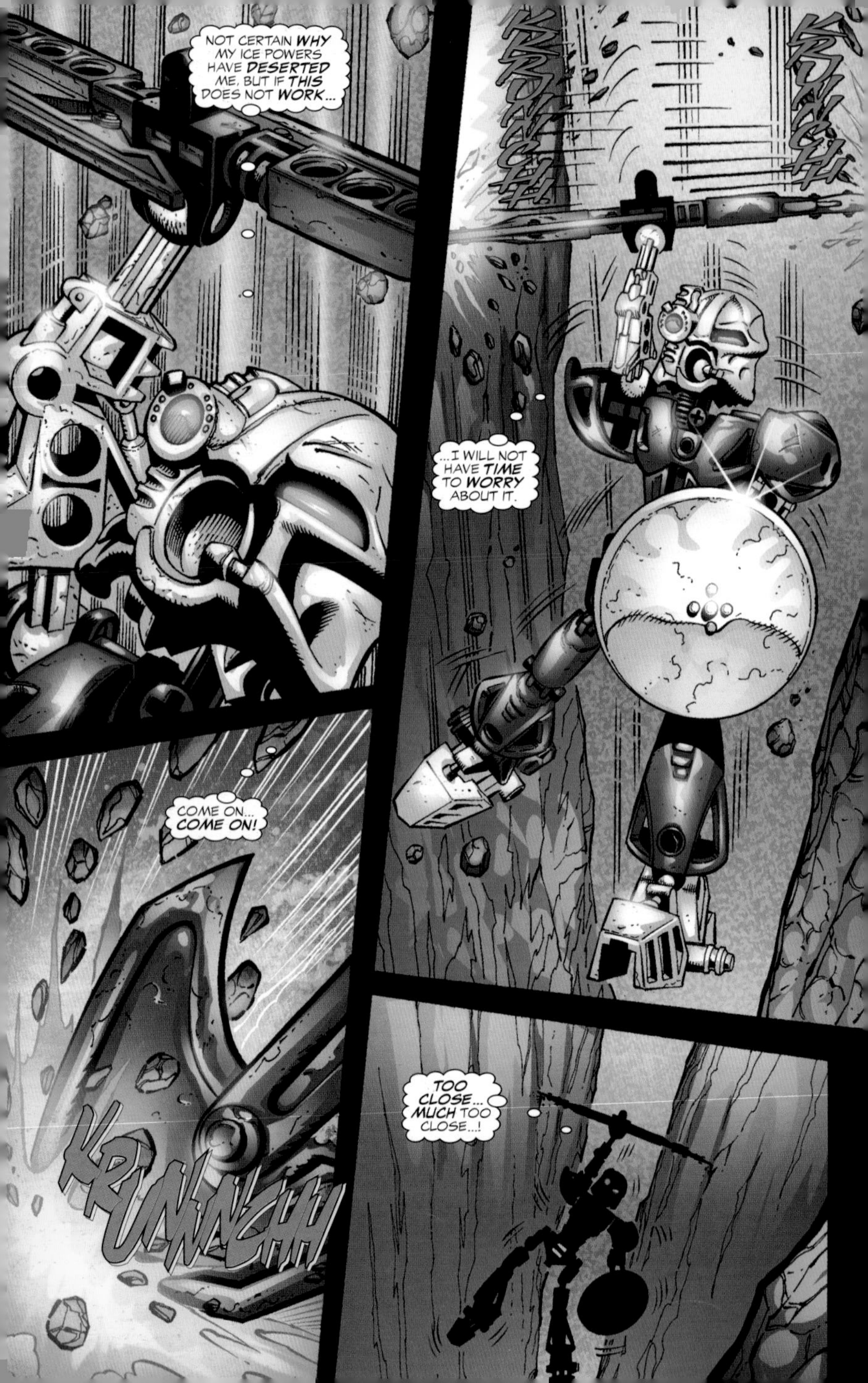
NOT CERTAIN **WHY** MY ICE POWERS HAVE **DESERTED** ME, BUT IF **THIS** DOES NOT **WORK**...
...I WILL NOT HAVE **TIME** TO **WORRY** ABOUT IT.
COME ON... **COME ON!**
KRUNNCHH
TOO CLOSE... **MUCH** TOO CLOSE...!

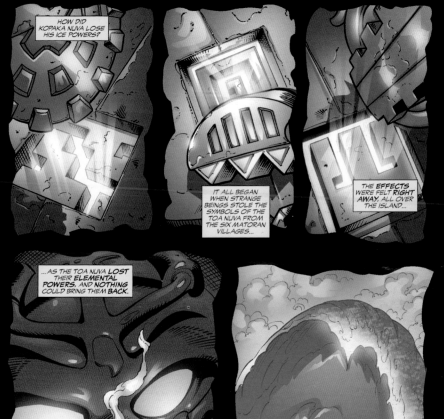

HOW DID KOPAKA NUVA LOSE HIS ICE POWERS?

IT ALL BEGAN WHEN STRANGE BEINGS STOLE THE SYMBOLS OF THE TOA NUVA FROM THE SIX MATORAN VILLAGES...

THE EFFECTS WERE FELT RIGHT AWAY, ALL OVER THE ISLAND...

...AS THE TOA NUVA LOST THEIR ELEMENTAL POWERS, AND NOTHING COULD BRING THEM BACK.

SUDDENLY, PROBLEMS THEY COULD HAVE SOLVED EASILY THE DAY BEFORE THREATENED TO BECOME DISASTERS!

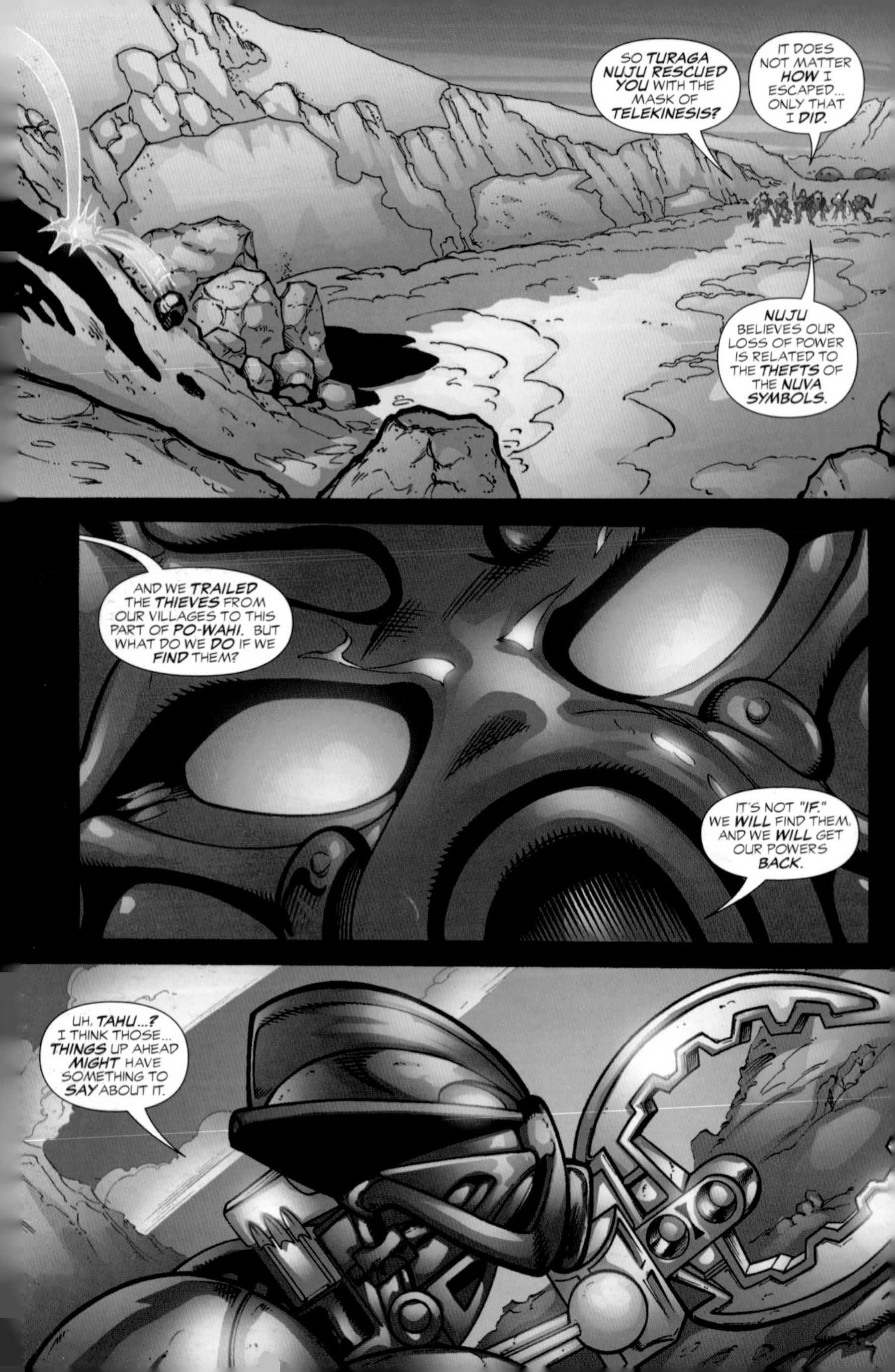

SO TURAGA NUJU RESCUED YOU WITH THE MASK OF TELEKINESIS?
IT DOES NOT MATTER HOW I ESCAPED... ONLY THAT I DID.
NUJU BELIEVES OUR LOSS OF POWER IS RELATED TO THE THEFTS OF THE NUVA SYMBOLS.
AND WE TRAILED THE THIEVES FROM OUR VILLAGES TO THIS PART OF PO-WAHI. BUT WHAT DO WE DO IF WE FIND THEM?
IT'S NOT "IF." WE WILL FIND THEM, AND WE WILL GET OUR POWERS BACK.
UH, TAHU...? I THINK THOSE... THINGS UP AHEAD MIGHT HAVE SOMETHING TO SAY ABOUT IT.

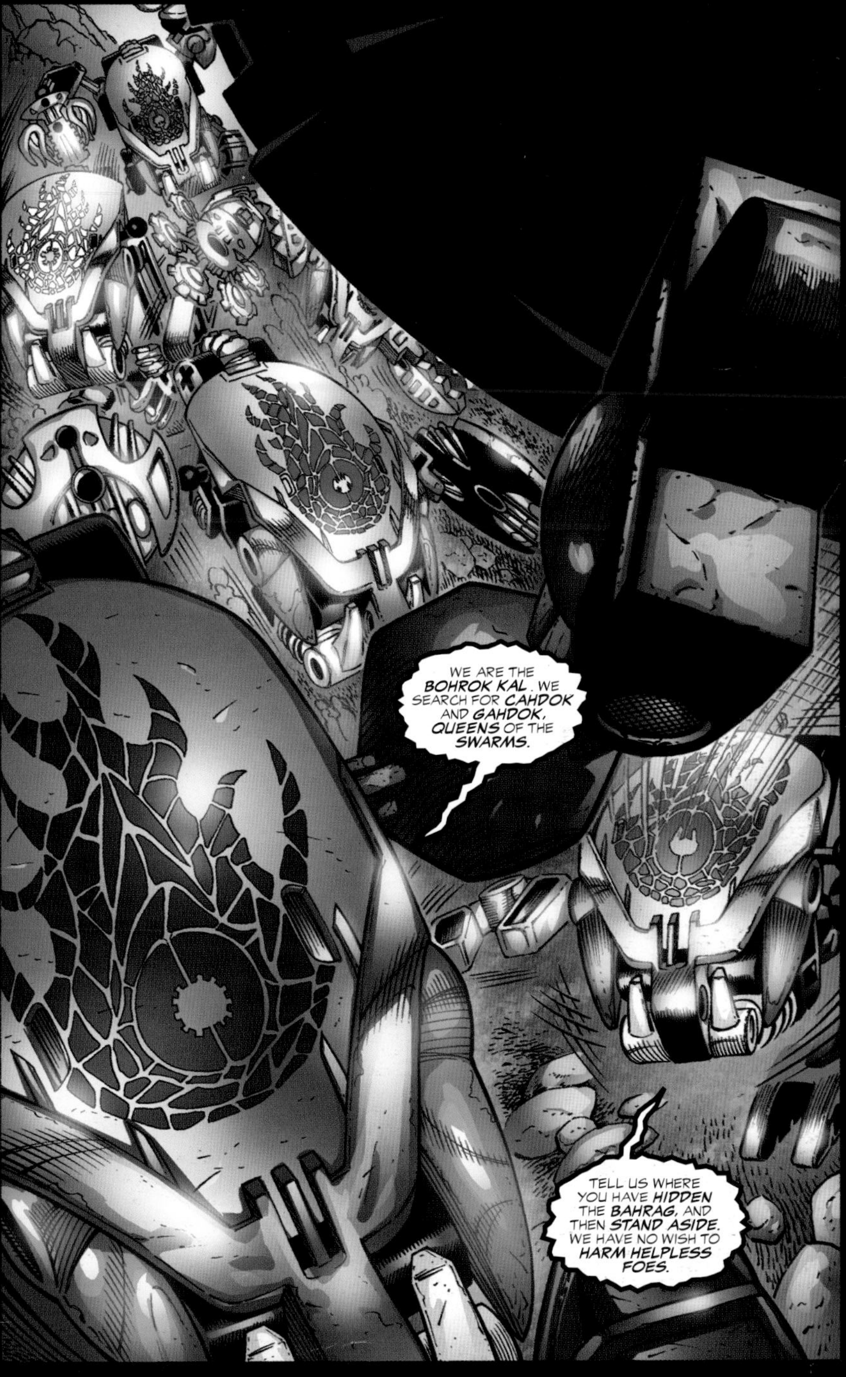
WE ARE THE BOHROK KAL. WE SEARCH FOR CAHDOK AND GAHDOK, QUEENS OF THE SWARMS.
TELL US WHERE YOU HAVE HIDDEN THE BAHRAG, AND THEN STAND ASIDE. WE HAVE NO WISH TO HARM HELPLESS FOES.

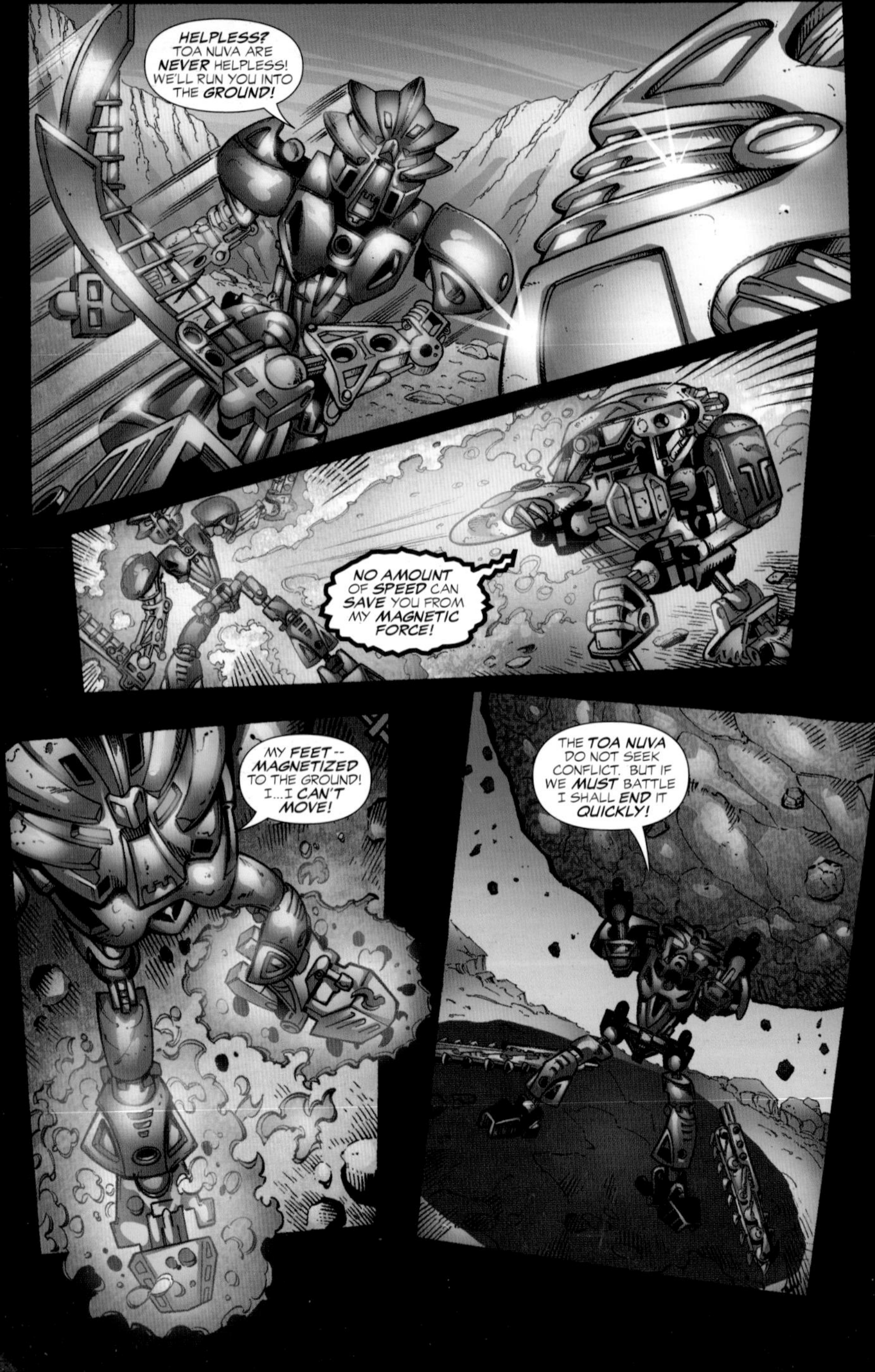
HELPLESS? TOA NUVA ARE NEVER HELPLESS! WE'LL RUN YOU INTO THE GROUND!
NO AMOUNT OF SPEED CAN SAVE YOU FROM MY MAGNETIC FORCE!
MY FEET -- MAGNETIZED TO THE GROUND! I...I CAN'T MOVE!
THE TOA NUVA DO NOT SEEK CONFLICT. BUT IF WE MUST BATTLE I SHALL END IT QUICKLY!

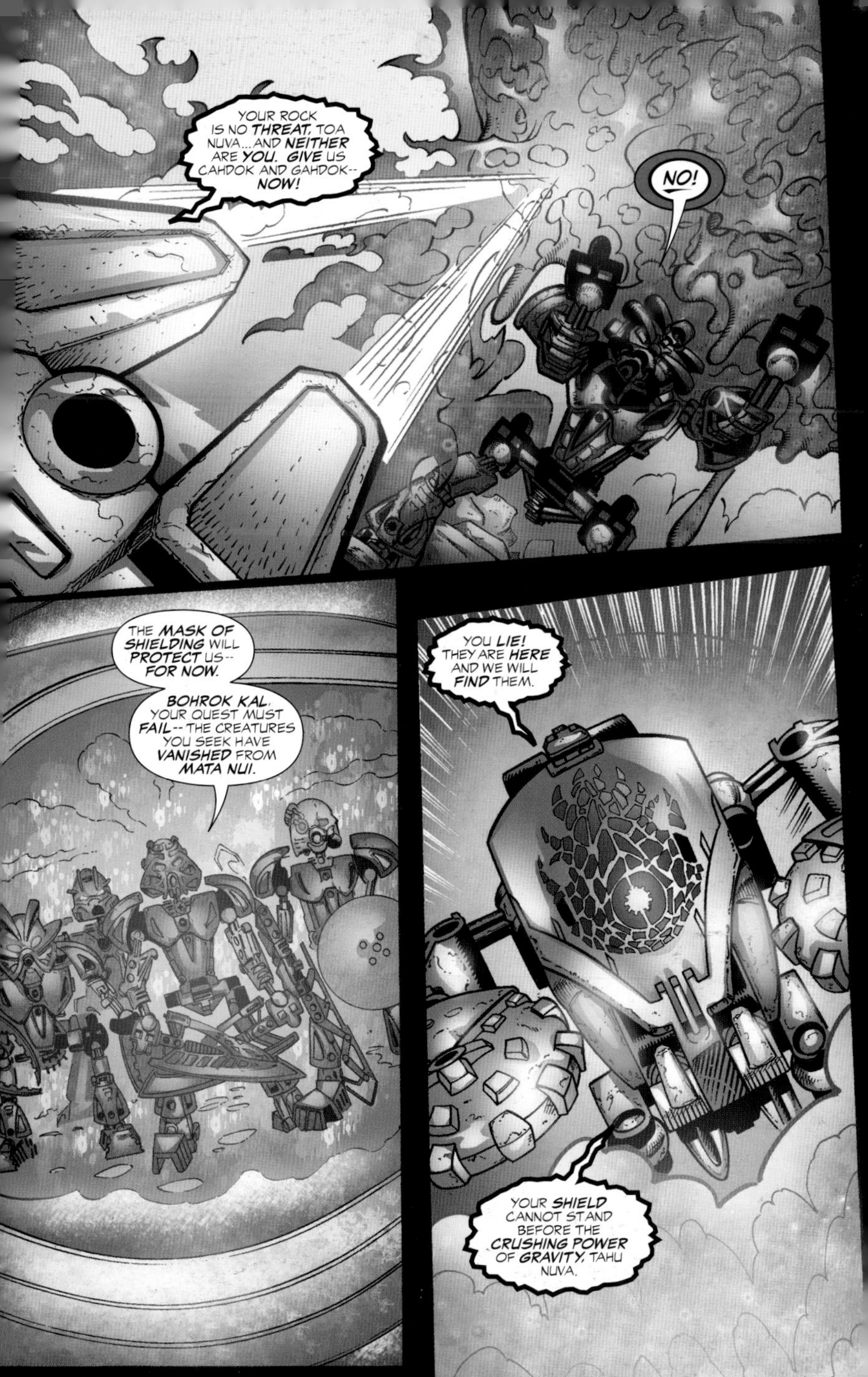
YOUR ROCK IS NO THREAT, TOA NUVA... AND NEITHER ARE YOU. GIVE US CAHDOK AND GAHDOK-- NOW!
NO!
THE MASK OF SHIELDING WILL PROTECT US-- FOR NOW.
BOHROK KAL, YOUR QUEST MUST FAIL-- THE CREATURES YOU SEEK HAVE VANISHED FROM MATA NUI.
YOU LIE! THEY ARE HERE AND WE WILL FIND THEM.
YOUR SHIELD CANNOT STAND BEFORE THE CRUSHING POWER OF GRAVITY, TAHU NUVA.

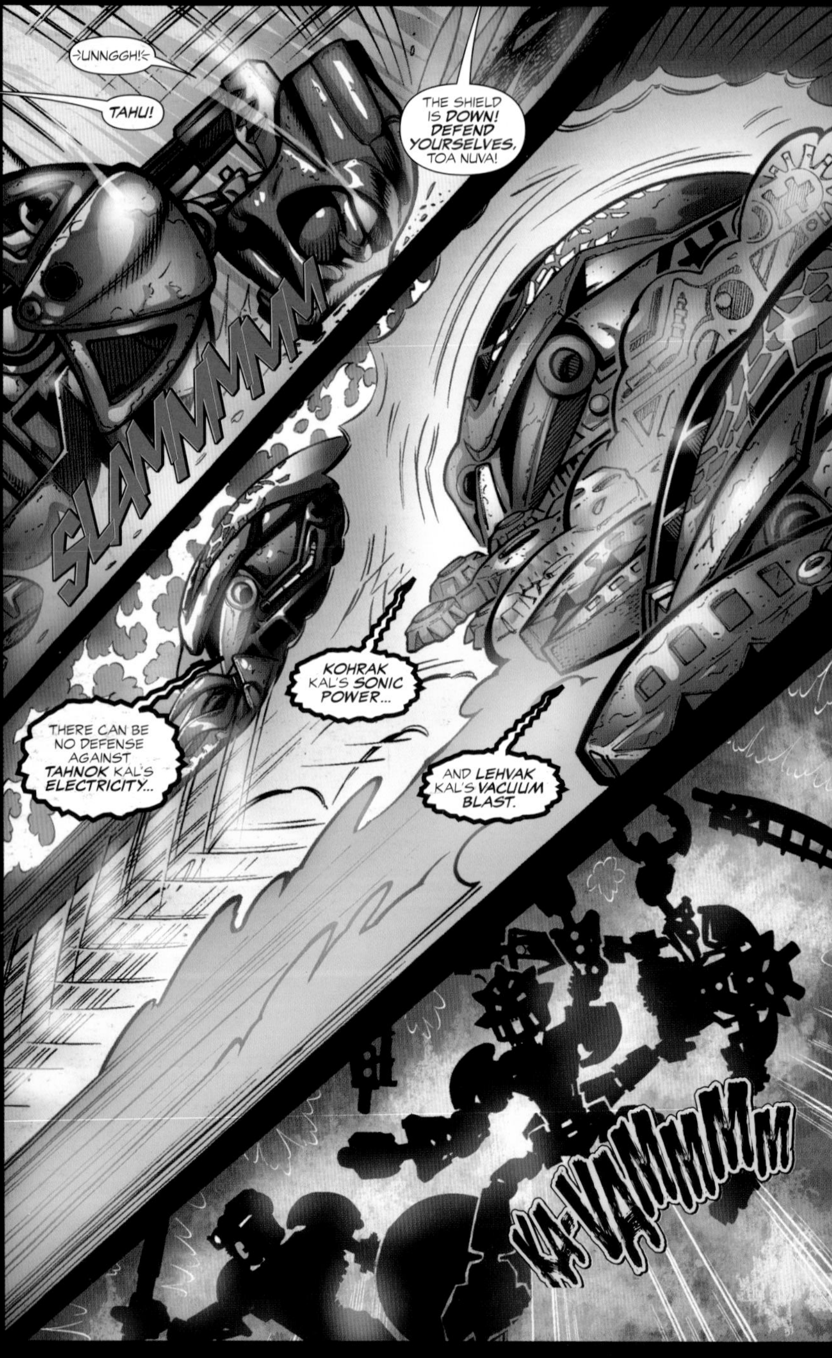
UNNGGH!
TAHU!
THE SHIELD IS DOWN! DEFEND YOURSELVES, TOA NUVA!
SLAMMMMM
KOHRAK KAL'S SONIC POWER...
THERE CAN BE NO DEFENSE AGAINST TAHNOK KAL'S ELECTRICITY...
AND LEHVAK KAL'S VACUUM BLAST.
KA-VAMMMMM

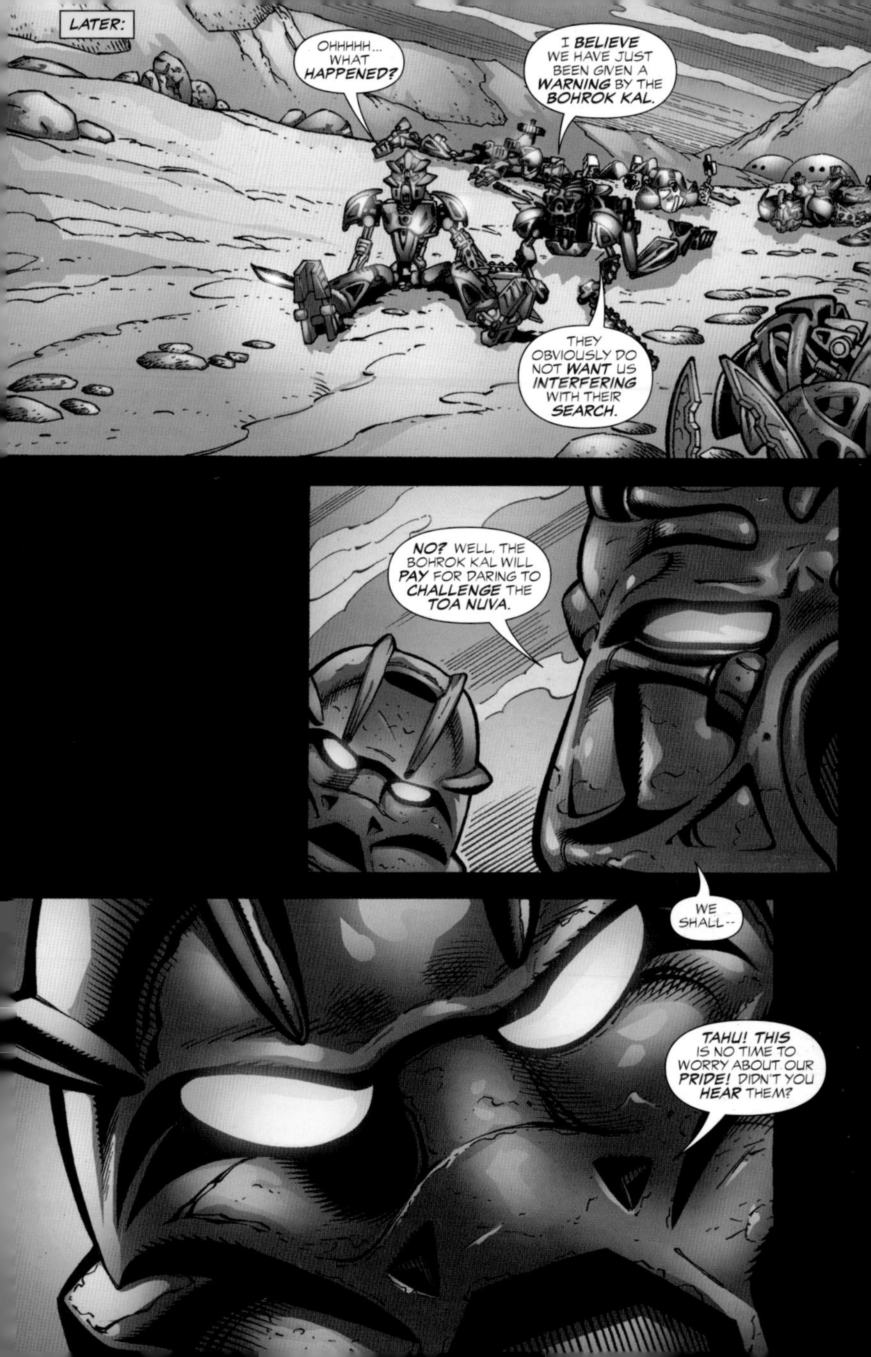

LATER:
OHHHHH... WHAT HAPPENED?
I BELIEVE WE HAVE JUST BEEN GIVEN A WARNING BY THE BOHROK KAL.
THEY OBVIOUSLY DO NOT WANT US INTERFERING WITH THEIR SEARCH.
NO? WELL, THE BOHROK KAL WILL PAY FOR DARING TO CHALLENGE THE TOA NUVA.
WE SHALL--
TAHU! THIS IS NO TIME TO WORRY ABOUT OUR PRIDE! DIDN'T YOU HEAR THEM?

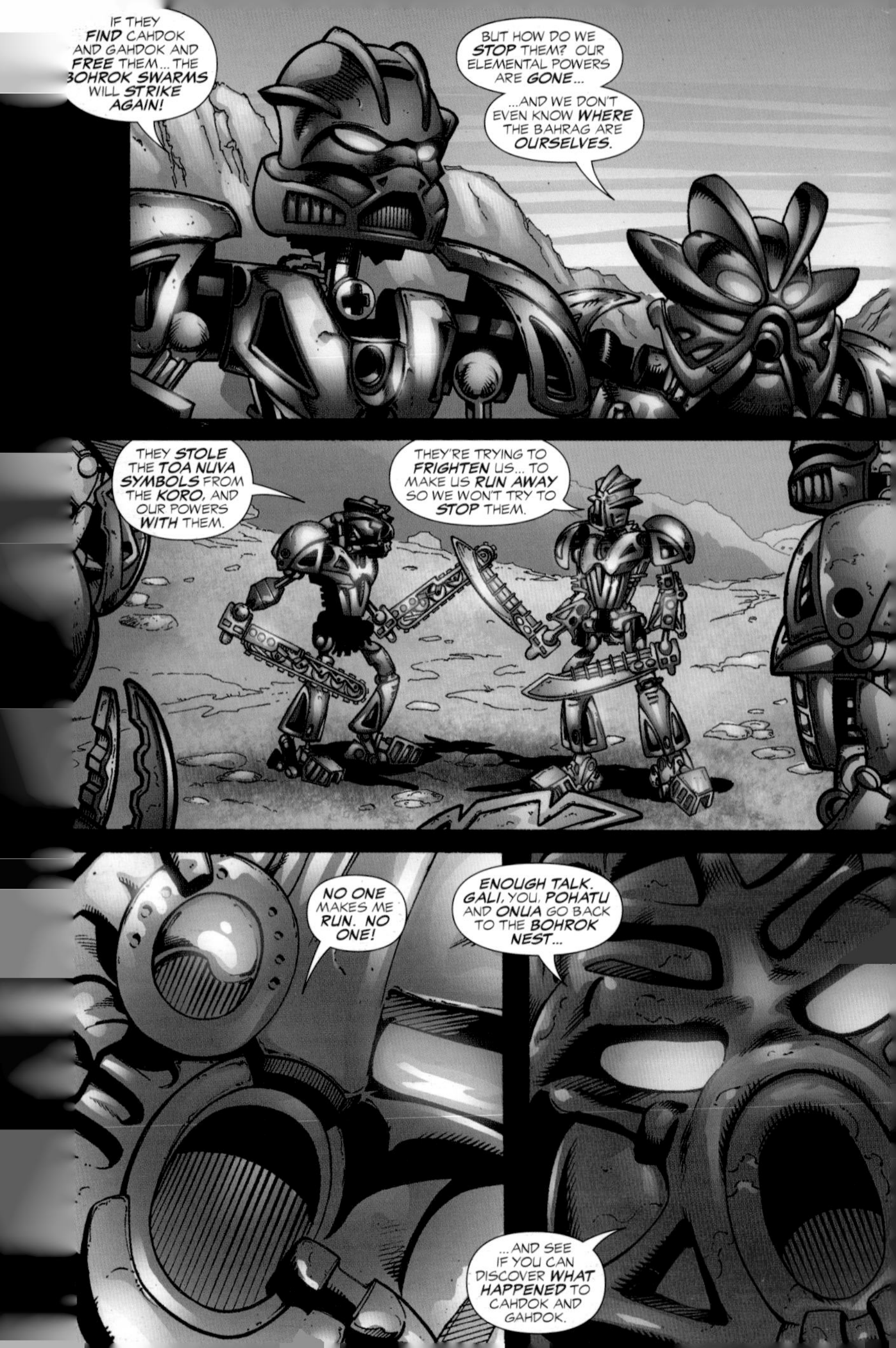
IF THEY FIND CAHDOK AND GAHDOK AND FREE THEM... THE BOHROK SWARMS WILL STRIKE AGAIN!
BUT HOW DO WE STOP THEM? OUR ELEMENTAL POWERS ARE GONE...
...AND WE DON'T EVEN KNOW WHERE THE BAHRAG ARE OURSELVES.
THEY STOLE THE TOA NUVA SYMBOLS FROM THE KORO, AND OUR POWERS WITH THEM.
THEY'RE TRYING TO FRIGHTEN US... TO MAKE US RUN AWAY SO WE WON'T TRY TO STOP THEM.
NO ONE MAKES ME RUN. NO ONE!
ENOUGH TALK. GALI, YOU, POHATU AND ONUA GO BACK TO THE BOHROK NEST...
...AND SEE IF YOU CAN DISCOVER WHAT HAPPENED TO CAHDOK AND GAHDOK.

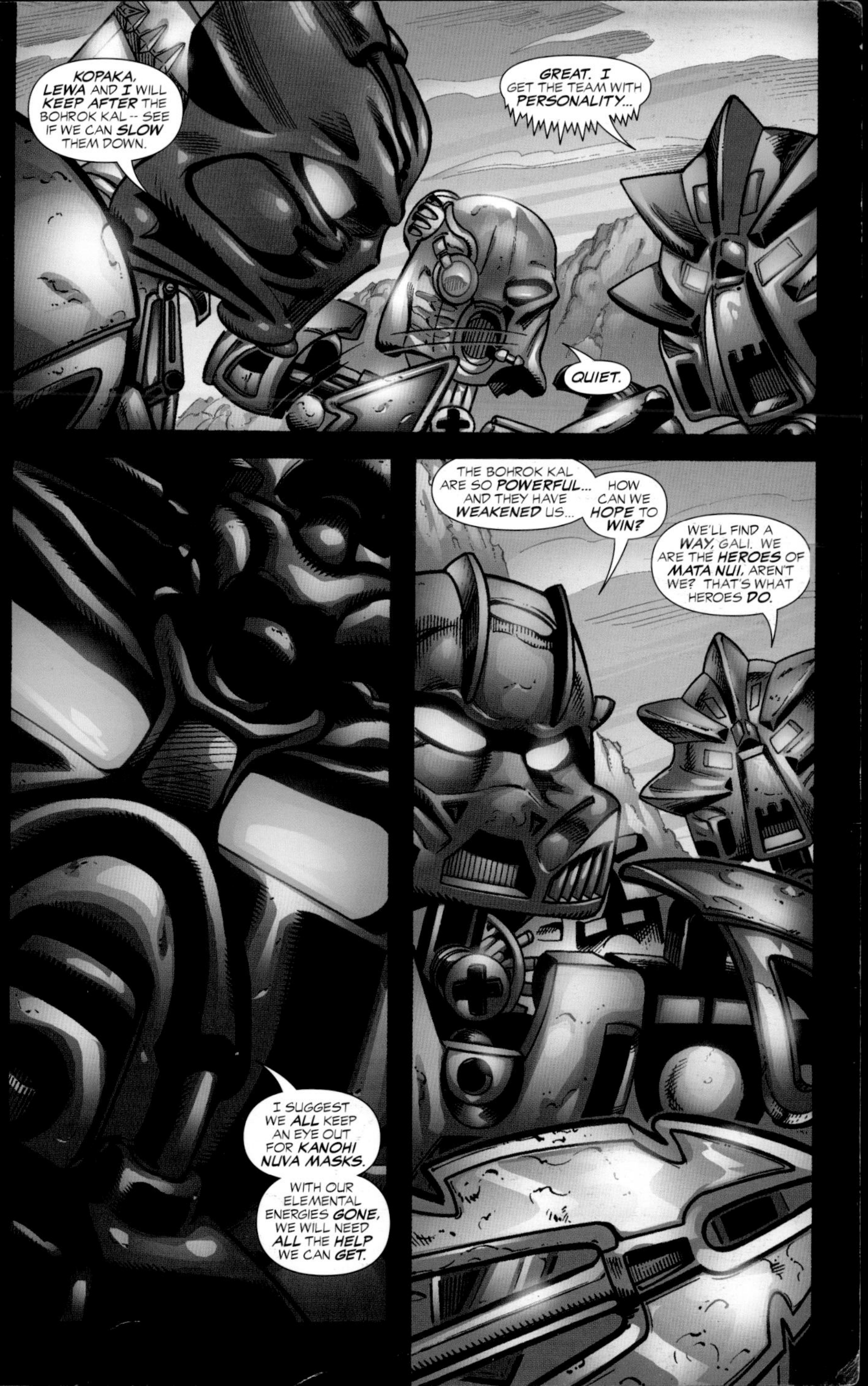
KOPAKA, LEWA AND I WILL KEEP AFTER THE BOHROK KAL -- SEE IF WE CAN SLOW THEM DOWN.
GREAT. I GET THE TEAM WITH PERSONALITY...
QUIET.
THE BOHROK KAL ARE SO POWERFUL... AND THEY HAVE WEAKENED US...
HOW CAN WE HOPE TO WIN?
WE'LL FIND A WAY, GALI. WE ARE THE HEROES OF MATA NUI, AREN'T WE? THAT'S WHAT HEROES DO.
I SUGGEST WE ALL KEEP AN EYE OUT FOR KANOHI NUVA MASKS.
WITH OUR ELEMENTAL ENERGIES GONE, WE WILL NEED ALL THE HELP WE CAN GET.

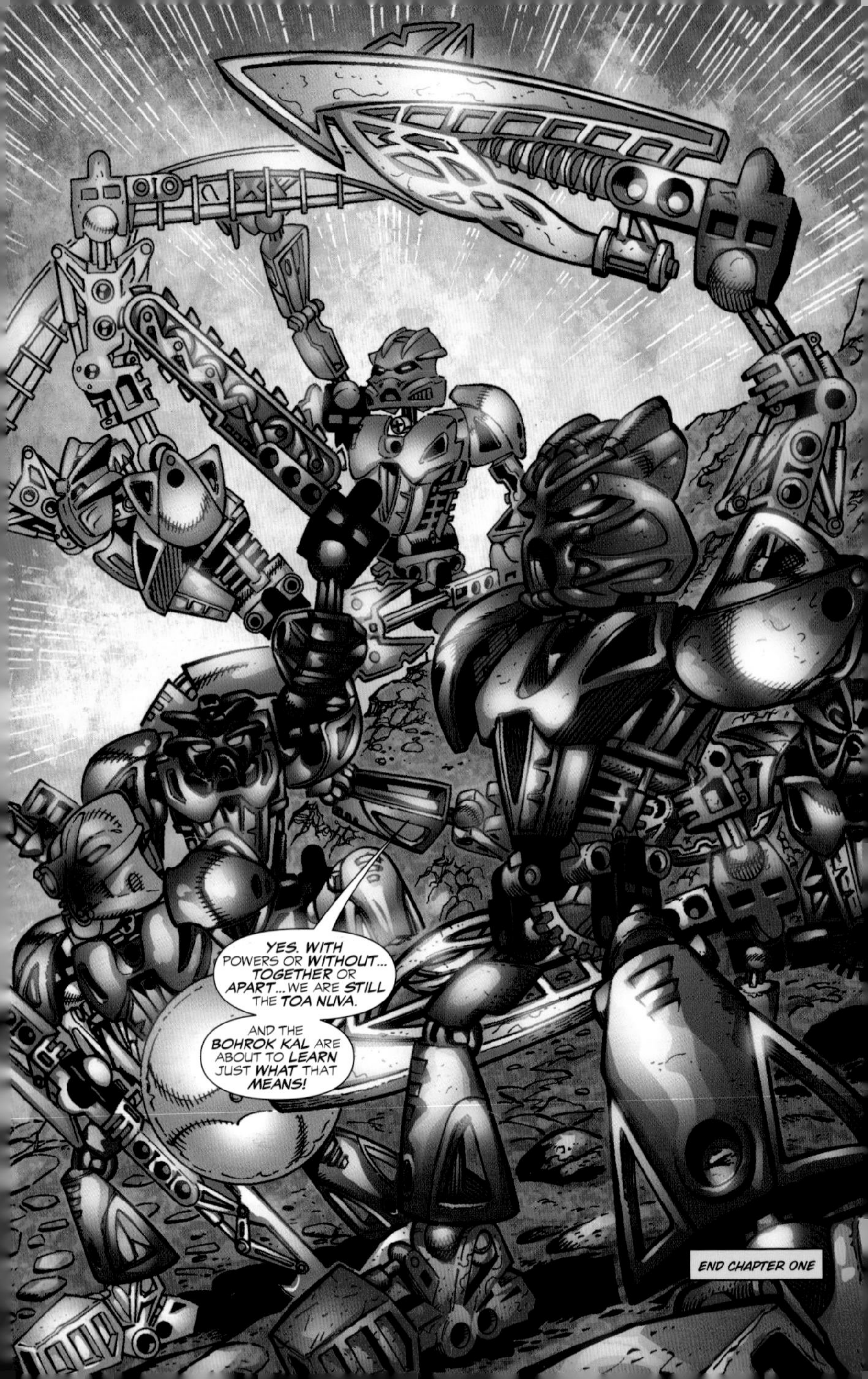
YES. WITH POWERS OR WITHOUT... TOGETHER OR APART...WE ARE STILL THE TOA NUVA.
AND THE BOHROK KAL ARE ABOUT TO LEARN JUST WHAT THAT MEANS!
END CHAPTER ONE

CHALLENGE OF THE RAHKSHI
CHAPTER TWO

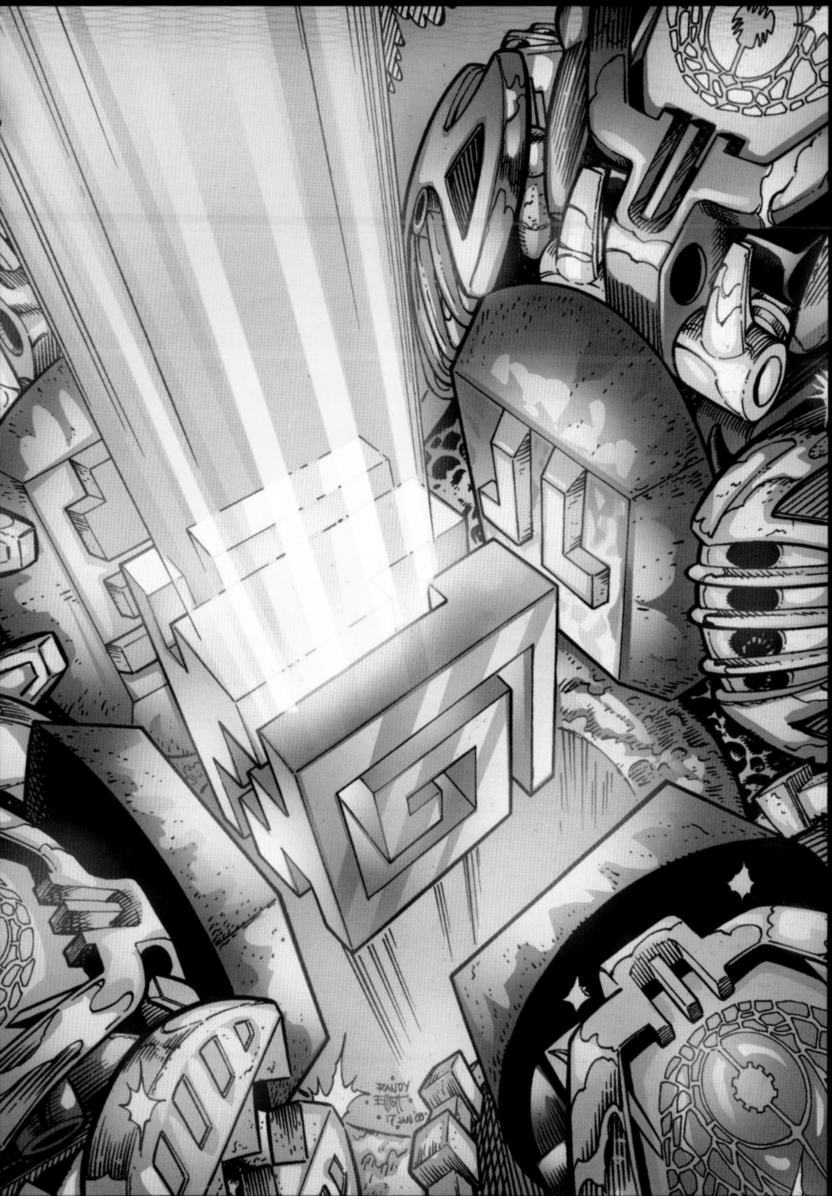
RANDY
ELLIOTT
17 JAN 03

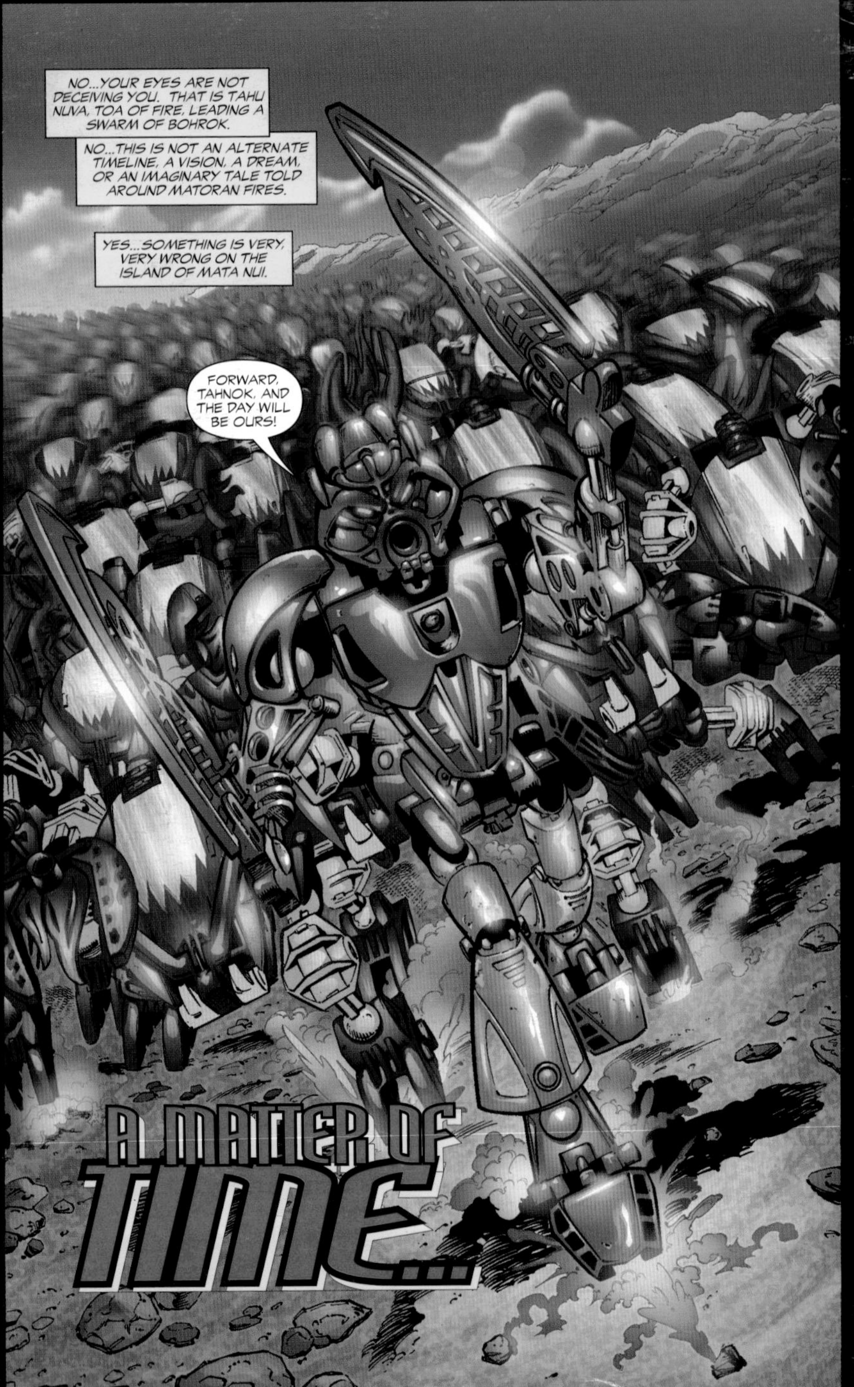
NO...YOUR EYES ARE NOT DECEIVING YOU. THAT IS TAHU NUVA, TOA OF FIRE, LEADING A SWARM OF BOHROK.
NO...THIS IS NOT AN ALTERNATE TIMELINE, A VISION, A DREAM, OR AN IMAGINARY TALE TOLD AROUND MATORAN FIRES.
YES...SOMETHING IS VERY, VERY WRONG ON THE ISLAND OF MATA NUI.
FORWARD, TAHNOK, AND THE DAY WILL BE OURS!
A MATTER OF TIME...

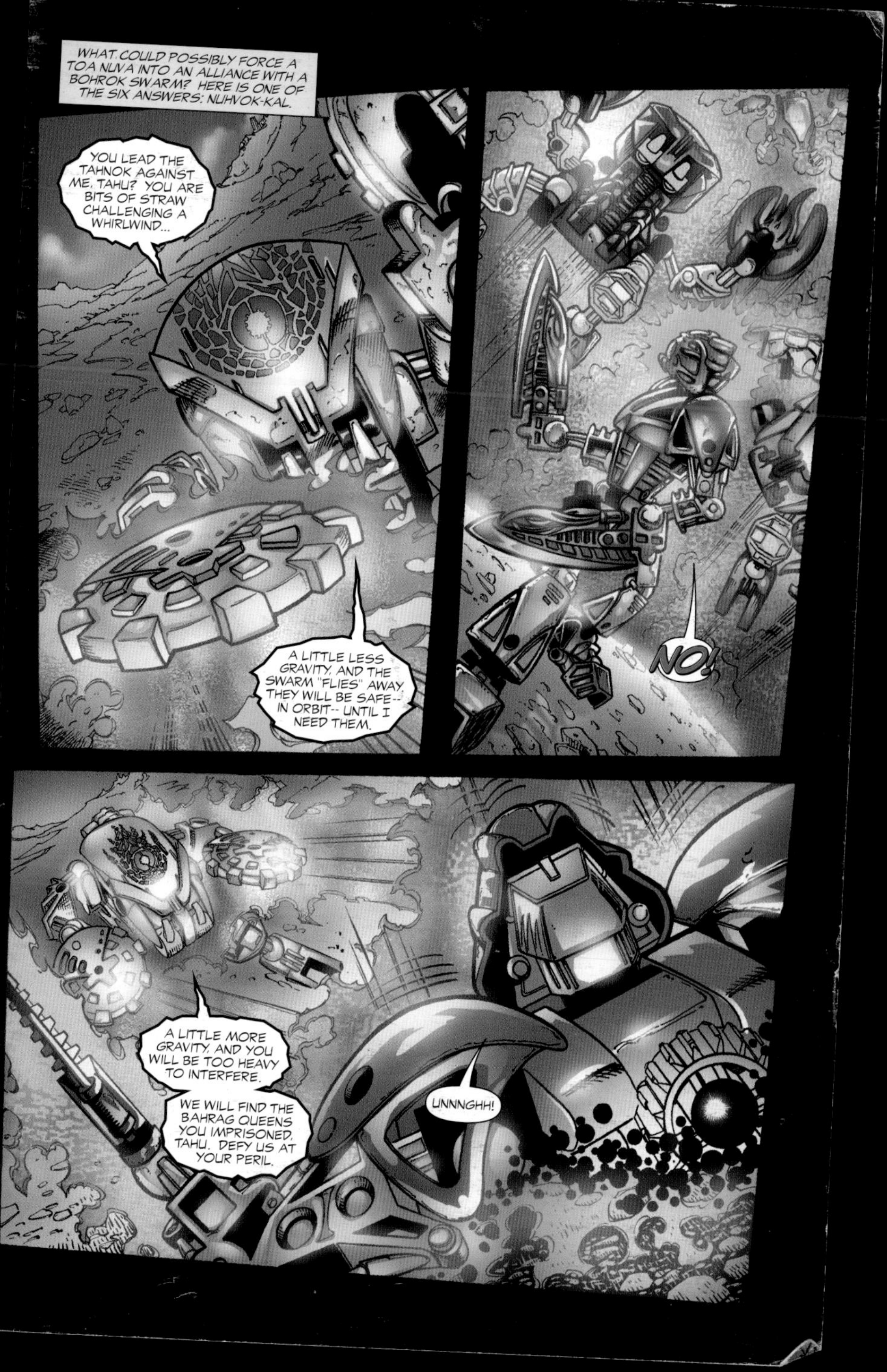
WHAT COULD POSSIBLY FORCE A TOA NUVA INTO AN ALLIANCE WITH A BOHROK SWARM? HERE IS ONE OF THE SIX ANSWERS: NUHVOK-KAL.
YOU LEAD THE TAHNOK AGAINST ME, TAHU? YOU ARE BITS OF STRAW CHALLENGING A WHIRLWIND...
A LITTLE LESS GRAVITY, AND THE SWARM "FLIES" AWAY. THEY WILL BE SAFE-- IN ORBIT-- UNTIL I NEED THEM.
NO!
A LITTLE MORE GRAVITY, AND YOU WILL BE TOO HEAVY TO INTERFERE.
WE WILL FIND THE BAHRAG QUEENS YOU IMPRISONED, TAHU. DEFY US AT YOUR PERIL.
UNNNGHH!

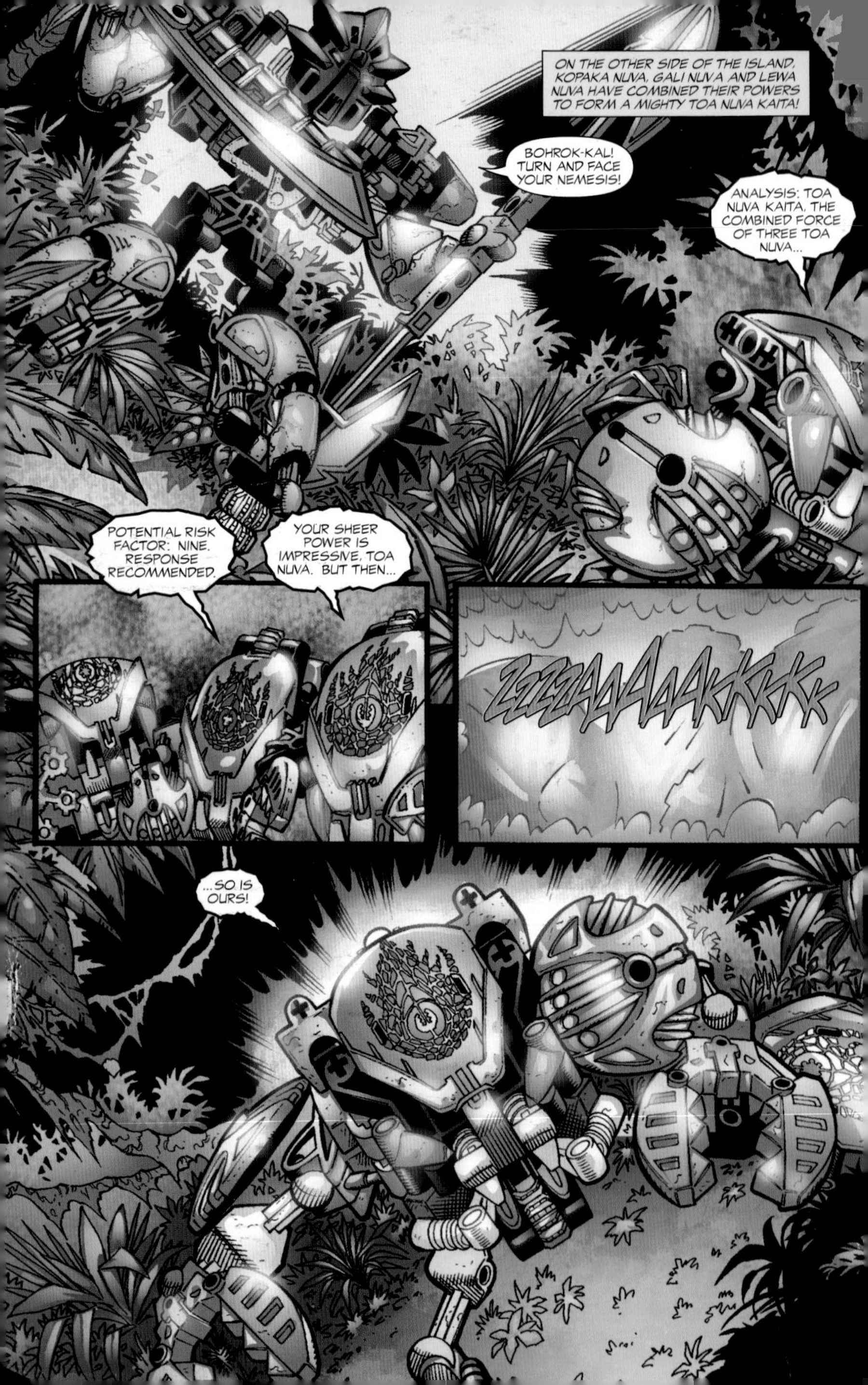
ON THE OTHER SIDE OF THE ISLAND, KOPAKA NUVA, GALI NUVA AND LEWA NUVA HAVE COMBINED THEIR POWERS TO FORM A MIGHTY TOA NUVA KAITA!
BOHROK-KAL! TURN AND FACE YOUR NEMESIS!
ANALYSIS: TOA NUVA KAITA, THE COMBINED FORCE OF THREE TOA NUVA...
POTENTIAL RISK FACTOR: NINE. RESPONSE RECOMMENDED.
YOUR SHEER POWER IS IMPRESSIVE, TOA NUVA. BUT THEN...
ZZZZAAAAAKKKKKK
...SO IS OURS!

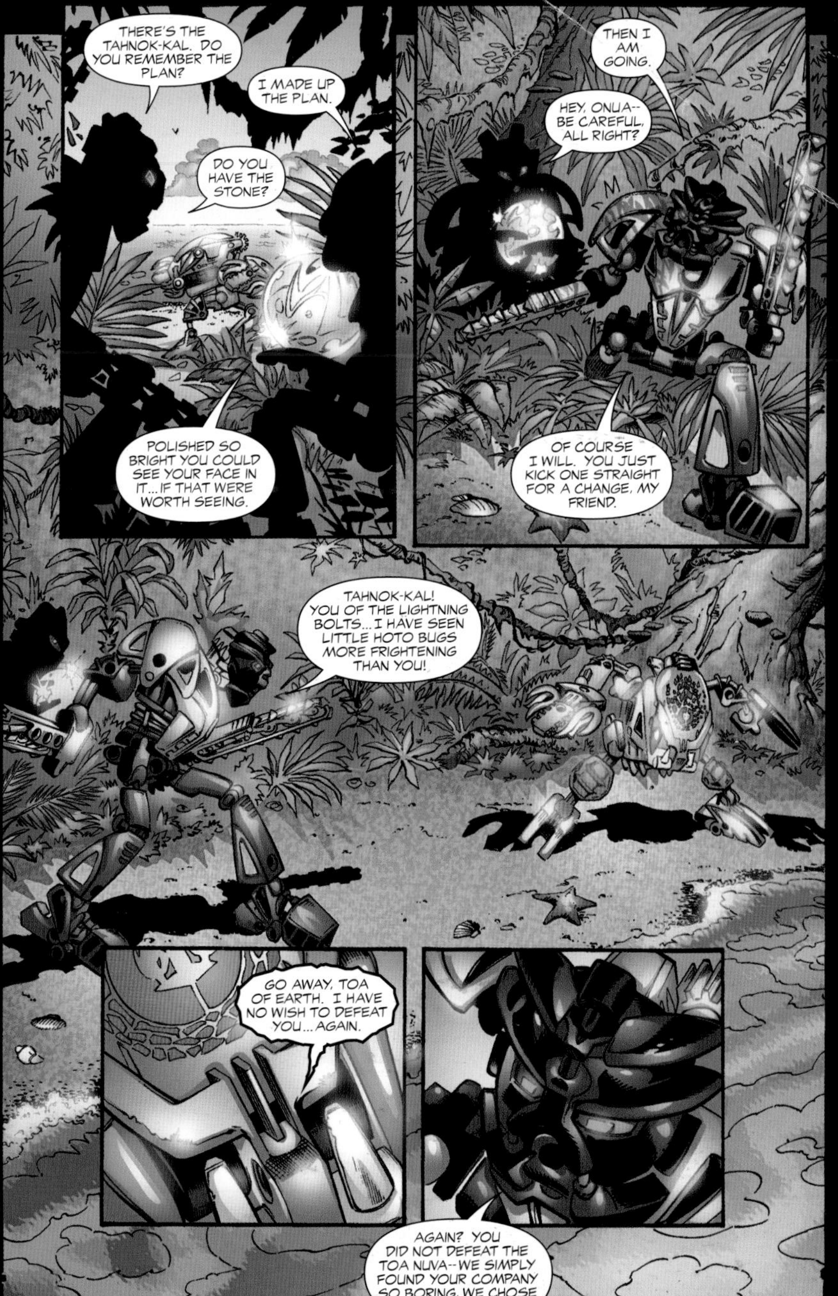
THERE'S THE TAHNOK-KAL. DO YOU REMEMBER THE PLAN?
I MADE UP THE PLAN.
DO YOU HAVE THE STONE?
POLISHED SO BRIGHT YOU COULD SEE YOUR FACE IN IT... IF THAT WERE WORTH SEEING.
THEN I AM GOING.
HEY, ONUA-- BE CAREFUL, ALL RIGHT?
OF COURSE I WILL. YOU JUST KICK ONE STRAIGHT FOR A CHANGE, MY FRIEND.
TAHNOK-KAL! YOU OF THE LIGHTNING BOLTS... I HAVE SEEN LITTLE HOTO BUGS MORE FRIGHTENING THAN YOU!
GO AWAY, TOA OF EARTH. I HAVE NO WISH TO DEFEAT YOU... AGAIN.
AGAIN? YOU DID NOT DEFEAT THE TOA NUVA--WE SIMPLY FOUND YOUR COMPANY SO BORING, WE CHOSE TO TAKE A NAP.

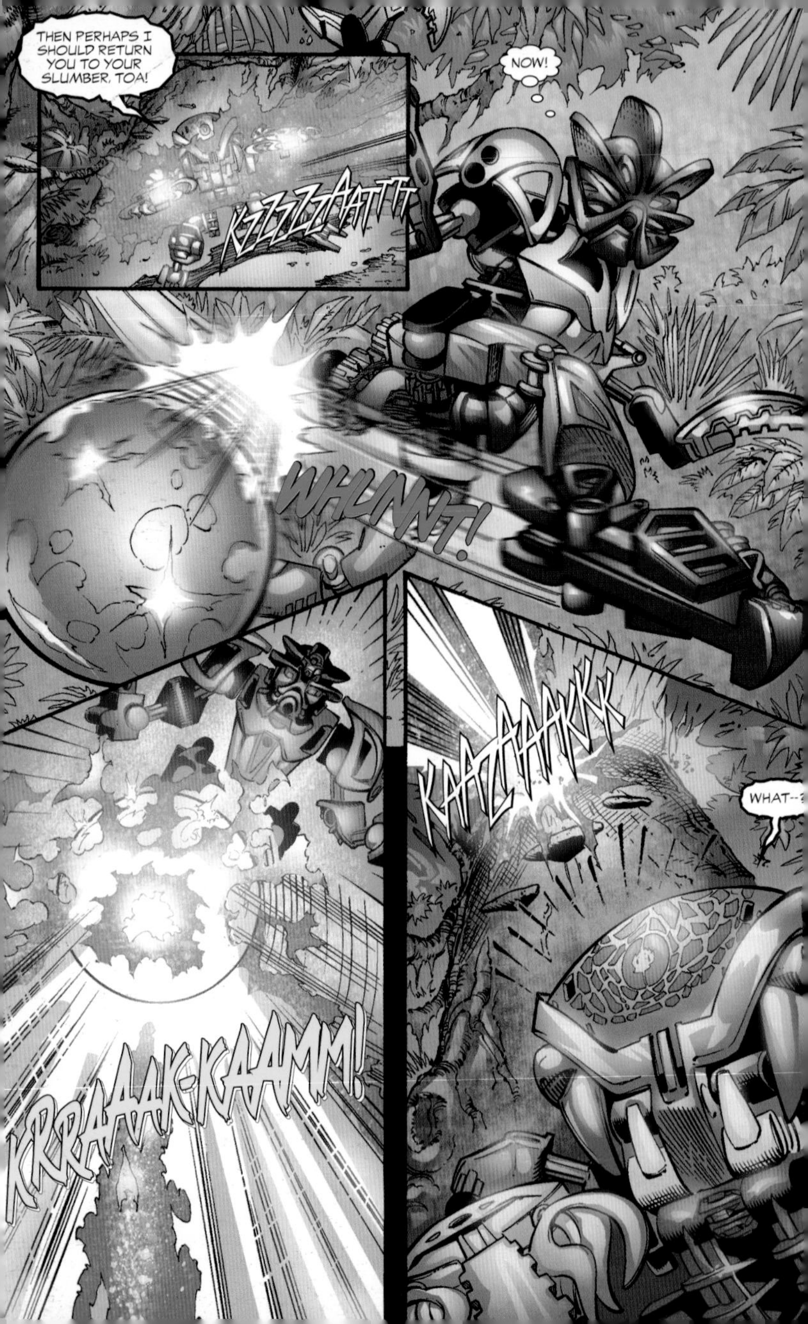
THEN PERHAPS I SHOULD RETURN YOU TO YOUR SLUMBER, TOA!
KZZZZZZAATTTT
NOW!
WHUNNT!
KRRAAAK-KAAMM!
KAAZAAAKKK
WHAT--?

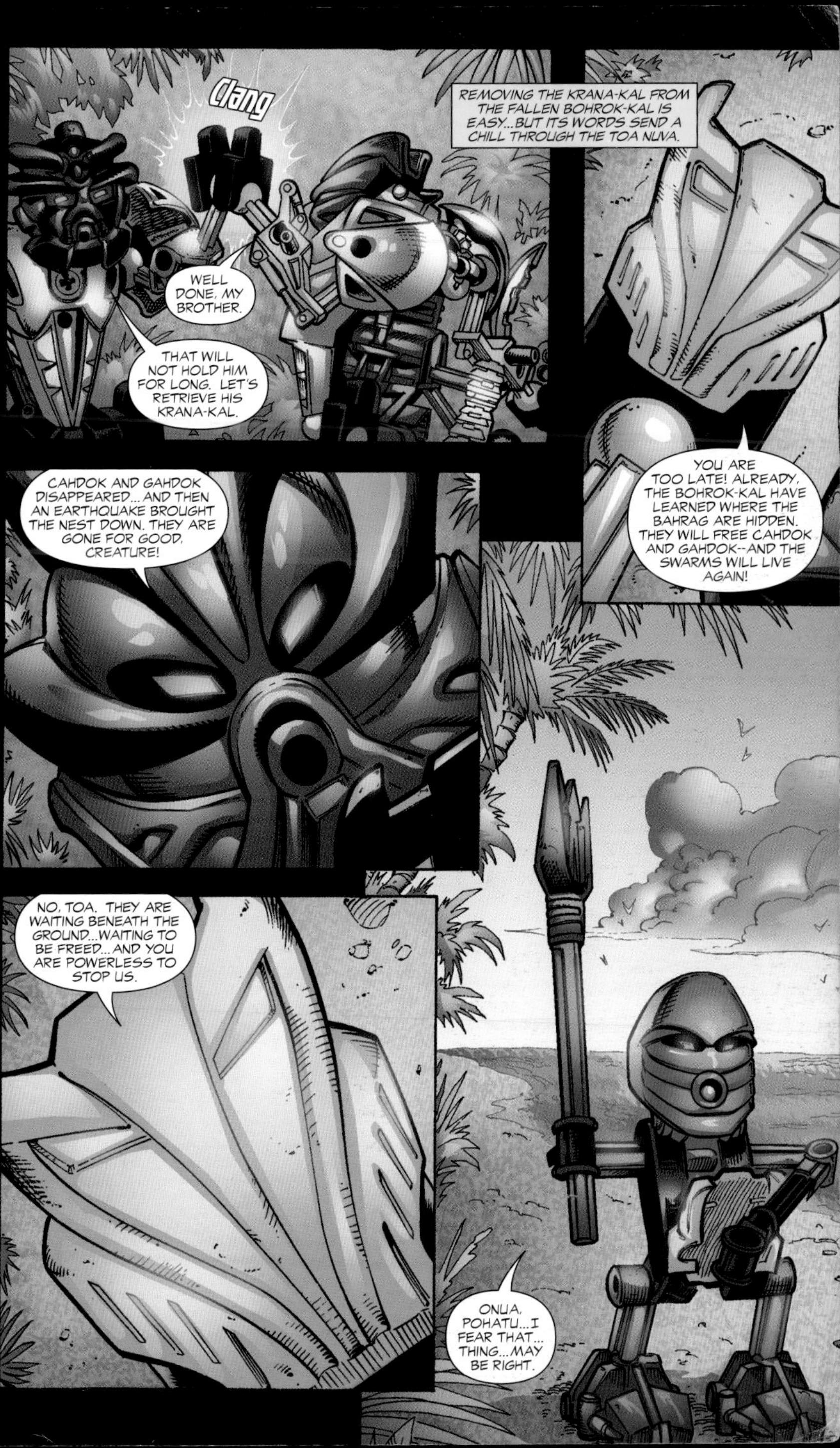
Clang
WELL DONE, MY BROTHER.
THAT WILL NOT HOLD HIM FOR LONG. LET'S RETRIEVE HIS KRANA-KAL.
REMOVING THE KRANA-KAL FROM THE FALLEN BOHROK-KAL IS EASY...BUT ITS WORDS SEND A CHILL THROUGH THE TOA NUVA.
YOU ARE TOO LATE! ALREADY, THE BOHROK-KAL HAVE LEARNED WHERE THE BAHRAG ARE HIDDEN. THEY WILL FREE CAHDOK AND GAHDOK--AND THE SWARMS WILL LIVE AGAIN!
CAHDOK AND GAHDOK DISAPPEARED... AND THEN AN EARTHQUAKE BROUGHT THE NEST DOWN. THEY ARE GONE FOR GOOD, CREATURE!
NO, TOA. THEY ARE WAITING BENEATH THE GROUND...WAITING TO BE FREED...AND YOU ARE POWERLESS TO STOP US.
ONUA, POHATU...I FEAR THAT... THING...MAY BE RIGHT.

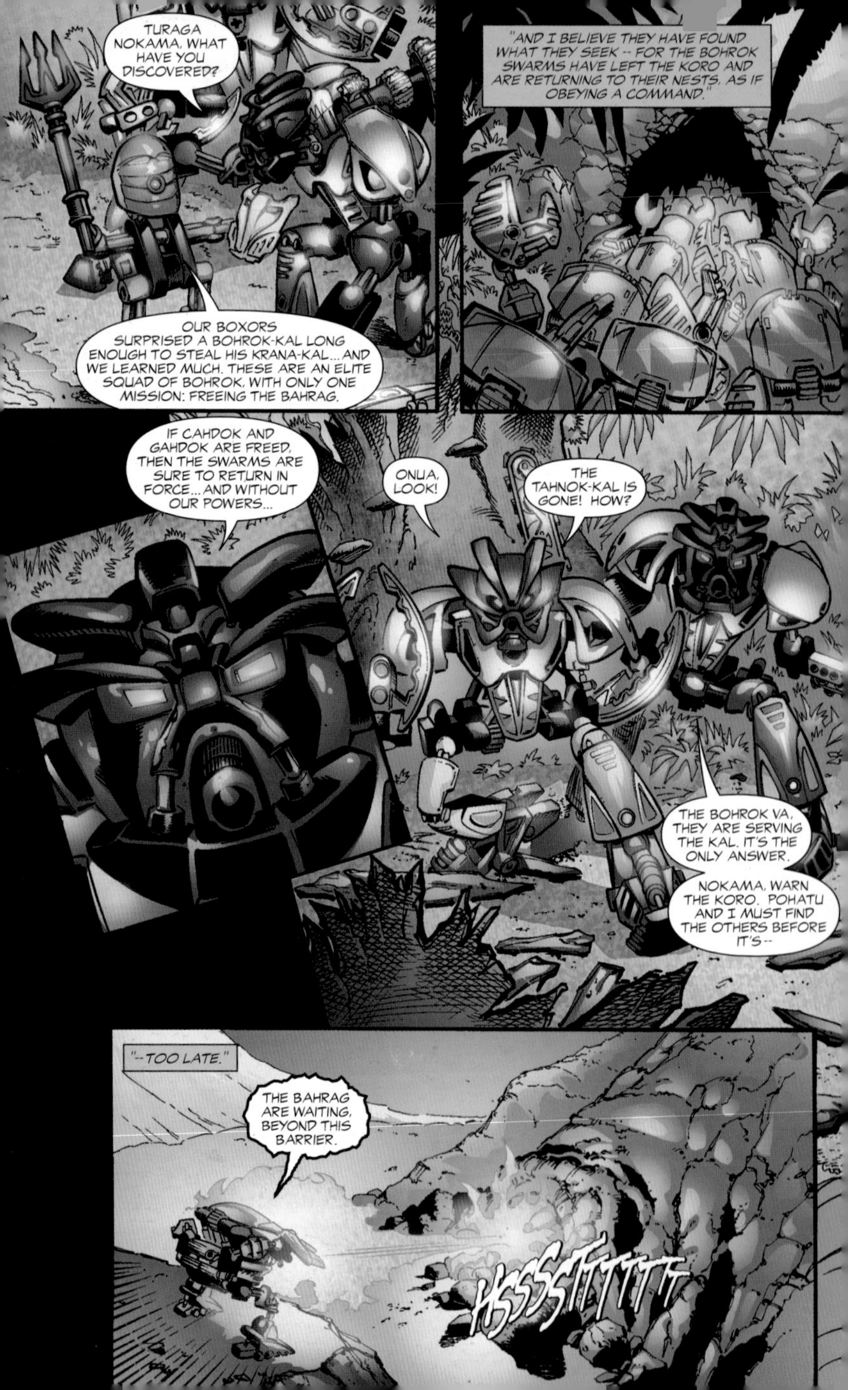
TURAGA NOKAMA, WHAT HAVE YOU DISCOVERED?
OUR BOXORS SURPRISED A BOHROK-KAL LONG ENOUGH TO STEAL HIS KRANA-KAL... AND WE LEARNED MUCH. THESE ARE AN ELITE SQUAD OF BOHROK, WITH ONLY ONE MISSION: FREEING THE BAHRAG.
"AND I BELIEVE THEY HAVE FOUND WHAT THEY SEEK -- FOR THE BOHROK SWARMS HAVE LEFT THE KORO AND ARE RETURNING TO THEIR NESTS, AS IF OBEYING A COMMAND."
IF CAHDOK AND GAHDOK ARE FREED, THEN THE SWARMS ARE SURE TO RETURN IN FORCE... AND WITHOUT OUR POWERS...
ONUA, LOOK!
THE TAHNOK-KAL IS GONE! HOW?
THE BOHROK VA, THEY ARE SERVING THE KAL. IT'S THE ONLY ANSWER.
NOKAMA, WARN THE KORO. POHATU AND I MUST FIND THE OTHERS BEFORE IT'S--
"--TOO LATE."
THE BAHRAG ARE WAITING, BEYOND THIS BARRIER.
HSSSSTTTTTT

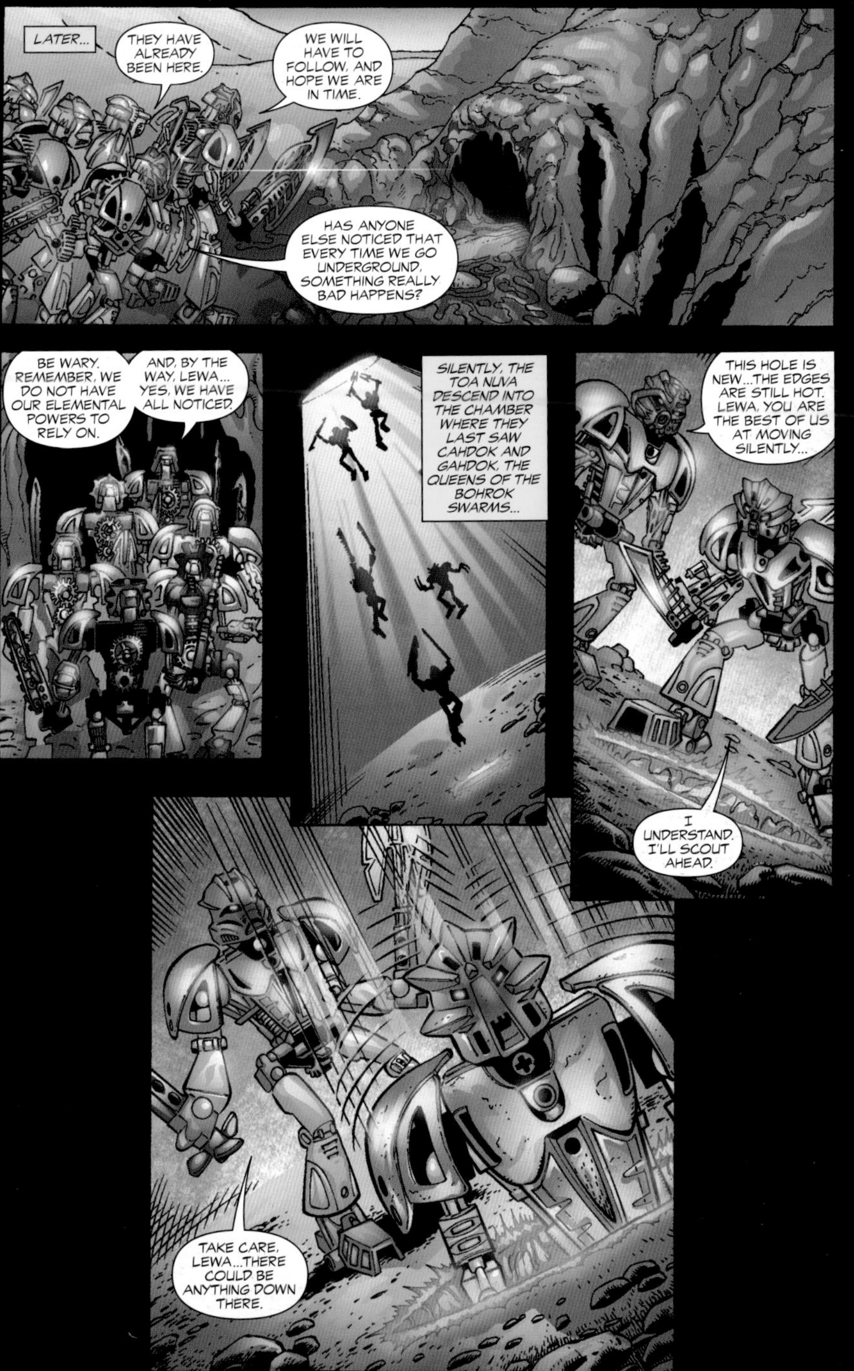
LATER...
THEY HAVE ALREADY BEEN HERE.
WE WILL HAVE TO FOLLOW, AND HOPE WE ARE IN TIME.
HAS ANYONE ELSE NOTICED THAT EVERY TIME WE GO UNDERGROUND, SOMETHING REALLY BAD HAPPENS?
BE WARY. REMEMBER, WE DO NOT HAVE OUR ELEMENTAL POWERS TO RELY ON.
AND, BY THE WAY, LEWA... YES, WE HAVE ALL NOTICED.
SILENTLY, THE TOA NUVA DESCEND INTO THE CHAMBER WHERE THEY LAST SAW CAHDOK AND GAHDOK, THE QUEENS OF THE BOHROK SWARMS...
THIS HOLE IS NEW...THE EDGES ARE STILL HOT. LEWA, YOU ARE THE BEST OF US AT MOVING SILENTLY...
I UNDERSTAND. I'LL SCOUT AHEAD.
TAKE CARE, LEWA...THERE COULD BE ANYTHING DOWN THERE.

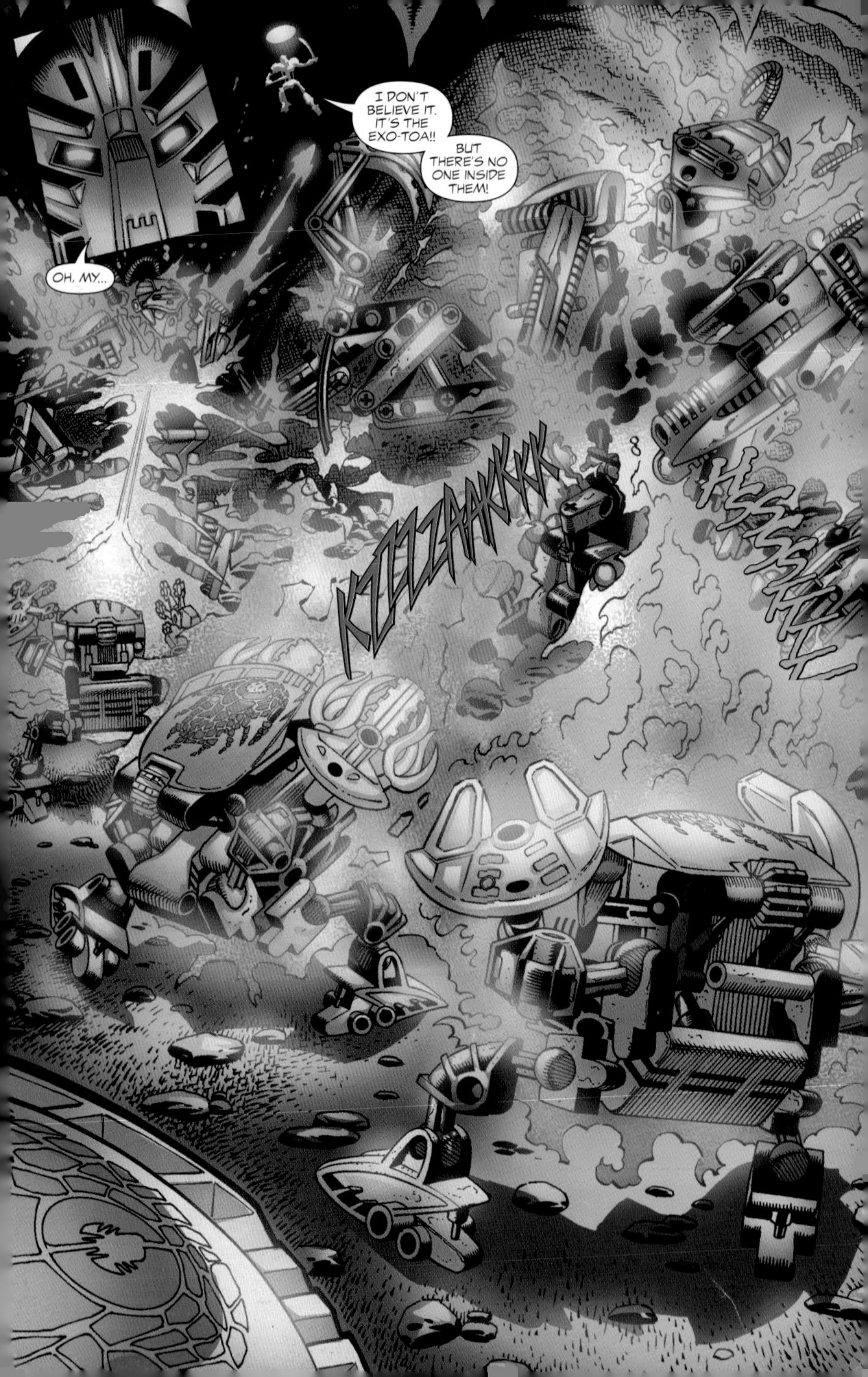
I DON'T BELIEVE IT. IT'S THE EXO-TOA!!
BUT THERE'S NO ONE INSIDE THEM!
OH, MY...
KZZZZAAKKKK
HSSSSKKKK

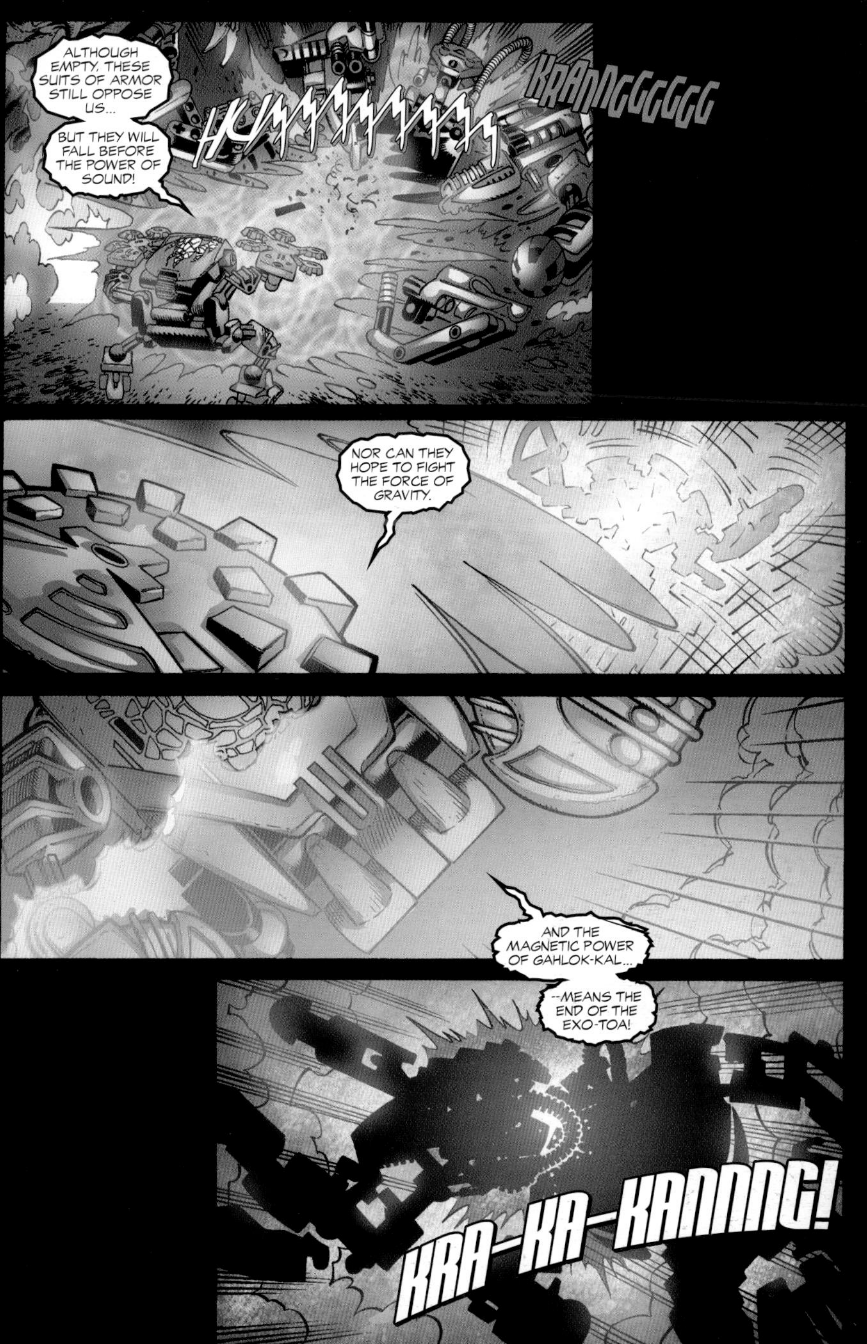
ALTHOUGH EMPTY, THESE SUITS OF ARMOR STILL OPPOSE US...
BUT THEY WILL FALL BEFORE THE POWER OF SOUND!
KRANNGGGGGG
NOR CAN THEY HOPE TO FIGHT THE FORCE OF GRAVITY.
AND THE MAGNETIC POWER OF GAHLOK-KAL...
--MEANS THE END OF THE EXO-TOA!
KRA-KA-KANNNG!

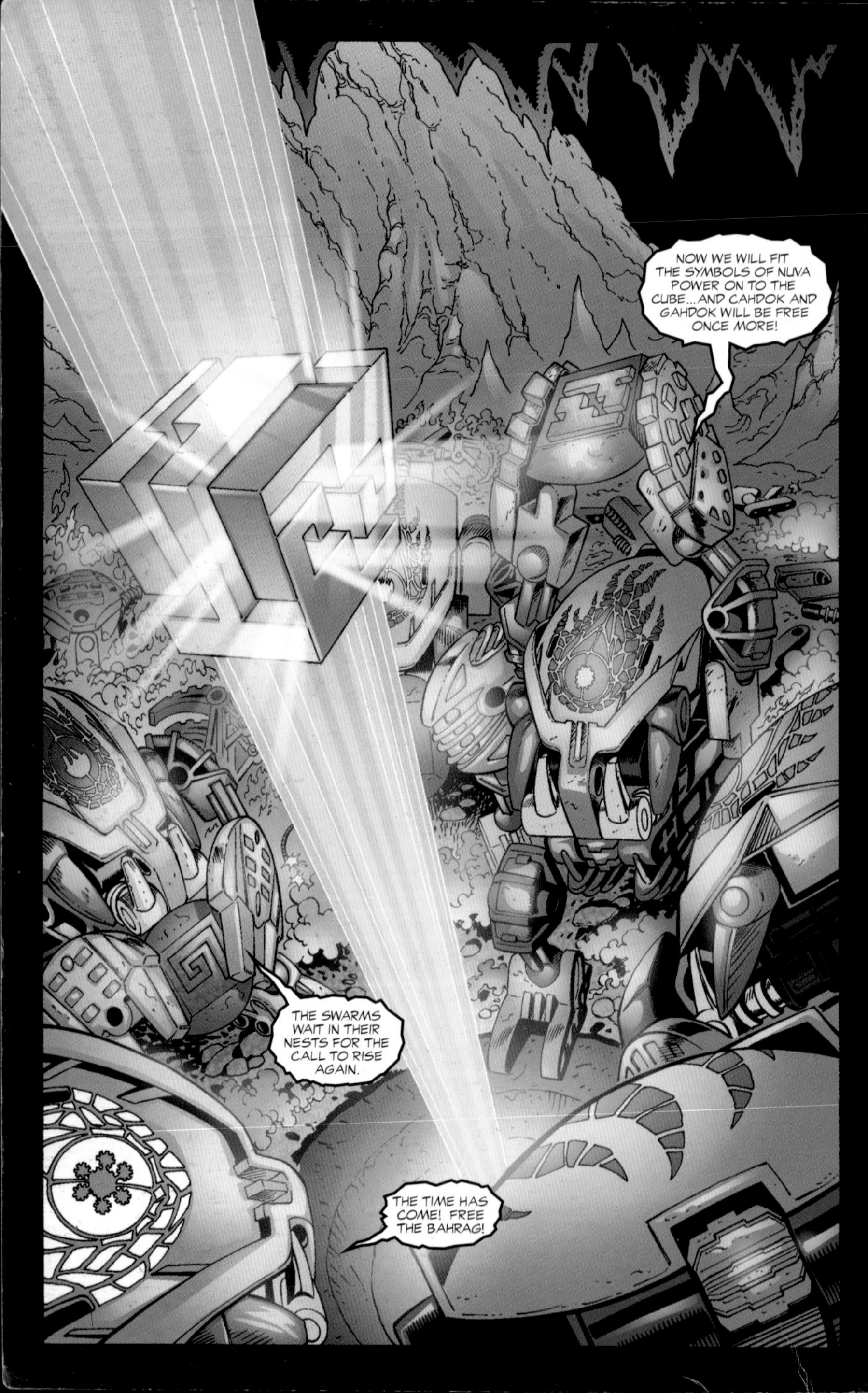
NOW WE WILL FIT THE SYMBOLS OF NUVA POWER ON TO THE CUBE... AND CAHDOK AND GAHDOK WILL BE FREE ONCE MORE!
THE SWARMS WAIT IN THEIR NESTS FOR THE CALL TO RISE AGAIN.
THE TIME HAS COME! FREE THE BAHRAG!

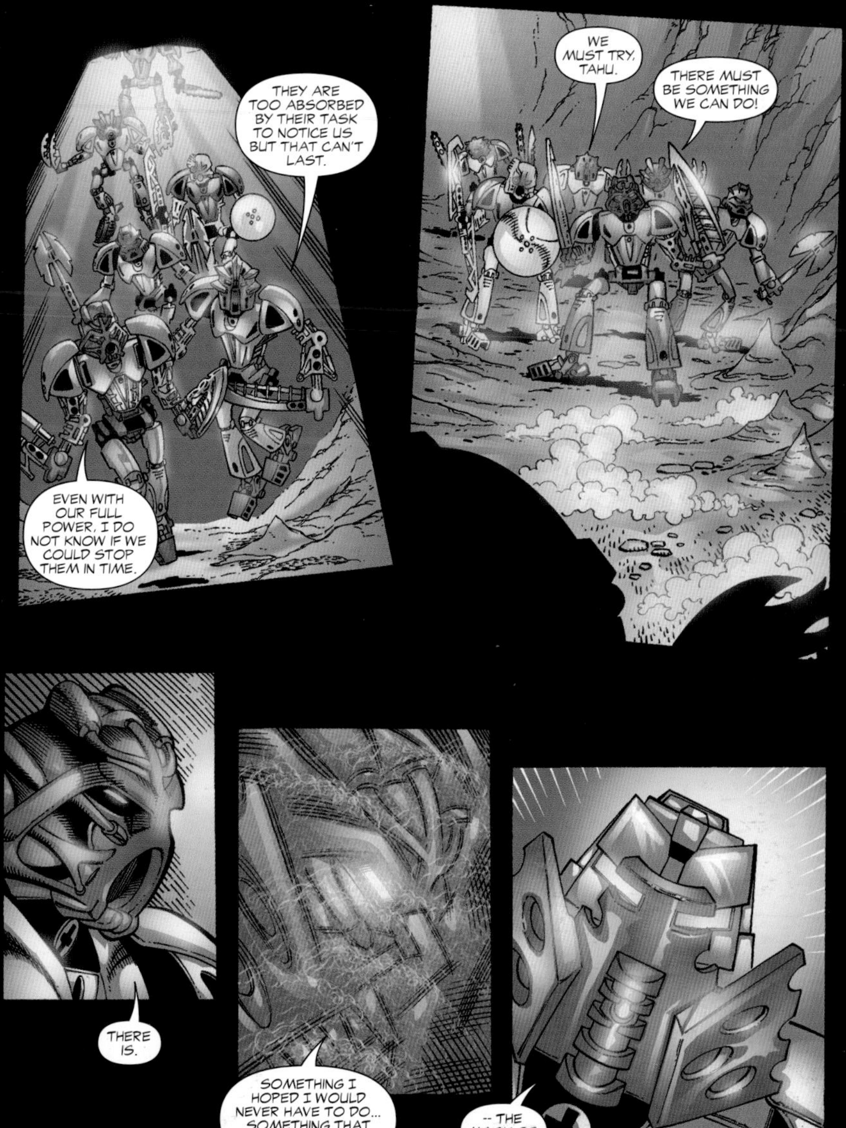
THEY ARE TOO ABSORBED BY THEIR TASK TO NOTICE US BUT THAT CAN'T LAST.
EVEN WITH OUR FULL POWER, I DO NOT KNOW IF WE COULD STOP THEM IN TIME.
WE MUST TRY, TAHU.
THERE MUST BE SOMETHING WE CAN DO!
THERE IS.
SOMETHING I HOPED I WOULD NEVER HAVE TO DO... SOMETHING THAT COULD MEAN THE END OF EVERYTHING.
I CALL UPON--
-- THE MASK OF TIME!

END CHAPTER TWO

CHALLENGE OF THE RAHKSHI
CHAPTER THREE

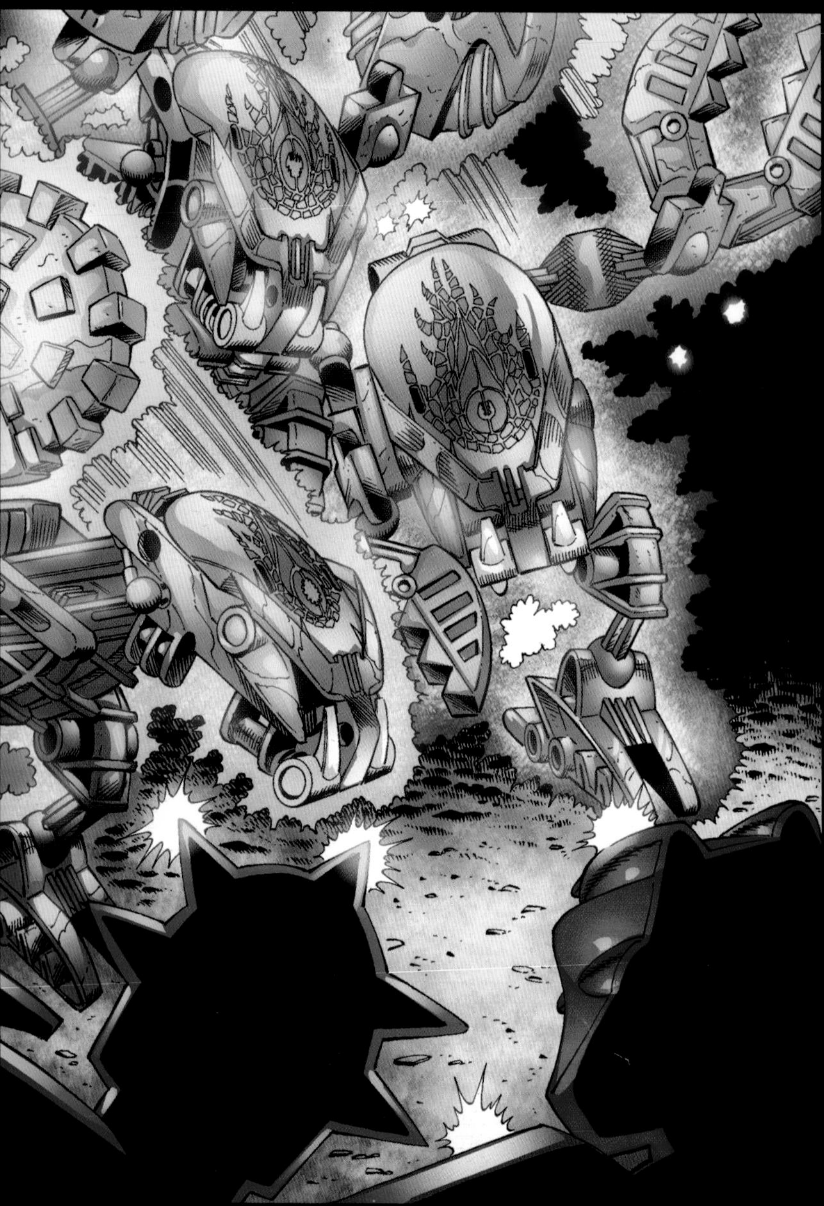

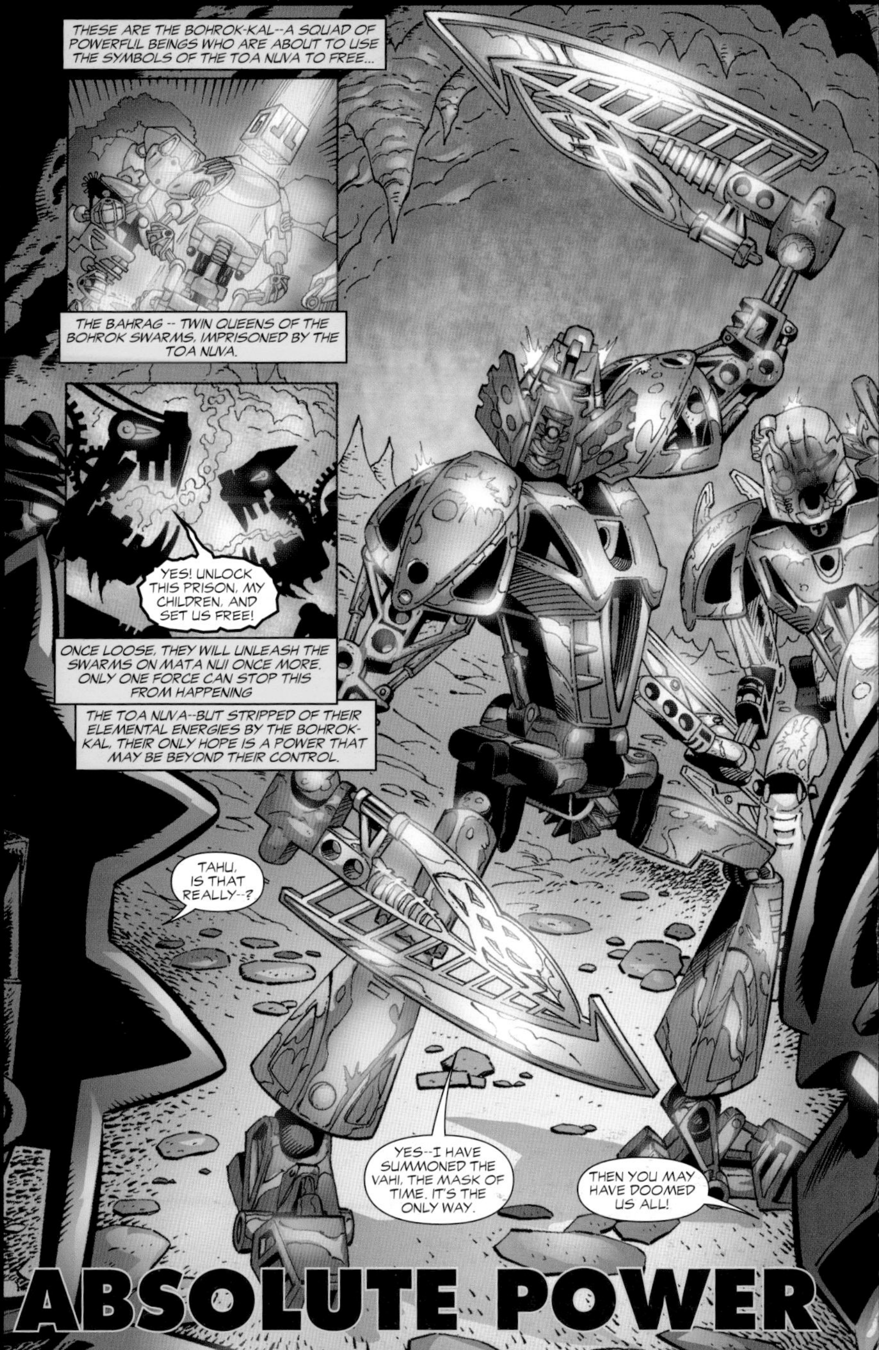
THESE ARE THE BOHROK-KAL--A SQUAD OF POWERFUL BEINGS WHO ARE ABOUT TO USE THE SYMBOLS OF THE TOA NUVA TO FREE...
THE BAHRAG -- TWIN QUEENS OF THE BOHROK SWARMS, IMPRISONED BY THE TOA NUVA.
YES! UNLOCK THIS PRISON, MY CHILDREN, AND SET US FREE!
ONCE LOOSE, THEY WILL UNLEASH THE SWARMS ON MATA NUI ONCE MORE. ONLY ONE FORCE CAN STOP THIS FROM HAPPENING
THE TOA NUVA--BUT STRIPPED OF THEIR ELEMENTAL ENERGIES BY THE BOHROK-KAL, THEIR ONLY HOPE IS A POWER THAT MAY BE BEYOND THEIR CONTROL.
TAHU, IS THAT REALLY--?
YES--I HAVE SUMMONED THE VAHI, THE MASK OF TIME. IT'S THE ONLY WAY.
THEN YOU MAY HAVE DOOMED US ALL!
ABSOLUTE POWER

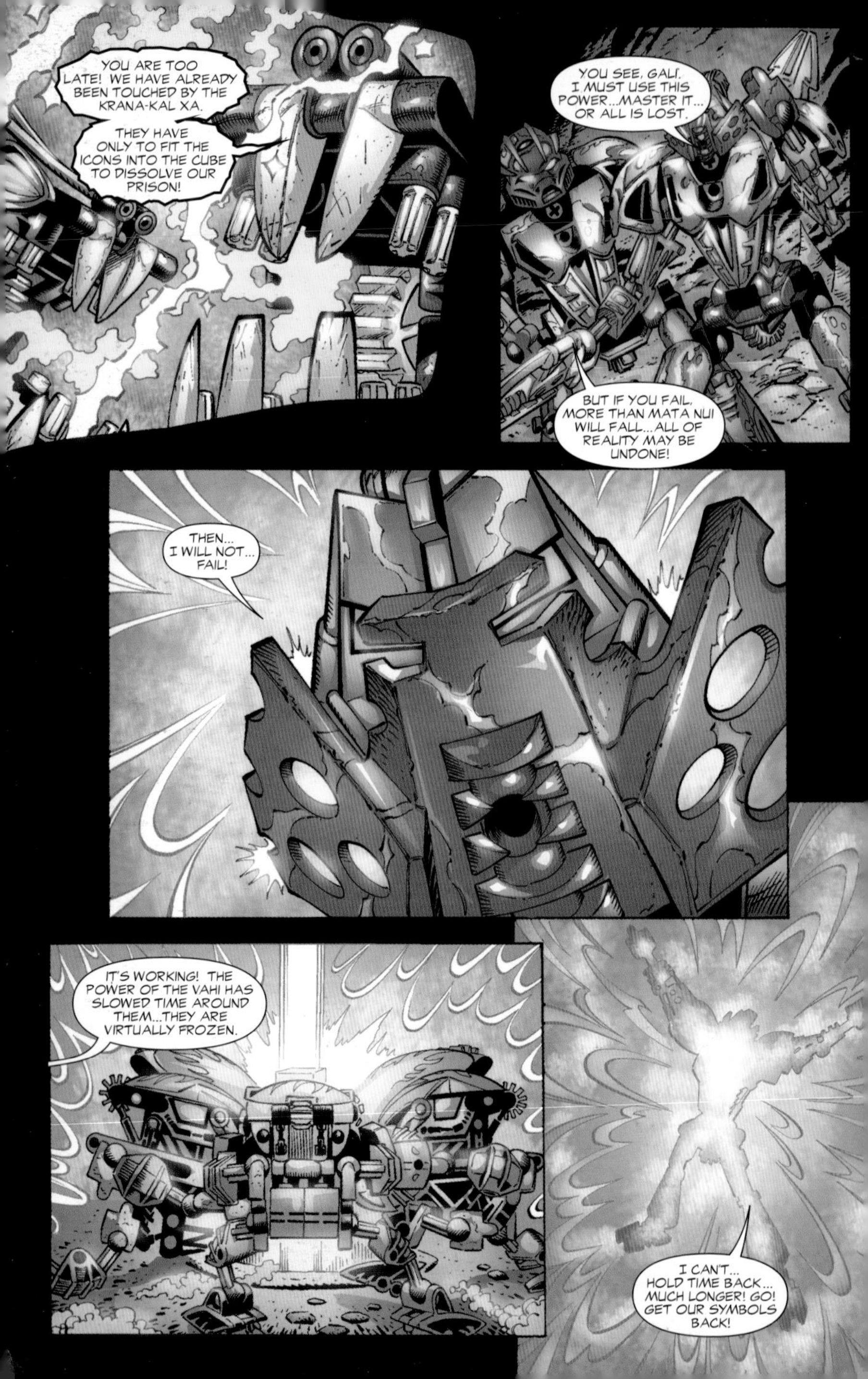
YOU ARE TOO LATE! WE HAVE ALREADY BEEN TOUCHED BY THE KRANA-KAL XA.
THEY HAVE ONLY TO FIT THE ICONS INTO THE CUBE TO DISSOLVE OUR PRISON!
YOU SEE, GALI. I MUST USE THIS POWER...MASTER IT... OR ALL IS LOST.
BUT IF YOU FAIL, MORE THAN MATA NUI WILL FALL...ALL OF REALITY MAY BE UNDONE!
THEN... I WILL NOT... FAIL!
IT'S WORKING! THE POWER OF THE VAHI HAS SLOWED TIME AROUND THEM...THEY ARE VIRTUALLY FROZEN.
I CAN'T... HOLD TIME BACK... MUCH LONGER! GO! GET OUR SYMBOLS BACK!

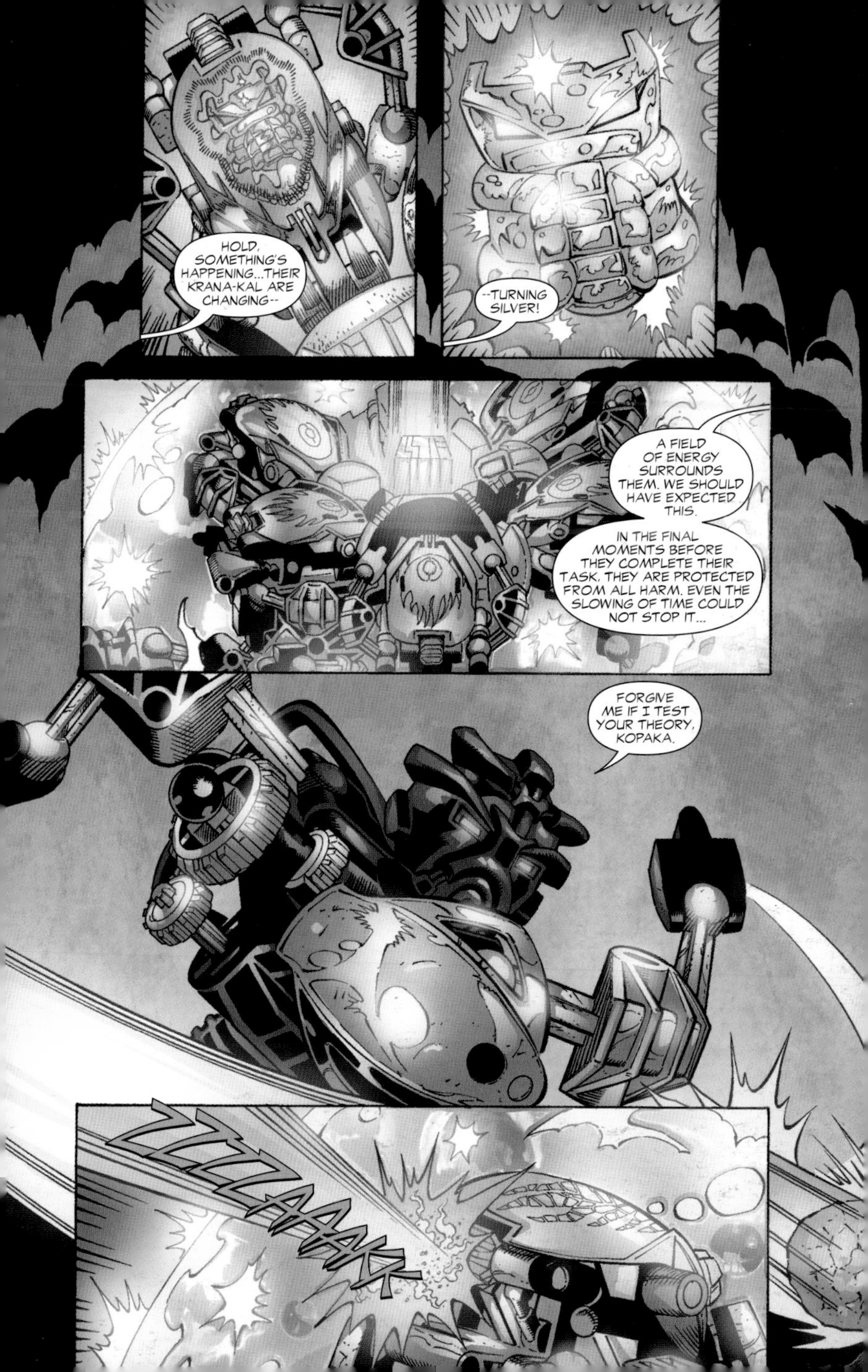
HOLD, SOMETHING'S HAPPENING...THEIR KRANA-KAL ARE CHANGING--
--TURNING SILVER!
A FIELD OF ENERGY SURROUNDS THEM. WE SHOULD HAVE EXPECTED THIS.
IN THE FINAL MOMENTS BEFORE THEY COMPLETE THEIR TASK, THEY ARE PROTECTED FROM ALL HARM. EVEN THE SLOWING OF TIME COULD NOT STOP IT...
FORGIVE ME IF I TEST YOUR THEORY, KOPAKA.
ZZZZAAAKK

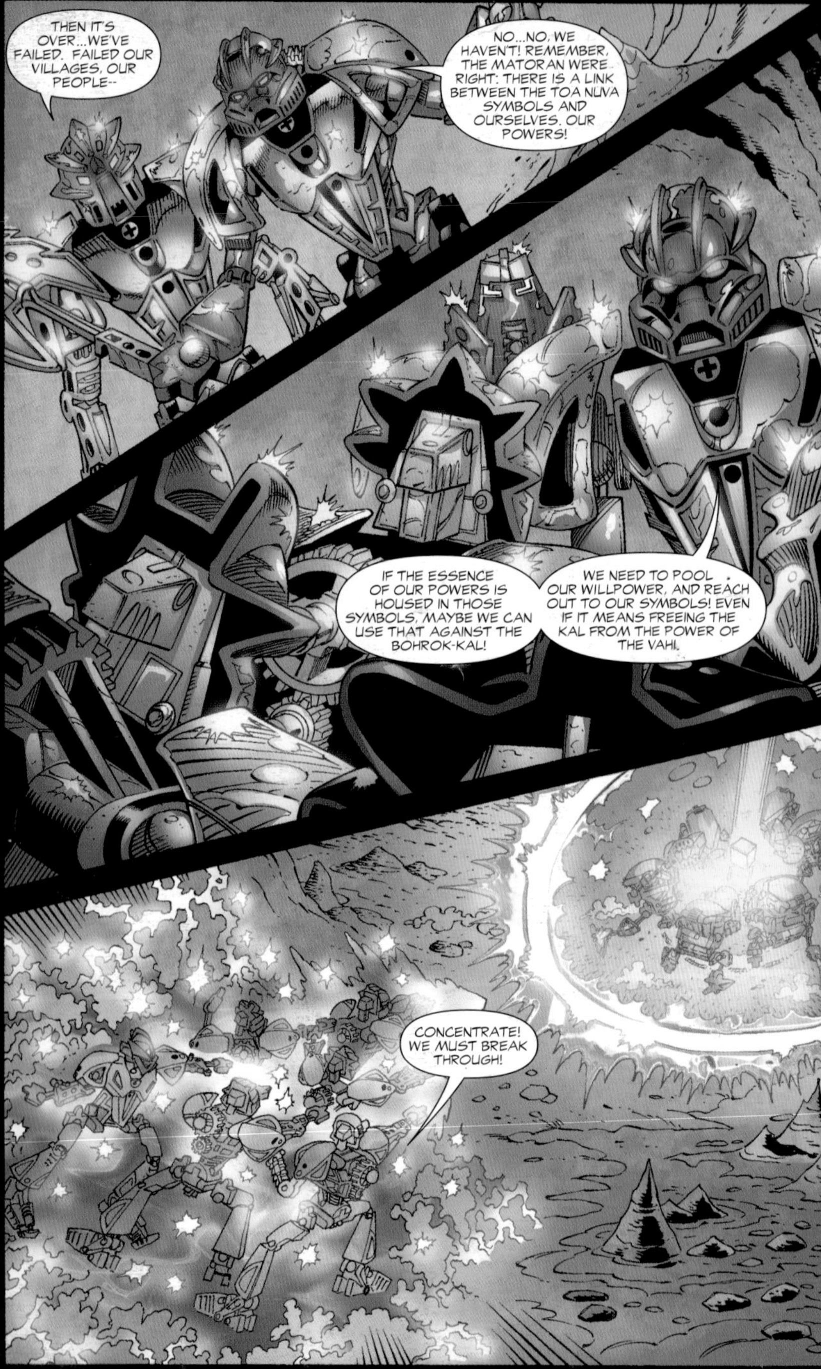
THEN IT'S OVER...WE'VE FAILED. FAILED OUR VILLAGES, OUR PEOPLE--
NO...NO, WE HAVEN'T! REMEMBER, THE MATORAN WERE RIGHT: THERE IS A LINK BETWEEN THE TOA NUVA SYMBOLS AND OURSELVES. OUR POWERS!
IF THE ESSENCE OF OUR POWERS IS HOUSED IN THOSE SYMBOLS, MAYBE WE CAN USE THAT AGAINST THE BOHROK-KAL!
WE NEED TO POOL OUR WILLPOWER, AND REACH OUT TO OUR SYMBOLS! EVEN IF IT MEANS FREEING THE KAL FROM THE POWER OF THE VAHI.
CONCENTRATE! WE MUST BREAK THROUGH!

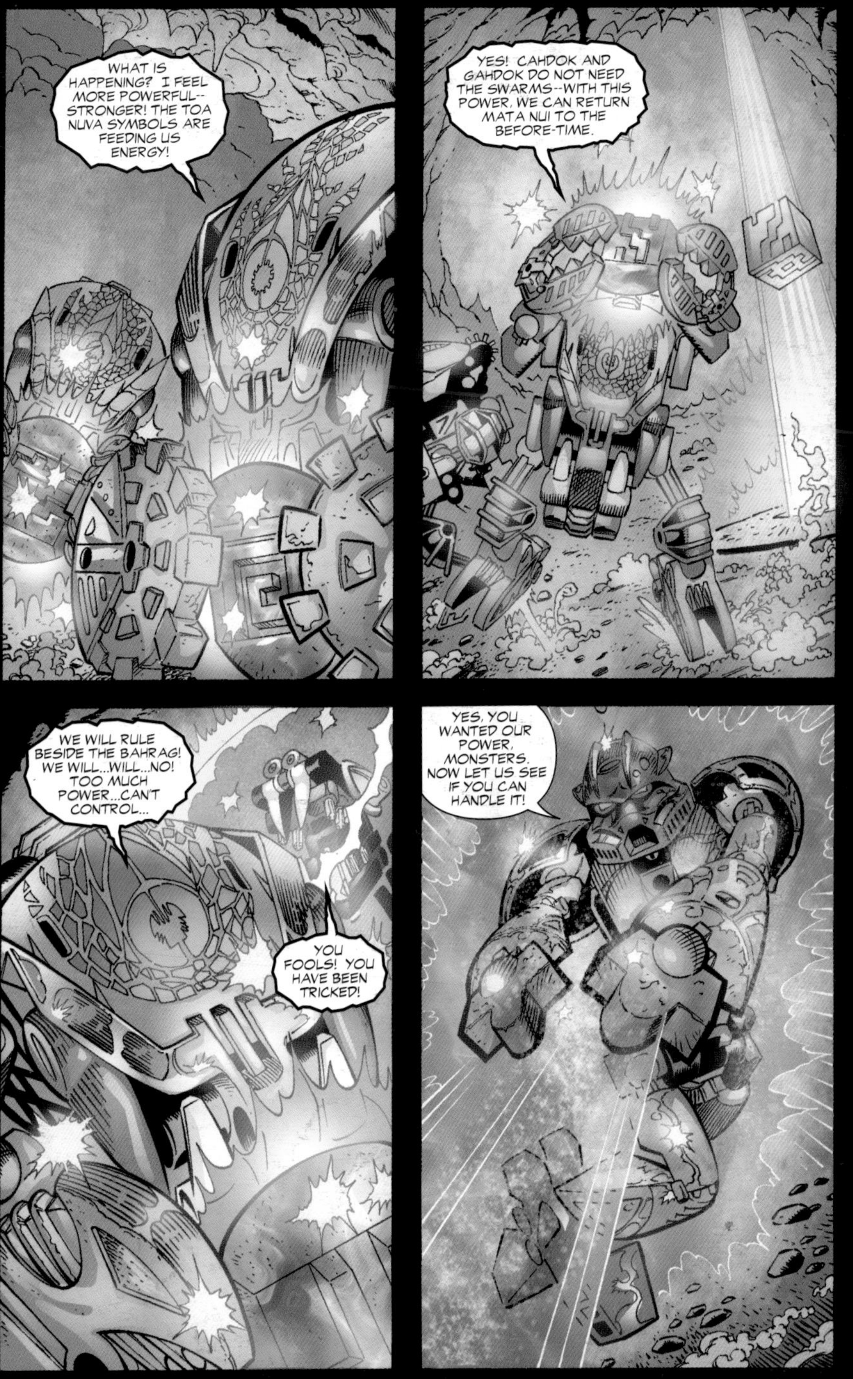
WHAT IS HAPPENING? I FEEL MORE POWERFUL-- STRONGER! THE TOA NUVA SYMBOLS ARE FEEDING US ENERGY!
YES! CAHDOK AND GAHDOK DO NOT NEED THE SWARMS--WITH THIS POWER, WE CAN RETURN MATA NUI TO THE BEFORE-TIME.
WE WILL RULE BESIDE THE BAHRAG! WE WILL...WILL...NO! TOO MUCH POWER...CAN'T CONTROL...
YOU FOOLS! YOU HAVE BEEN TRICKED!
YES, YOU WANTED OUR POWER, MONSTERS. NOW LET US SEE IF YOU CAN HANDLE IT!

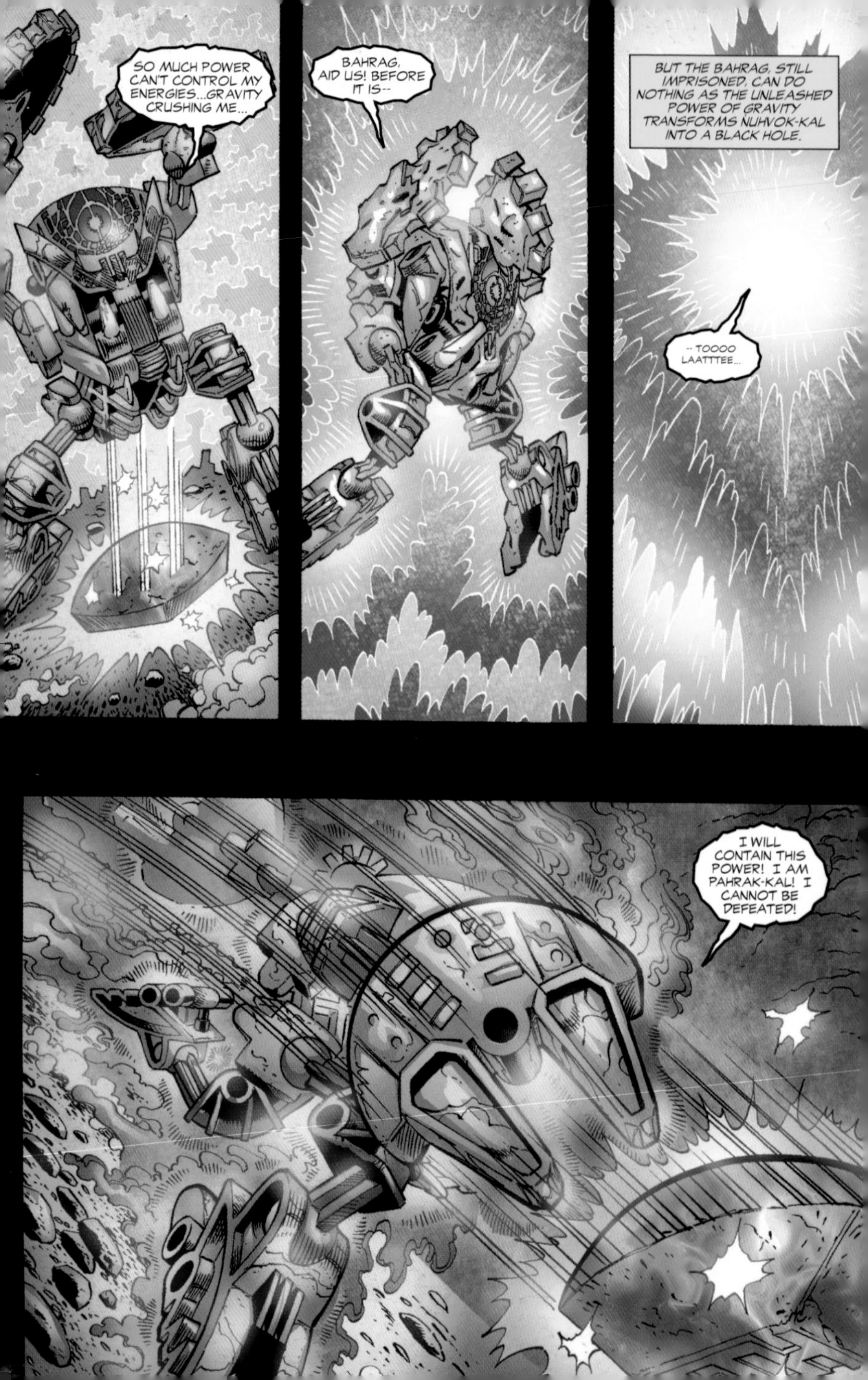
SO MUCH POWER CAN'T CONTROL MY ENERGIES...GRAVITY CRUSHING ME...
BAHRAG, AID US! BEFORE IT IS--
BUT THE BAHRAG, STILL IMPRISONED, CAN DO NOTHING AS THE UNLEASHED POWER OF GRAVITY TRANSFORMS NUHVOK-KAL INTO A BLACK HOLE.
-- TOOOO LAATTTEE...
I WILL CONTAIN THIS POWER! I AM PAHRAK-KAL! I CANNOT BE DEFEATED!

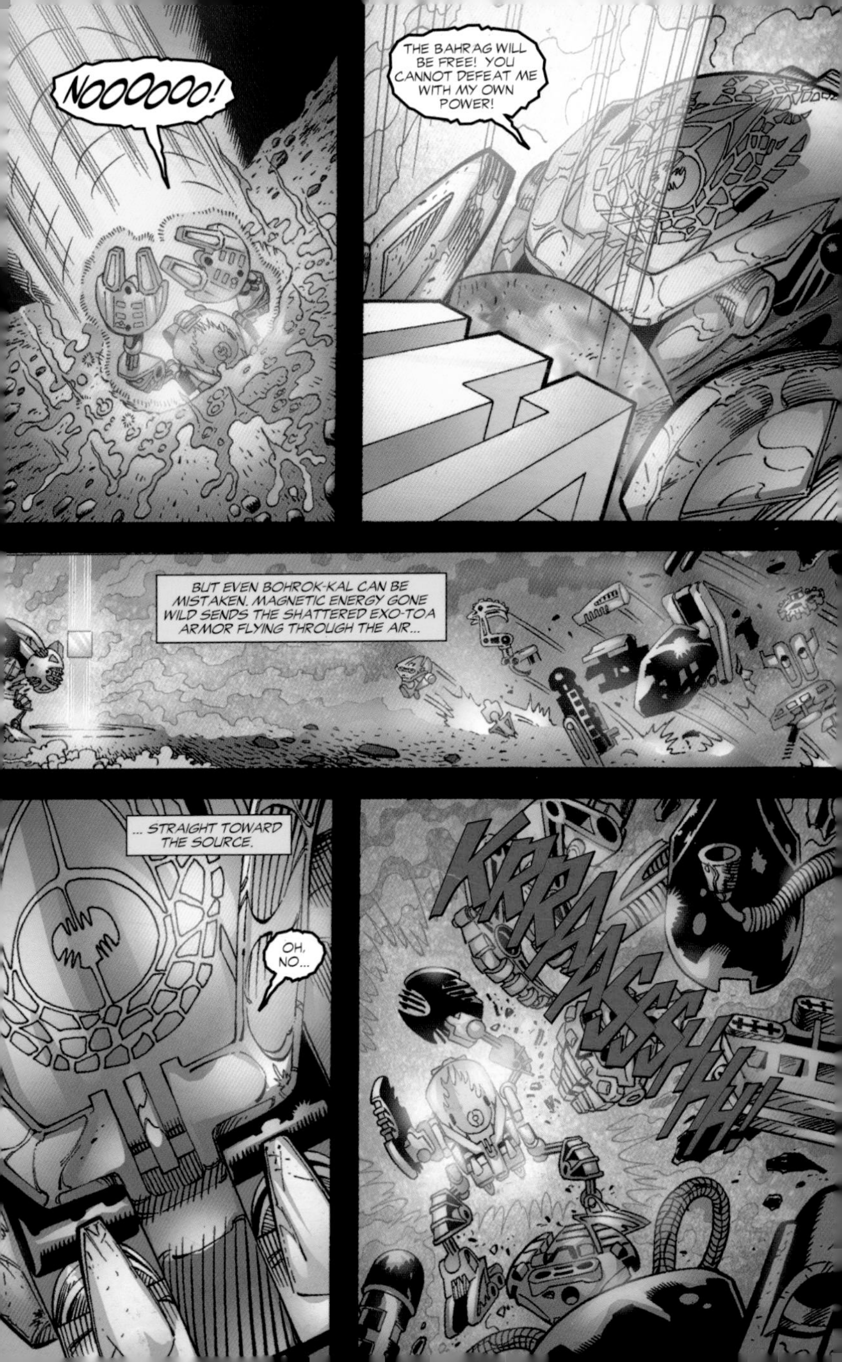
NOOOOOO!
THE BAHRAG WILL BE FREE! YOU CANNOT DEFEAT ME WITH MY OWN POWER!
BUT EVEN BOHROK-KAL CAN BE MISTAKEN. MAGNETIC ENERGY GONE WILD SENDS THE SHATTERED EXO-TOA ARMOR FLYING THROUGH THE AIR...
... STRAIGHT TOWARD THE SOURCE.
OH, NO...
KRRAASSHHH!

LEHVAK-KAL'S VACUUM POWER, UNCONTROLLED, SENDS HIM HURTLING TOWARD THE CEILING...

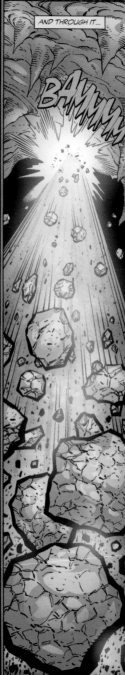

AND THROUGH IT...

BAMMMM

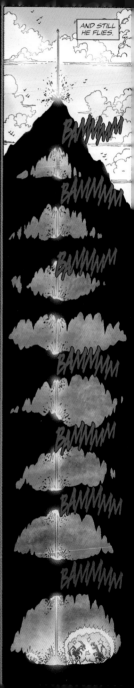

AND STILL HE FLIES.

BAMMMM

BAMMMM

BAMMMM

BAMMMM

BAMMMM

BAMMMM

BAMMMM

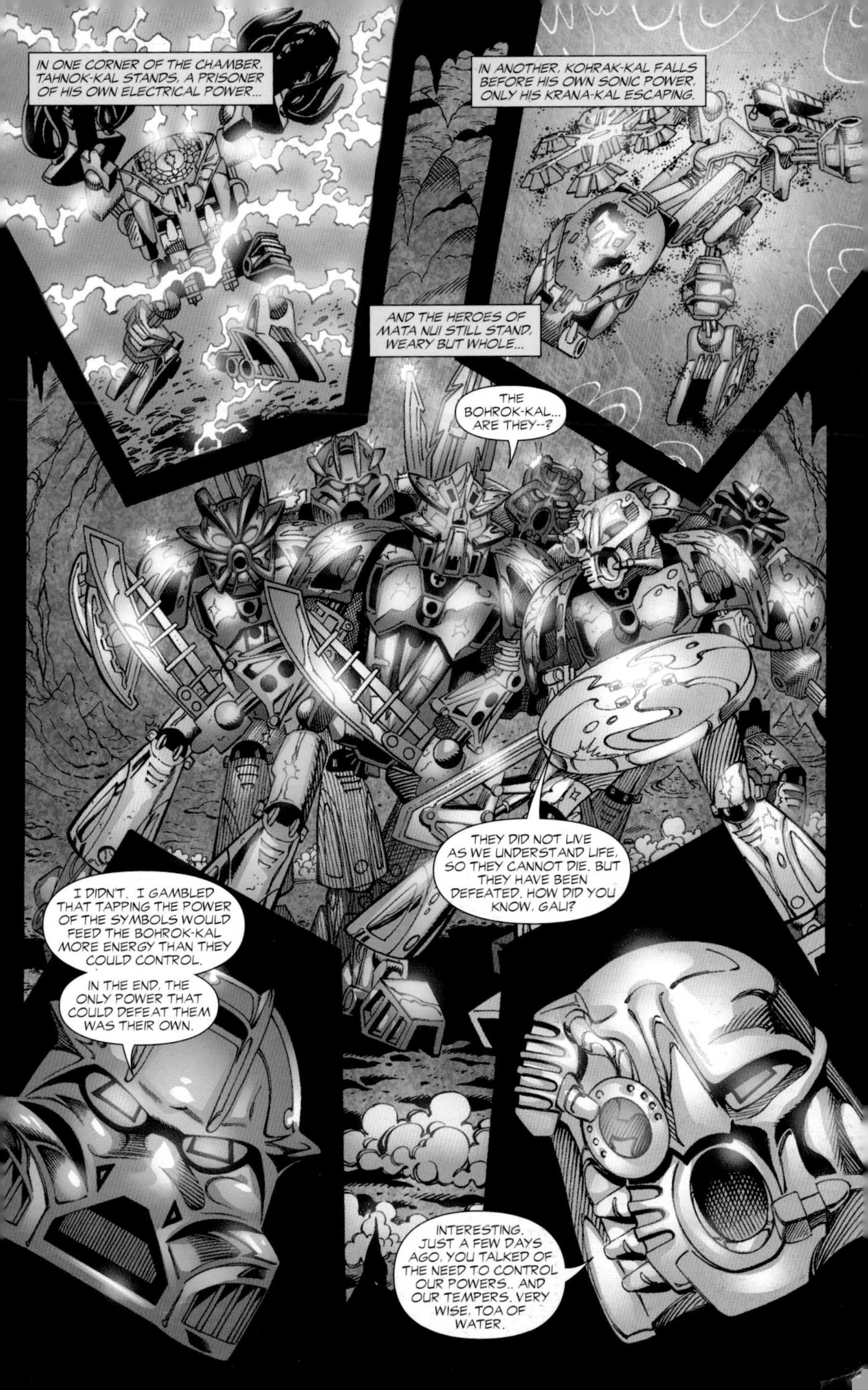
IN ONE CORNER OF THE CHAMBER, TAHNOK-KAL STANDS, A PRISONER OF HIS OWN ELECTRICAL POWER...
IN ANOTHER, KOHRAK-KAL FALLS BEFORE HIS OWN SONIC POWER, ONLY HIS KRANA-KAL ESCAPING.
AND THE HEROES OF MATA NUI STILL STAND, WEARY BUT WHOLE...
THE BOHROK-KAL... ARE THEY--?
THEY DID NOT LIVE AS WE UNDERSTAND LIFE, SO THEY CANNOT DIE. BUT THEY HAVE BEEN DEFEATED. HOW DID YOU KNOW, GALI?
I DIDN'T. I GAMBLED THAT TAPPING THE POWER OF THE SYMBOLS WOULD FEED THE BOHROK-KAL MORE ENERGY THAN THEY COULD CONTROL.
IN THE END, THE ONLY POWER THAT COULD DEFEAT THEM WAS THEIR OWN.
INTERESTING. JUST A FEW DAYS AGO, YOU TALKED OF THE NEED TO CONTROL OUR POWERS.. AND OUR TEMPERS. VERY WISE, TOA OF WATER.

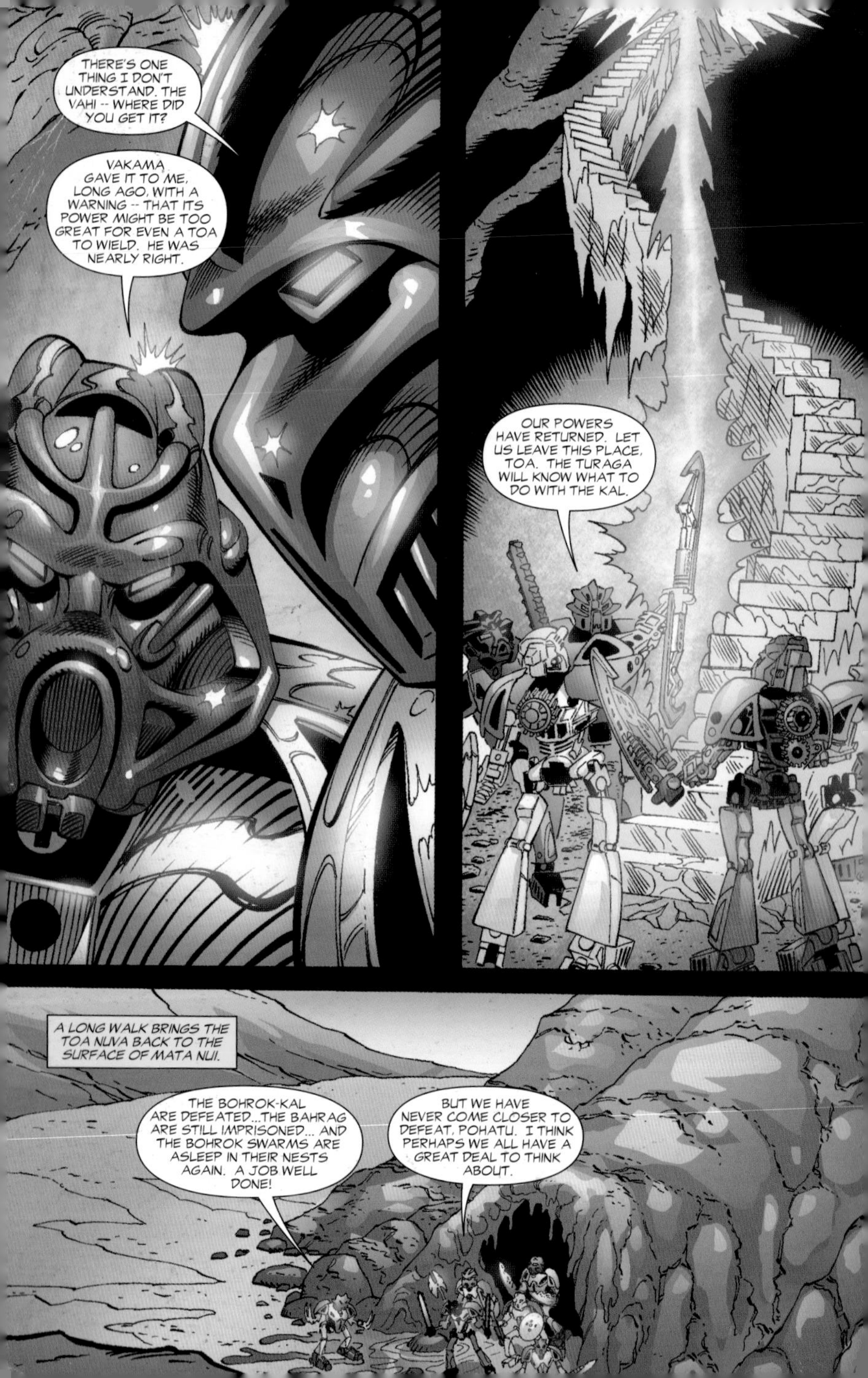
THERE'S ONE THING I DON'T UNDERSTAND. THE VAHI -- WHERE DID YOU GET IT?
VAKAMA GAVE IT TO ME, LONG AGO, WITH A WARNING -- THAT ITS POWER MIGHT BE TOO GREAT FOR EVEN A TOA TO WIELD. HE WAS NEARLY RIGHT.
OUR POWERS HAVE RETURNED. LET US LEAVE THIS PLACE, TOA. THE TURAGA WILL KNOW WHAT TO DO WITH THE KAL.
A LONG WALK BRINGS THE TOA NUVA BACK TO THE SURFACE OF MATA NUI.
THE BOHROK-KAL ARE DEFEATED...THE BAHRAG ARE STILL IMPRISONED... AND THE BOHROK SWARMS ARE ASLEEP IN THEIR NESTS AGAIN. A JOB WELL DONE!
BUT WE HAVE NEVER COME CLOSER TO DEFEAT, POHATU. I THINK PERHAPS WE ALL HAVE A GREAT DEAL TO THINK ABOUT.

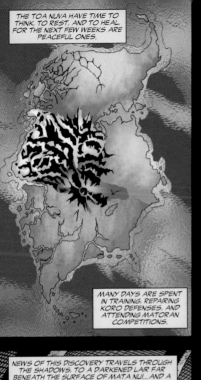

THE TOA NUVA HAVE TIME TO THINK, TO REST, AND TO HEAL FOR THE NEXT FEW WEEKS ARE PEACEFUL ONES.

MANY DAYS ARE SPENT IN TRAINING, REPAIRING KORO DEFENSES, AND ATTENDING MATORAN COMPETITIONS.

BUT THE PEACE IS NOT TO LAST FOR AN AMAZING DISCOVERY SENDS TWO MATORAN OFF IN SEARCH OF A LEGEND.*

*SEE IT ALL IN BIONICLE: THE MASK OF LIGHT DVD

NEWS OF THIS DISCOVERY TRAVELS THROUGH THE SHADOWS, TO A DARKENED LAIR FAR BENEATH THE SURFACE OF MATA NUI...AND A BEING EVEN THE TOA NUVA FEAR.

SO. AGAIN THE PROPHECIES OF THE MATORAN OPPOSE MY WILL.

I SET THE RAHI AGAINST THEM... I UNLEASHED THE BOHROK SWARMS...BUT STILL THEY REFUSED TO BREAK.

KKSSHHH!

NOW THEIR UNITY WILL BE POISONED...THEIR DUTY BROKEN... THEIR DESTINY SHATTERED.

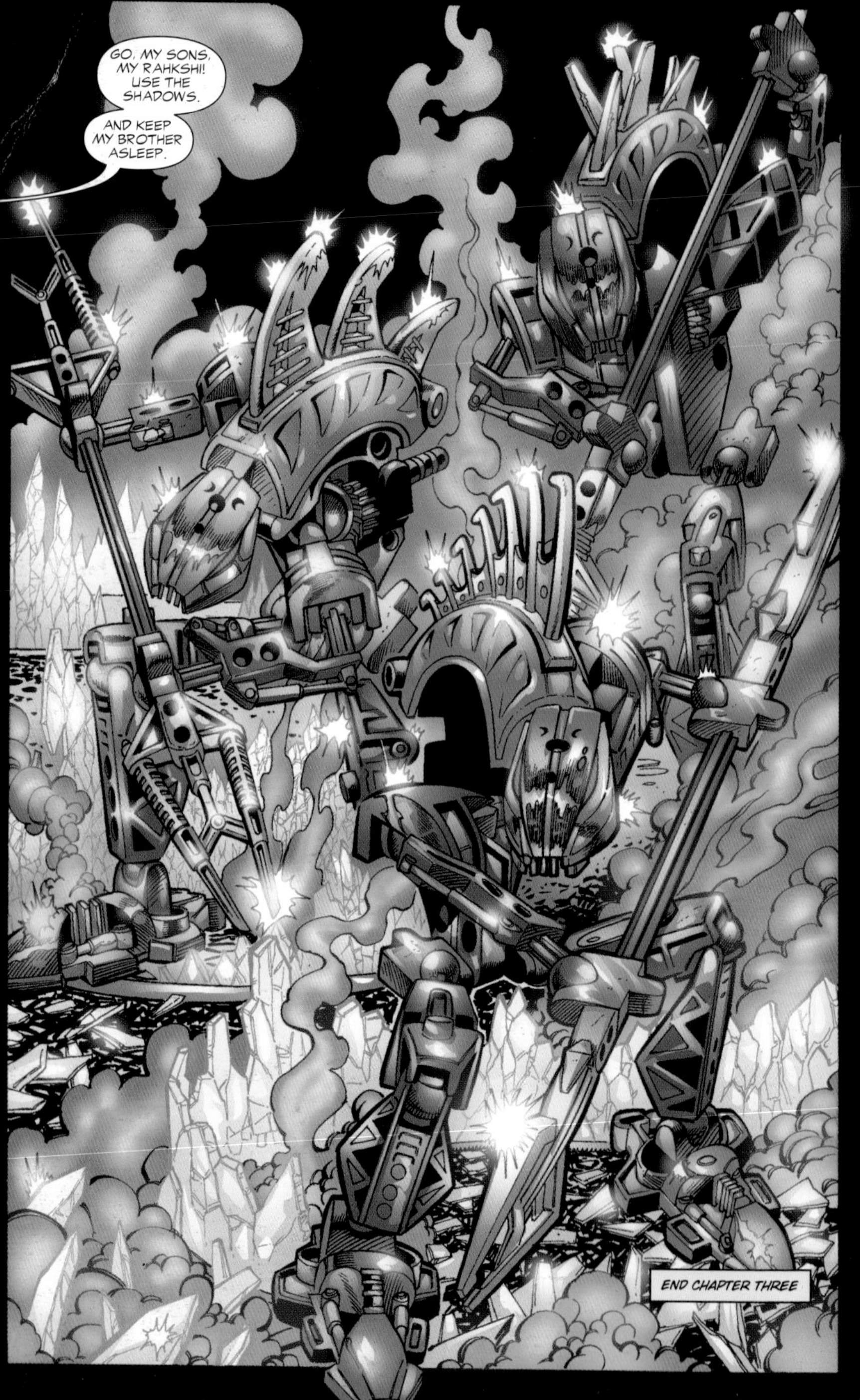
GO, MY SONS, MY RAHKSHI! USE THE SHADOWS.
AND KEEP MY BROTHER ASLEEP.
END CHAPTER THREE

RISE OF THE RAHKSHI
CHAPTER ONE

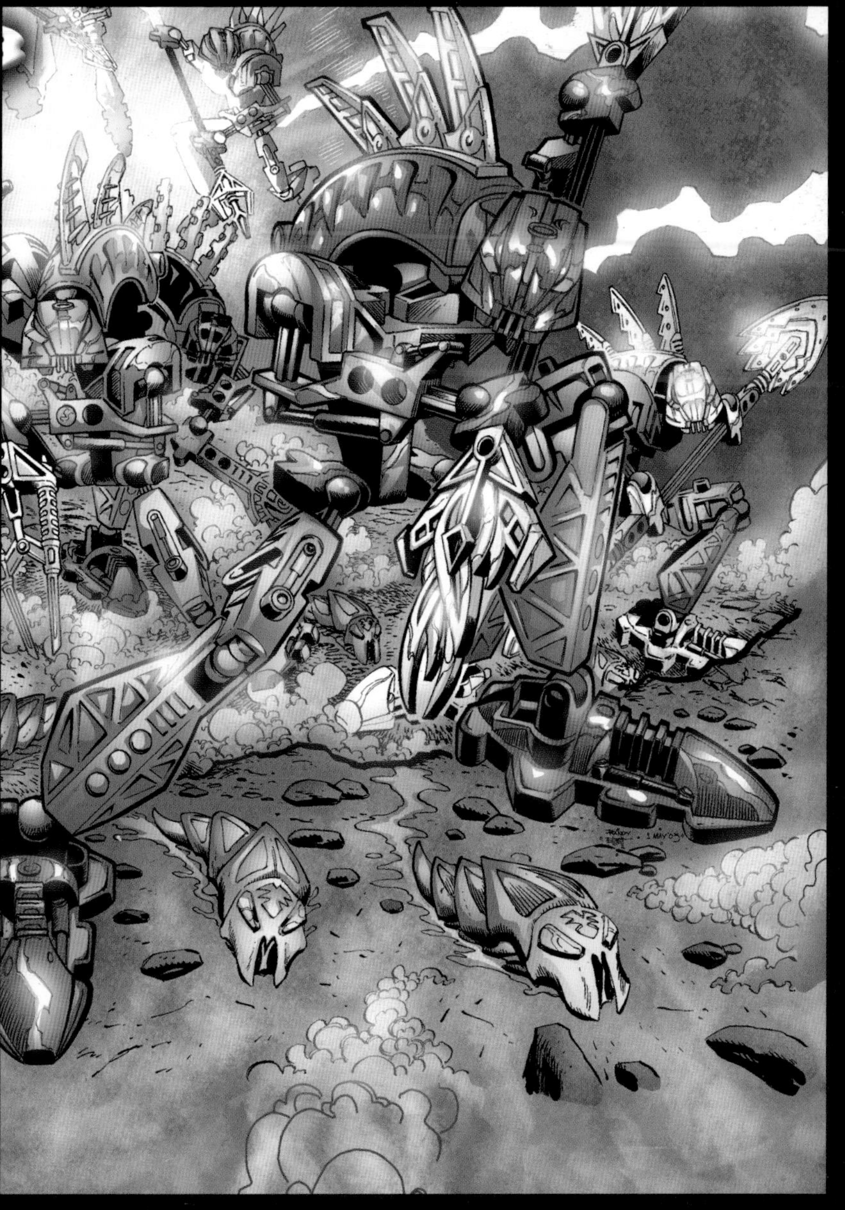

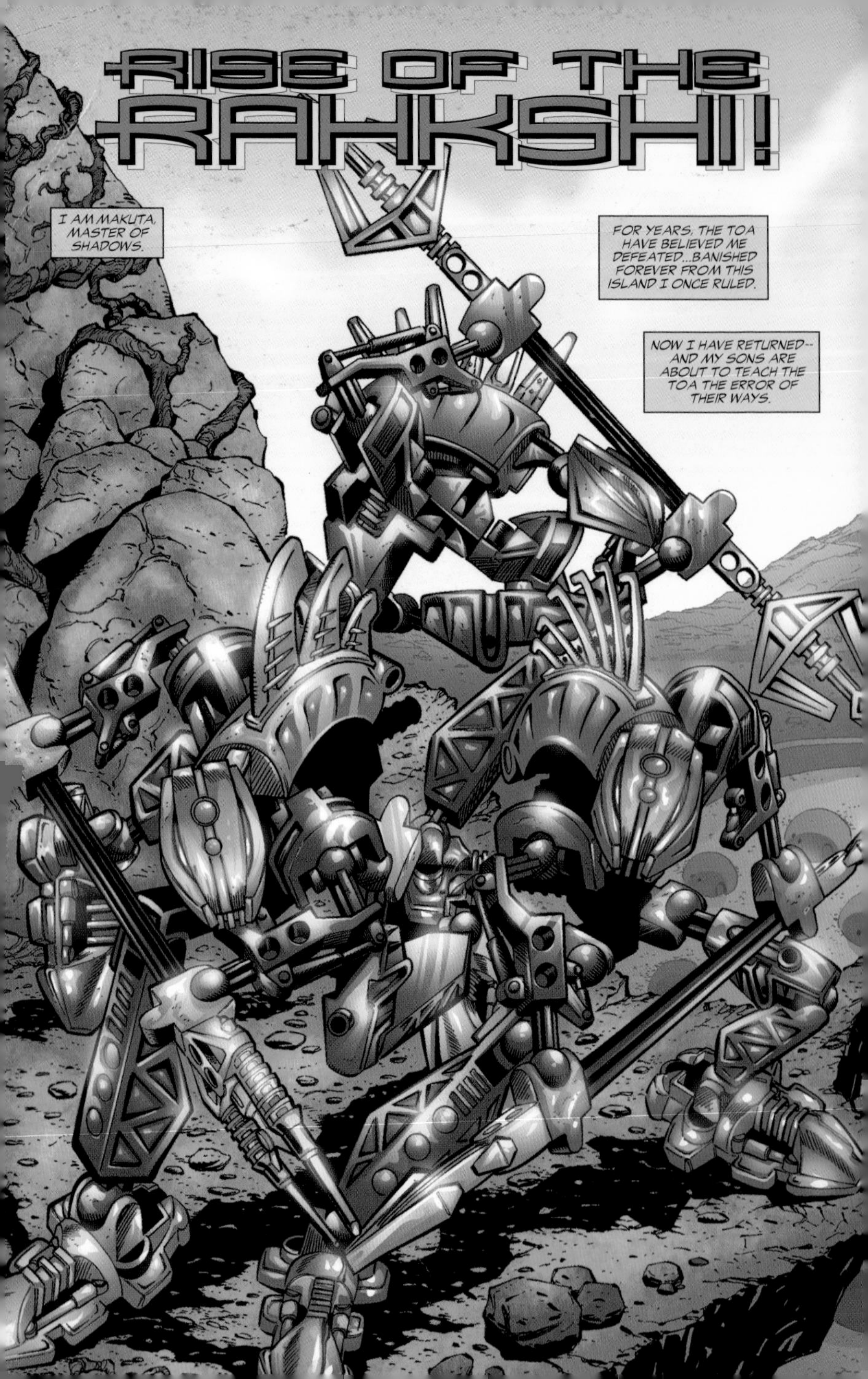
RISE OF THE RAHKSHI!
I AM MAKUTA, MASTER OF SHADOWS.
FOR YEARS, THE TOA HAVE BELIEVED ME DEFEATED...BANISHED FOREVER FROM THIS ISLAND I ONCE RULED.
NOW I HAVE RETURNED-- AND MY SONS ARE ABOUT TO TEACH THE TOA THE ERROR OF THEIR WAYS.

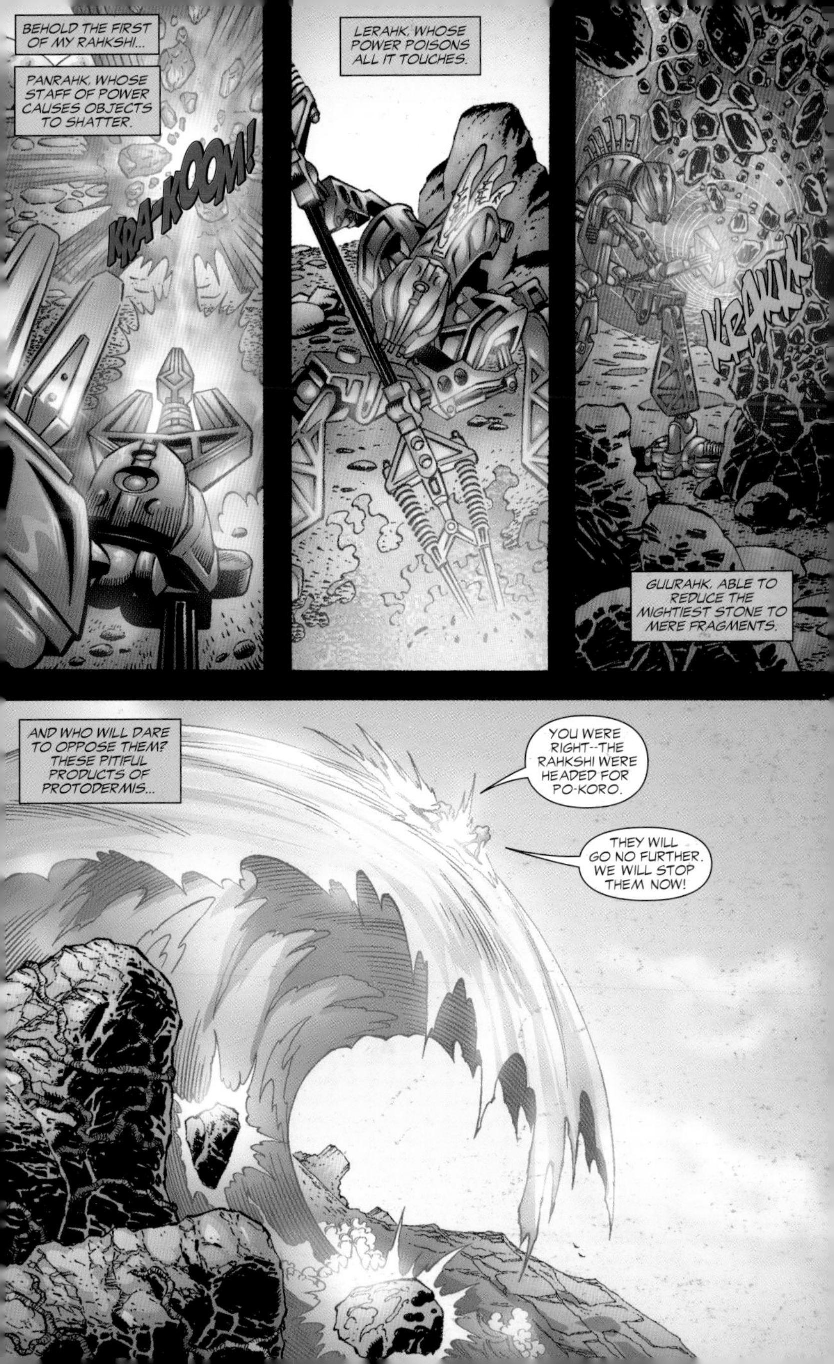
BEHOLD THE FIRST OF MY RAHKSHI...
PANRAHK, WHOSE STAFF OF POWER CAUSES OBJECTS TO SHATTER.
KRA-KOOM!
LERAHK, WHOSE POWER POISONS ALL IT TOUCHES.
GUURAHK, ABLE TO REDUCE THE MIGHTIEST STONE TO MERE FRAGMENTS.
AND WHO WILL DARE TO OPPOSE THEM? THESE PITIFUL PRODUCTS OF PROTODERMIS...
YOU WERE RIGHT--THE RAHKSHI WERE HEADED FOR PO-KORO.
THEY WILL GO NO FURTHER. WE WILL STOP THEM NOW!

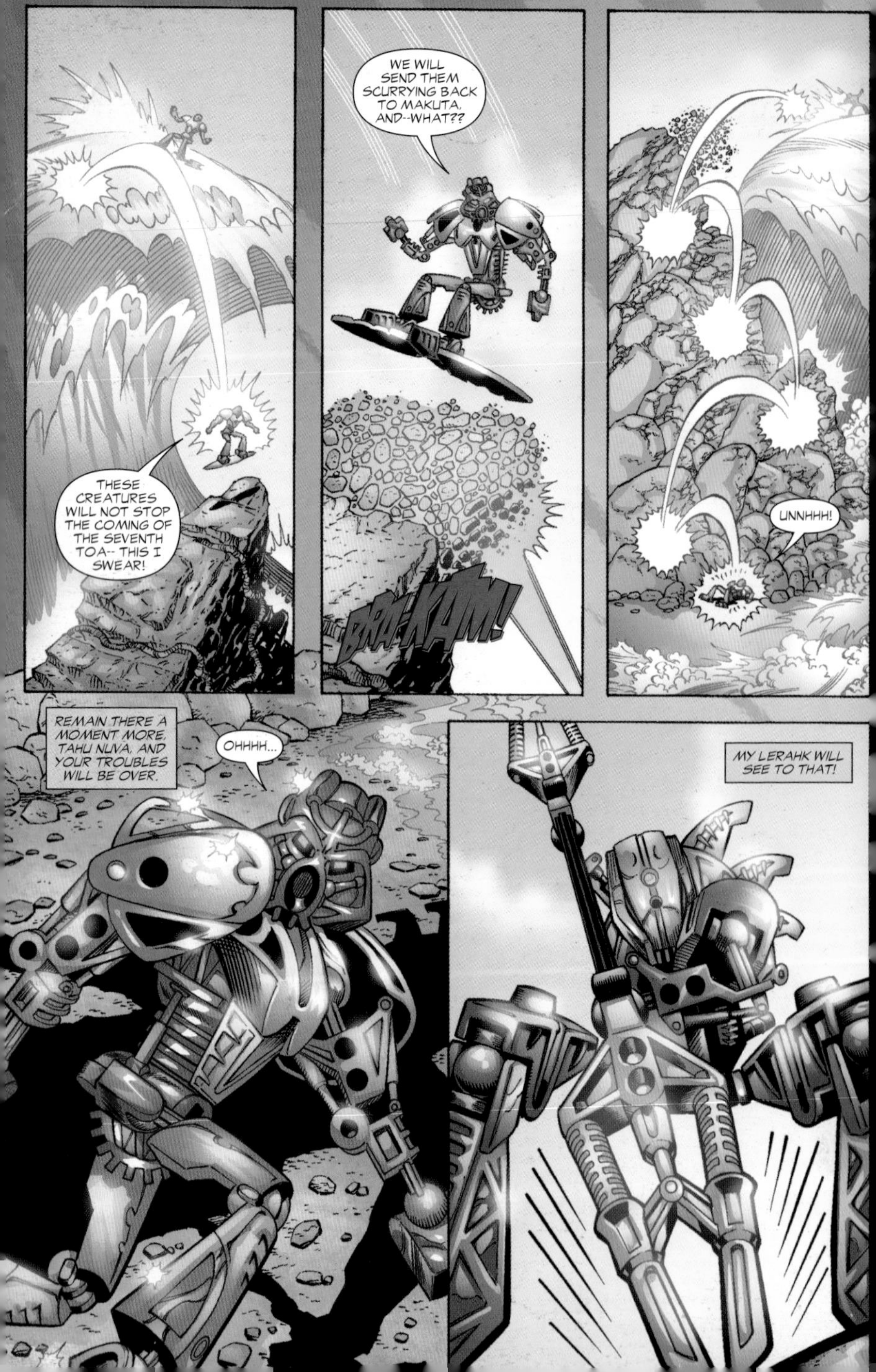
THESE CREATURES WILL NOT STOP THE COMING OF THE SEVENTH TOA-- THIS I SWEAR!
WE WILL SEND THEM SCURRYING BACK TO MAKUTA, AND--WHAT??
BRA-KAM!
UNNHHH!
REMAIN THERE A MOMENT MORE, TAHU NUVA, AND YOUR TROUBLES WILL BE OVER.
OHHHH...
MY LERAHK WILL SEE TO THAT!

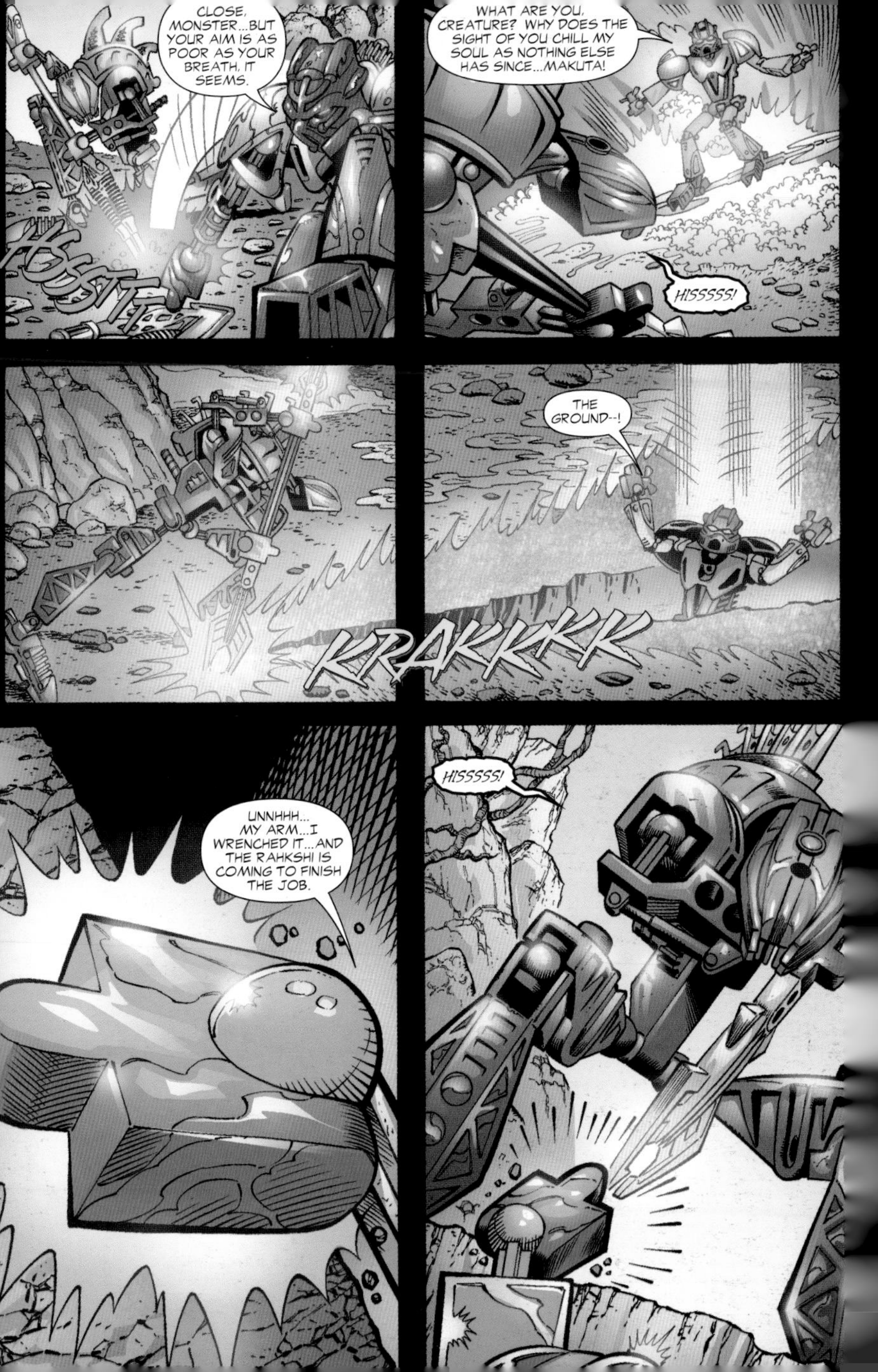
CLOSE, MONSTER...BUT YOUR AIM IS AS POOR AS YOUR BREATH, IT SEEMS.
HSSSTT
WHAT ARE YOU, CREATURE? WHY DOES THE SIGHT OF YOU CHILL MY SOUL AS NOTHING ELSE HAS SINCE...MAKUTA!
HISSSSS!
THE GROUND--!
KRAKKKK
UNNHHH... MY ARM...I WRENCHED IT...AND THE RAHKSHI IS COMING TO FINISH THE JOB.
HISSSSS!

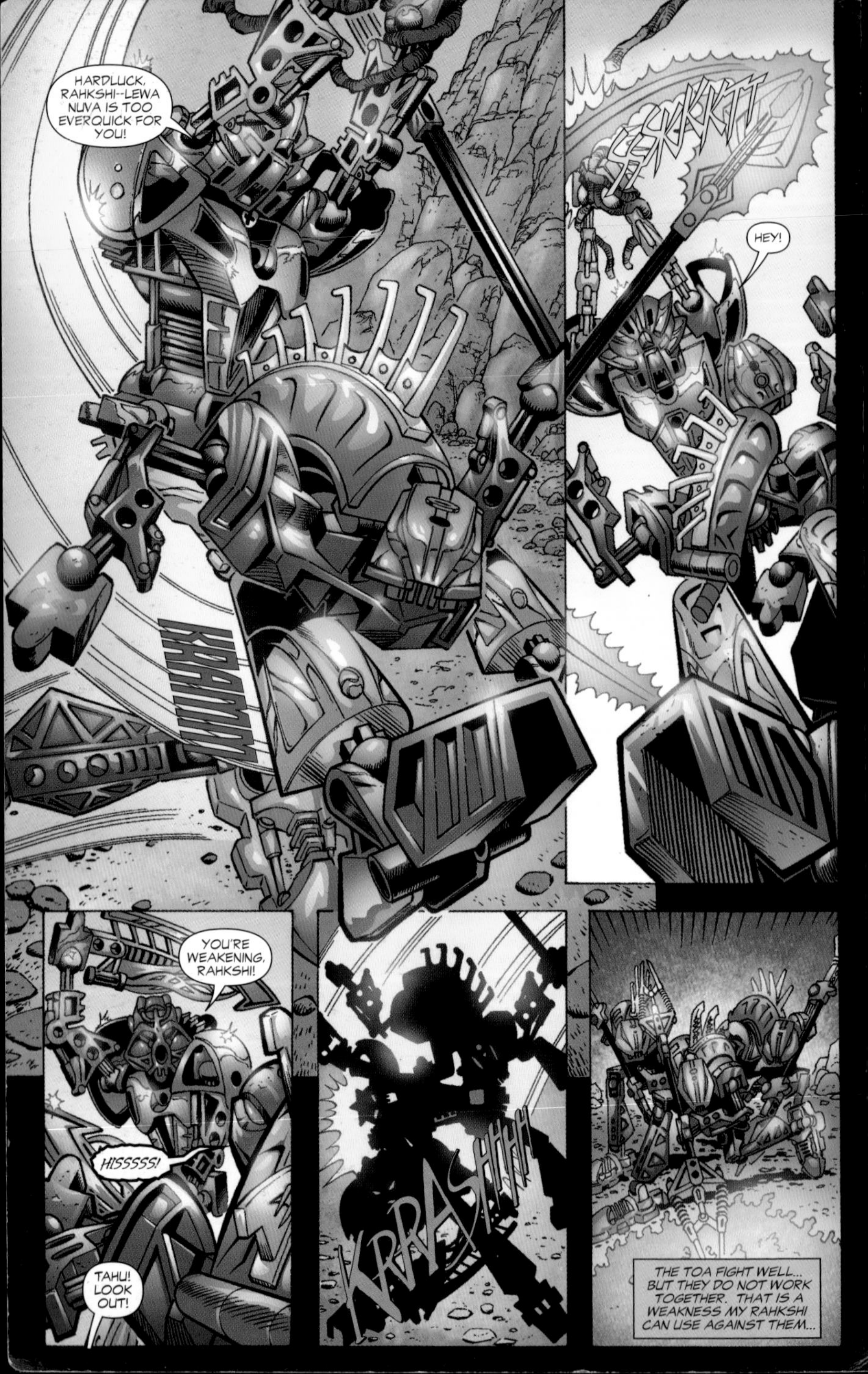

HARDLUCK, RAHKSHI--LEWA NUVA IS TOO EVERQUICK FOR YOU!
KRAKOOM
HEY!
YOU'RE WEAKENING, RAHKSHI!
HISSSSS!
TAHU! LOOK OUT!
KRRASHHH
THE TOA FIGHT WELL... BUT THEY DO NOT WORK TOGETHER. THAT IS A WEAKNESS MY RAHKSHI CAN USE AGAINST THEM...

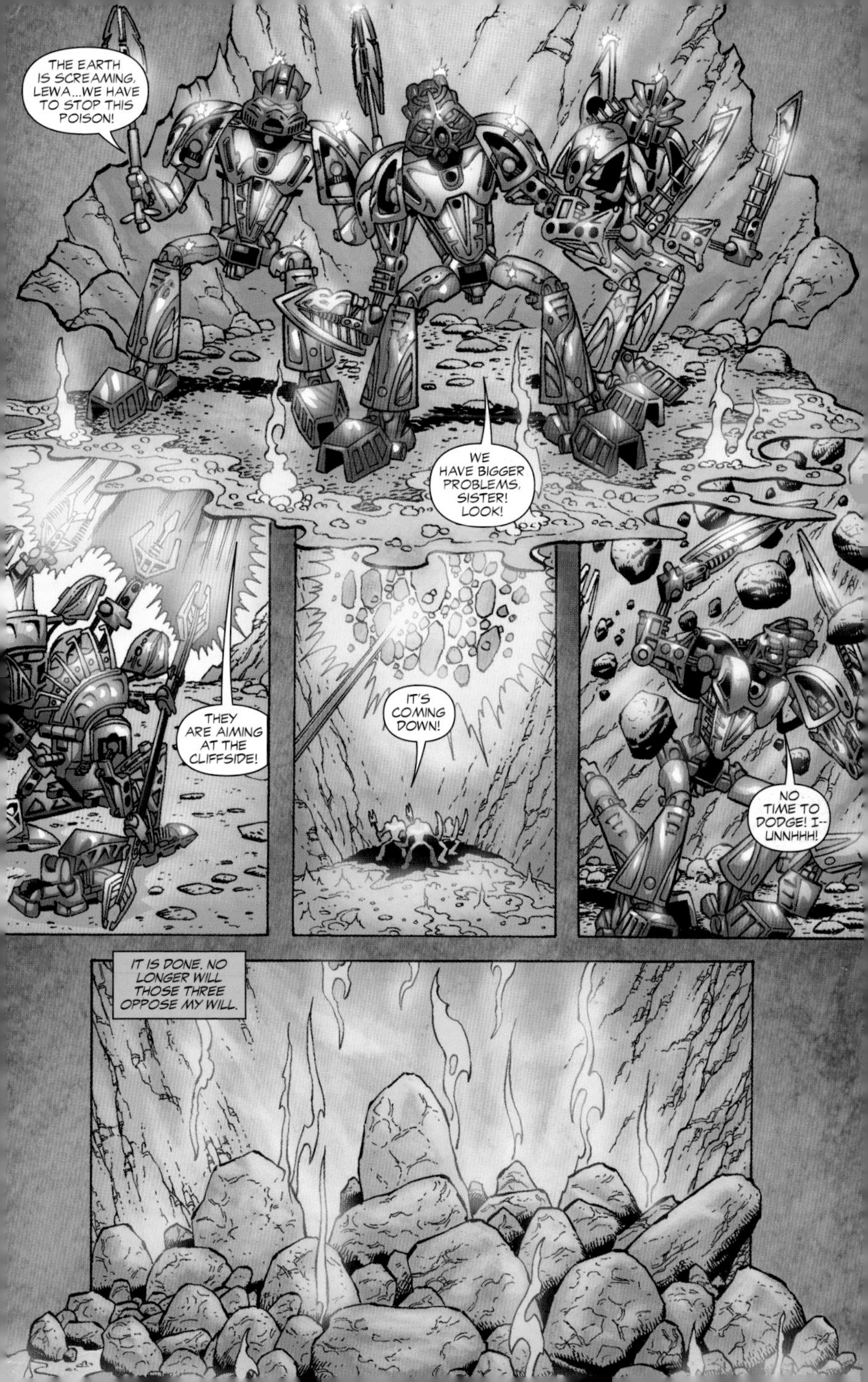
THE EARTH IS SCREAMING, LEWA...WE HAVE TO STOP THIS POISON!
WE HAVE BIGGER PROBLEMS, SISTER! LOOK!
THEY ARE AIMING AT THE CLIFFSIDE!
IT'S COMING DOWN!
NO TIME TO DODGE! I-- UNNHHH!
IT IS DONE. NO LONGER WILL THOSE THREE OPPOSE MY WILL.

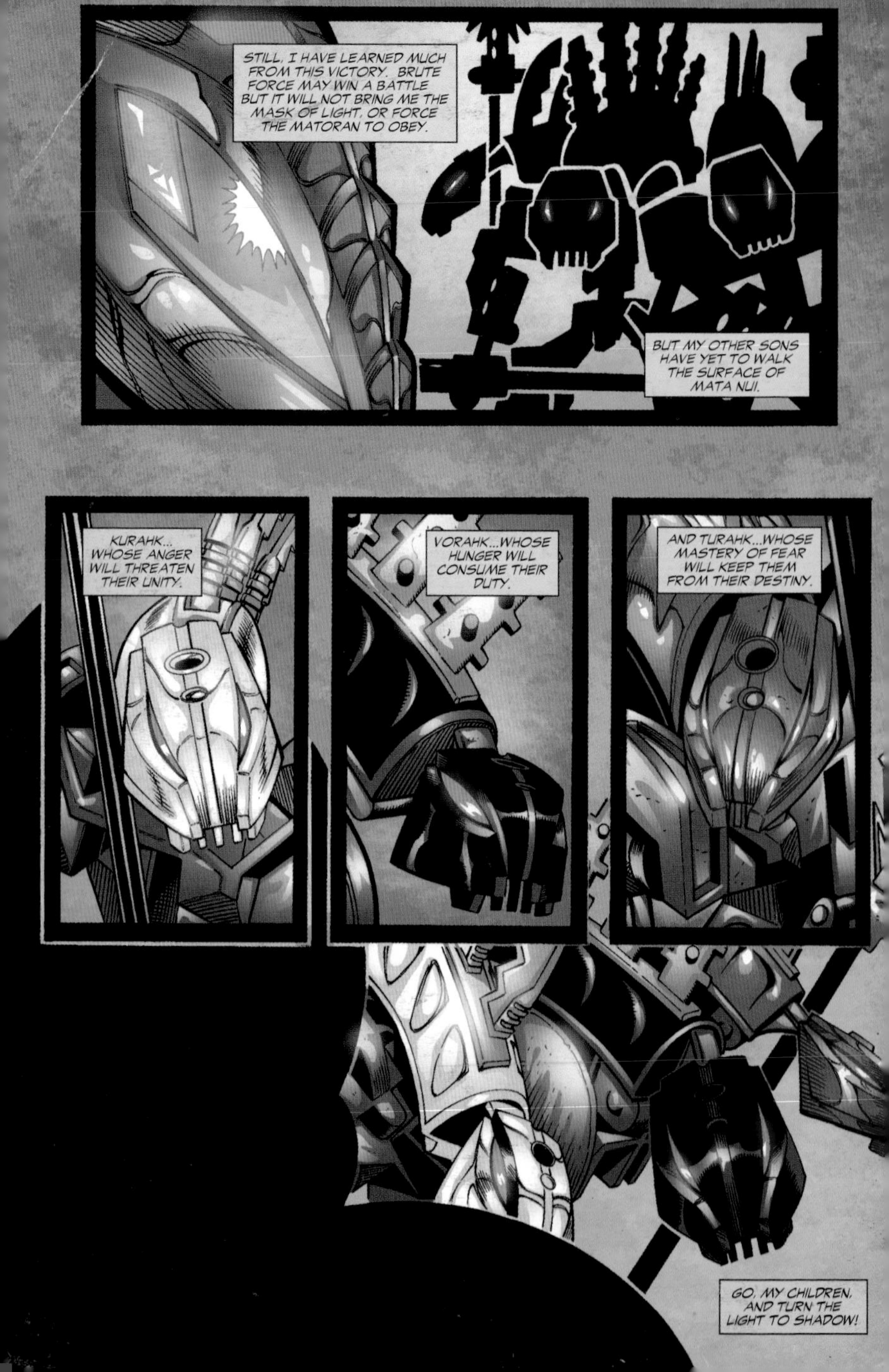
STILL, I HAVE LEARNED MUCH FROM THIS VICTORY. BRUTE FORCE MAY WIN A BATTLE BUT IT WILL NOT BRING ME THE MASK OF LIGHT, OR FORCE THE MATORAN TO OBEY.
BUT MY OTHER SONS HAVE YET TO WALK THE SURFACE OF MATA NUI.
KURAHK... WHOSE ANGER WILL THREATEN THEIR UNITY.
VORAHK...WHOSE HUNGER WILL CONSUME THEIR DUTY.
AND TURAHK...WHOSE MASTERY OF FEAR WILL KEEP THEM FROM THEIR DESTINY.
GO, MY CHILDREN, AND TURN THE LIGHT TO SHADOW!

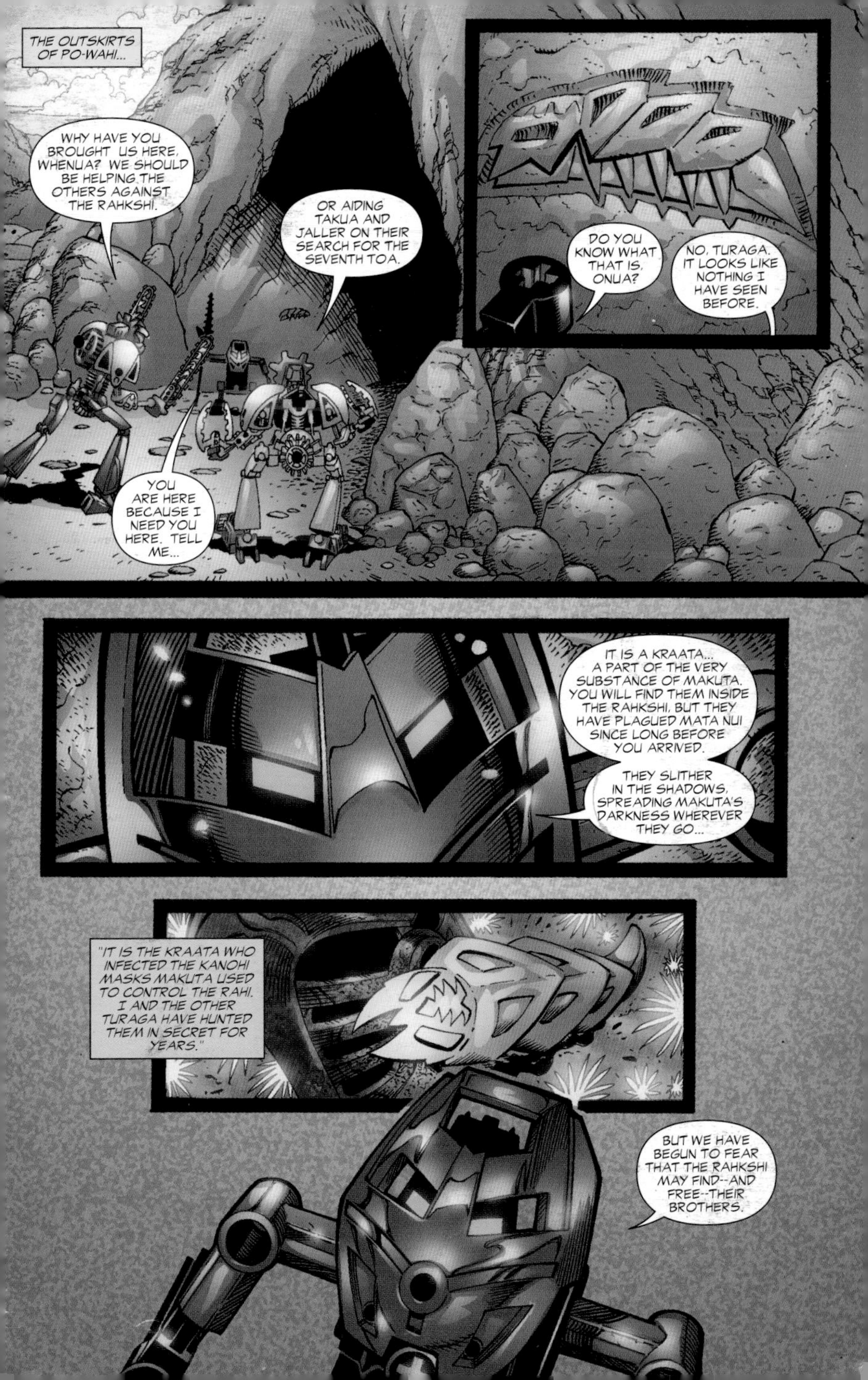
THE OUTSKIRTS OF PO-WAHI...
WHY HAVE YOU BROUGHT US HERE, WHENUA? WE SHOULD BE HELPING THE OTHERS AGAINST THE RAHKSHI.
OR AIDING TAKUA AND JALLER ON THEIR SEARCH FOR THE SEVENTH TOA.
YOU ARE HERE BECAUSE I NEED YOU HERE. TELL ME...
DO YOU KNOW WHAT THAT IS, ONUA?
NO, TURAGA. IT LOOKS LIKE NOTHING I HAVE SEEN BEFORE.
IT IS A KRAATA... A PART OF THE VERY SUBSTANCE OF MAKUTA. YOU WILL FIND THEM INSIDE THE RAHKSHI, BUT THEY HAVE PLAGUED MATA NUI SINCE LONG BEFORE YOU ARRIVED.
THEY SLITHER IN THE SHADOWS, SPREADING MAKUTA'S DARKNESS WHEREVER THEY GO...
"IT IS THE KRAATA WHO INFECTED THE KANOHI MASKS MAKUTA USED TO CONTROL THE RAHI. I AND THE OTHER TURAGA HAVE HUNTED THEM IN SECRET FOR YEARS."
BUT WE HAVE BEGUN TO FEAR THAT THE RAHKSHI MAY FIND--AND FREE--THEIR BROTHERS.

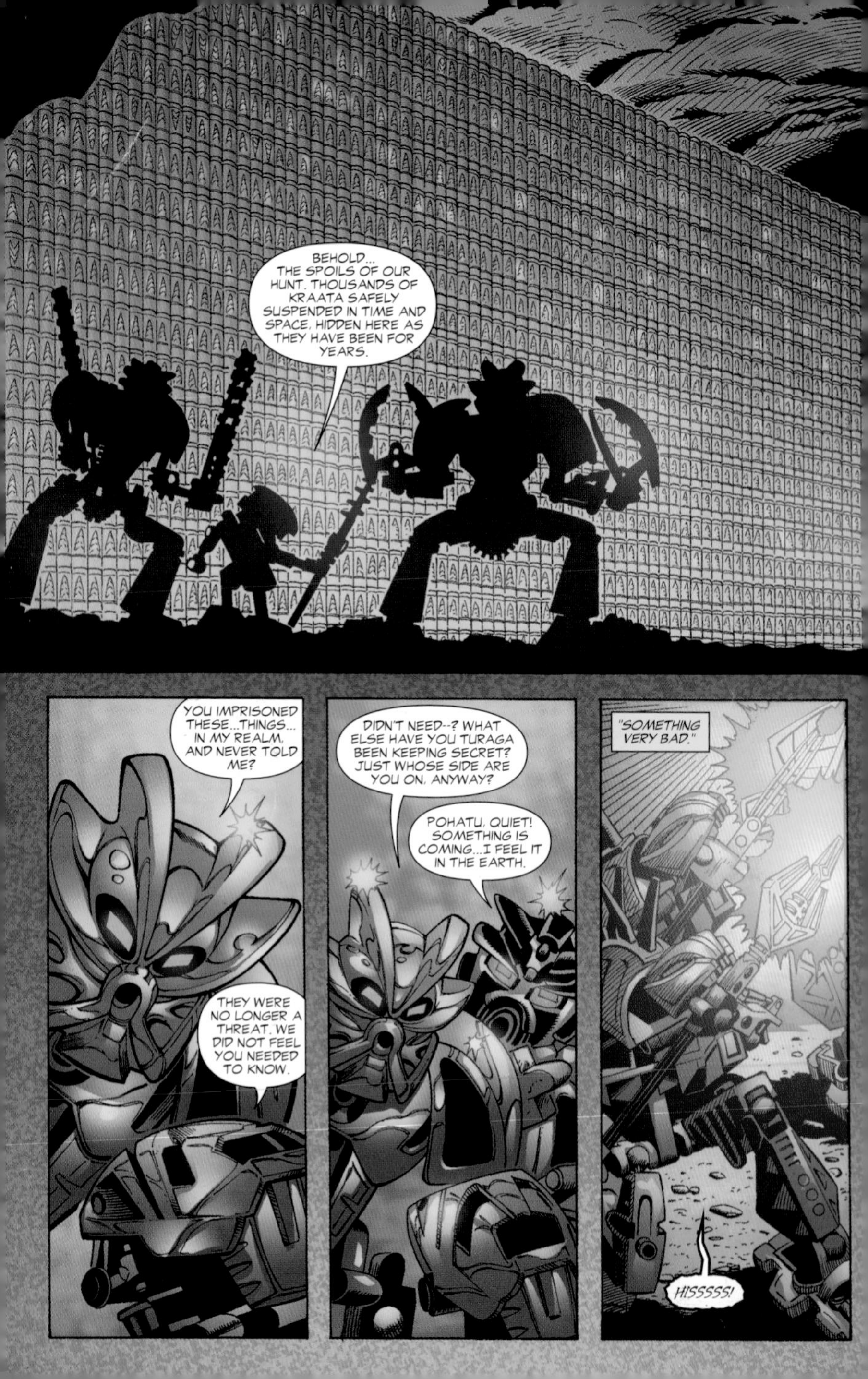
BEHOLD... THE SPOILS OF OUR HUNT. THOUSANDS OF KRAATA SAFELY SUSPENDED IN TIME AND SPACE, HIDDEN HERE AS THEY HAVE BEEN FOR YEARS.
YOU IMPRISONED THESE...THINGS... IN MY REALM, AND NEVER TOLD ME?
THEY WERE NO LONGER A THREAT. WE DID NOT FEEL YOU NEEDED TO KNOW.
DIDN'T NEED--? WHAT ELSE HAVE YOU TURAGA BEEN KEEPING SECRET? JUST WHOSE SIDE ARE YOU ON, ANYWAY?
POHATU, QUIET! SOMETHING IS COMING...I FEEL IT IN THE EARTH.
"SOMETHING VERY BAD."
HISSSSS!

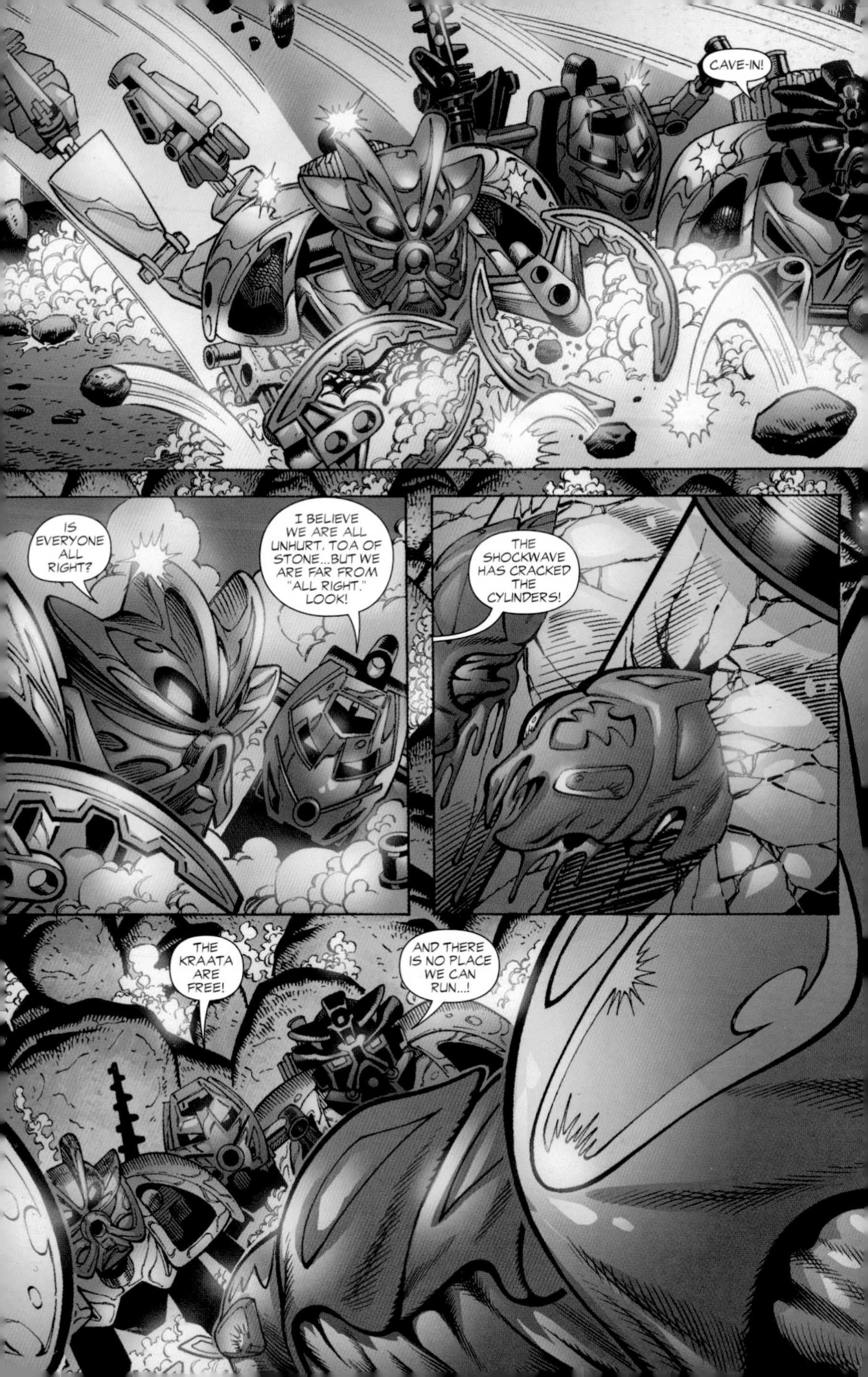
CAVE-IN!
IS EVERYONE ALL RIGHT?
I BELIEVE WE ARE ALL UNHURT, TOA OF STONE...BUT WE ARE FAR FROM "ALL RIGHT." LOOK!
THE SHOCKWAVE HAS CRACKED THE CYLINDERS!
THE KRAATA ARE FREE!
AND THERE IS NO PLACE WE CAN RUN...!

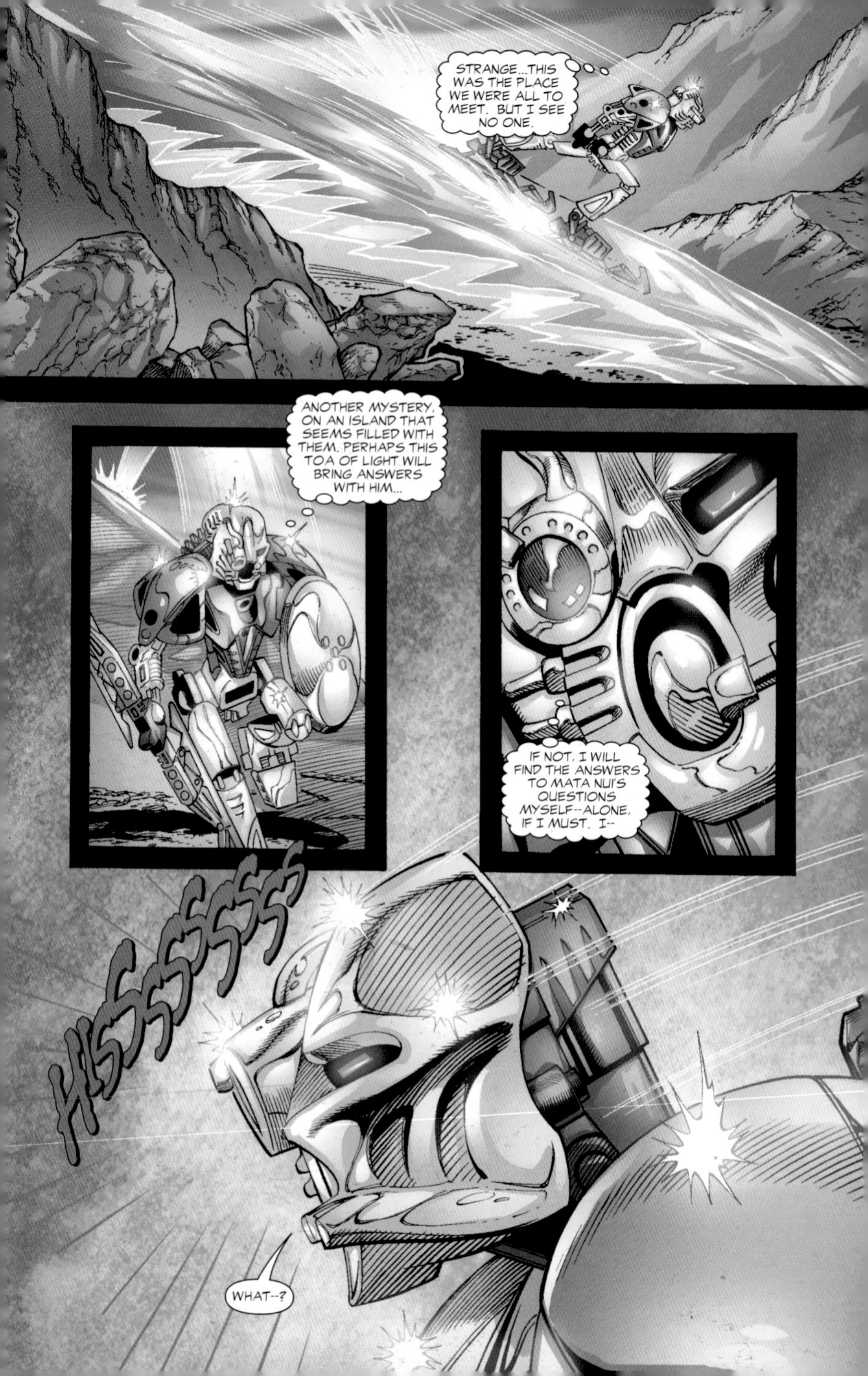
STRANGE...THIS WAS THE PLACE WE WERE ALL TO MEET. BUT I SEE NO ONE.
ANOTHER MYSTERY, ON AN ISLAND THAT SEEMS FILLED WITH THEM. PERHAPS THIS TOA OF LIGHT WILL BRING ANSWERS WITH HIM...
IF NOT, I WILL FIND THE ANSWERS TO MATA NUI'S QUESTIONS MYSELF--ALONE, IF I MUST. I--
HISSSSSSSS
WHAT--?

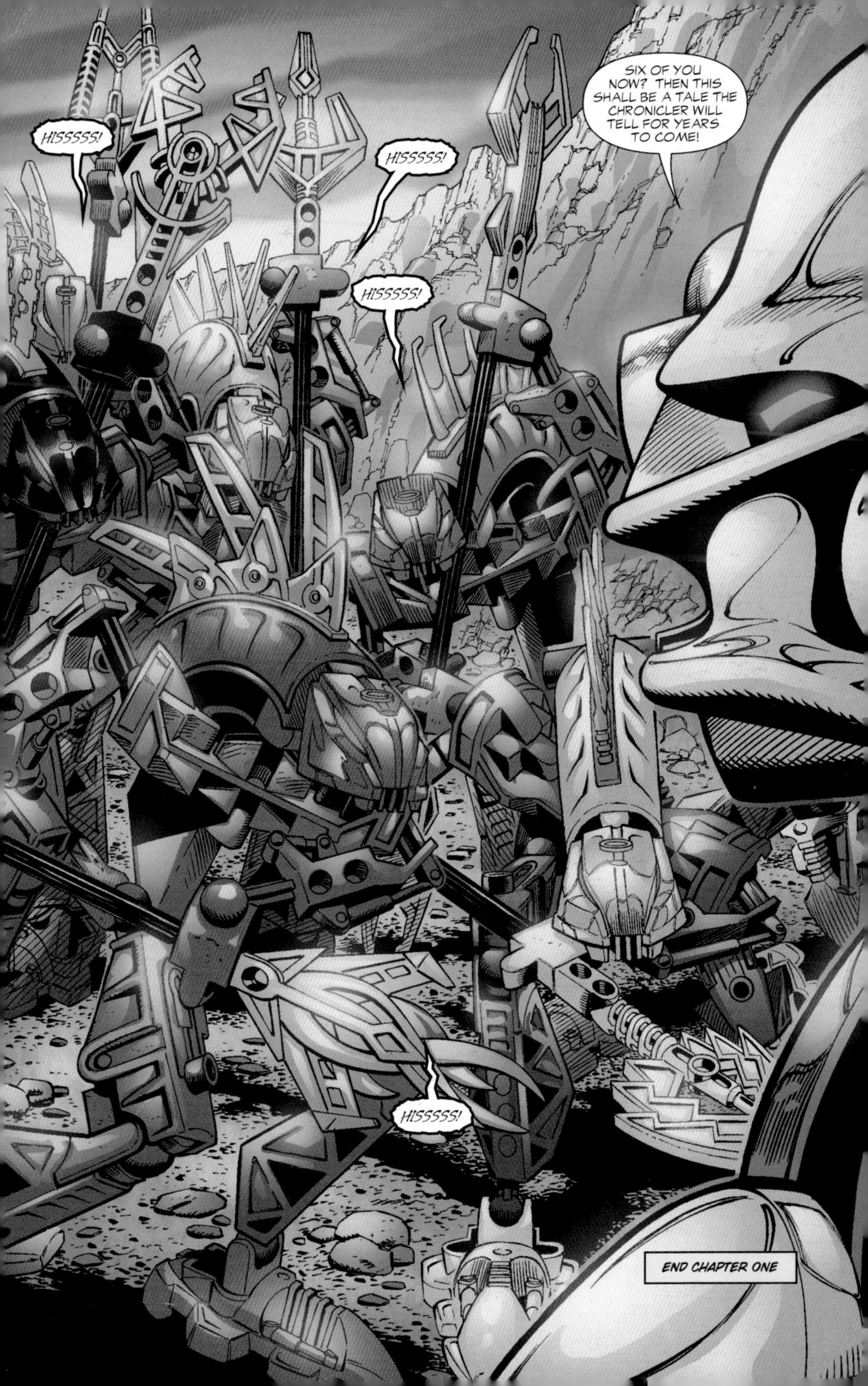
HISSSSS!
HISSSSS!
SIX OF YOU NOW? THEN THIS SHALL BE A TALE THE CHRONICLER WILL TELL FOR YEARS TO COME!
HISSSSS!
HISSSSS!
END CHAPTER ONE

RISE OF THE RAHKSHI
CHAPTER TWO

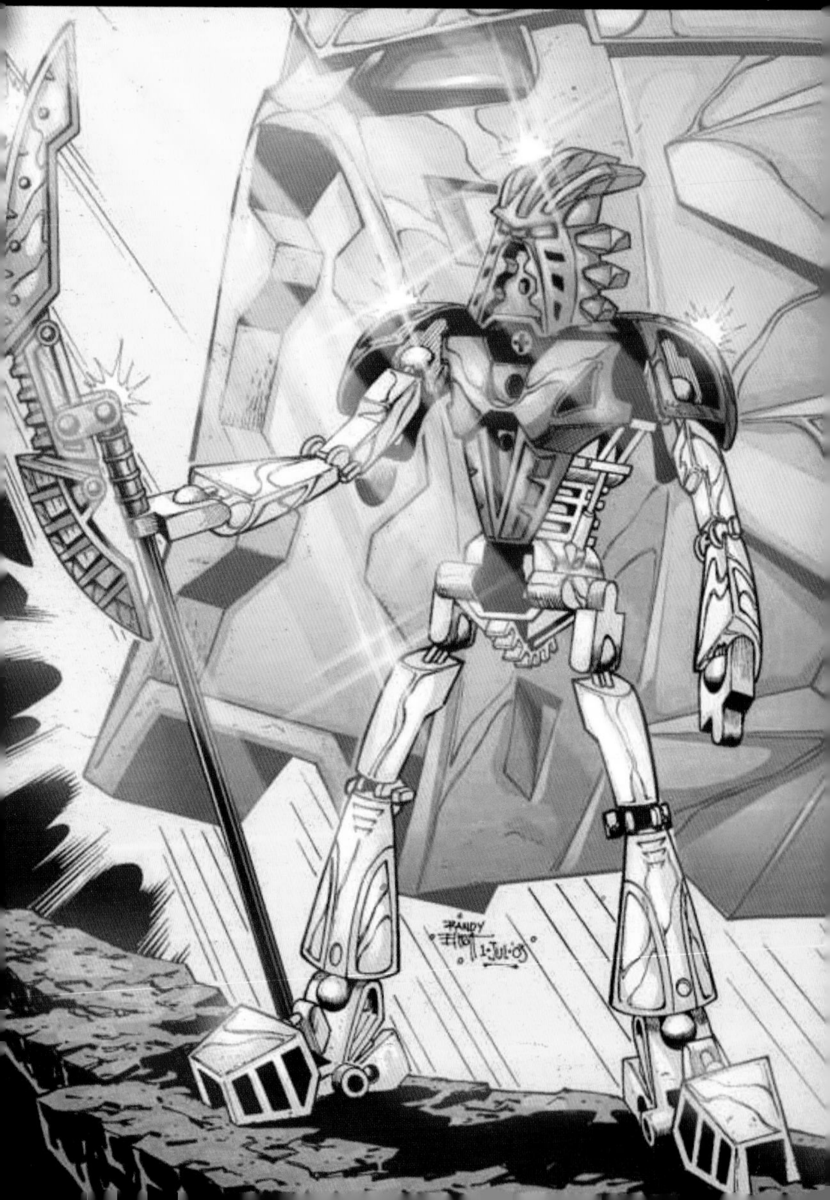

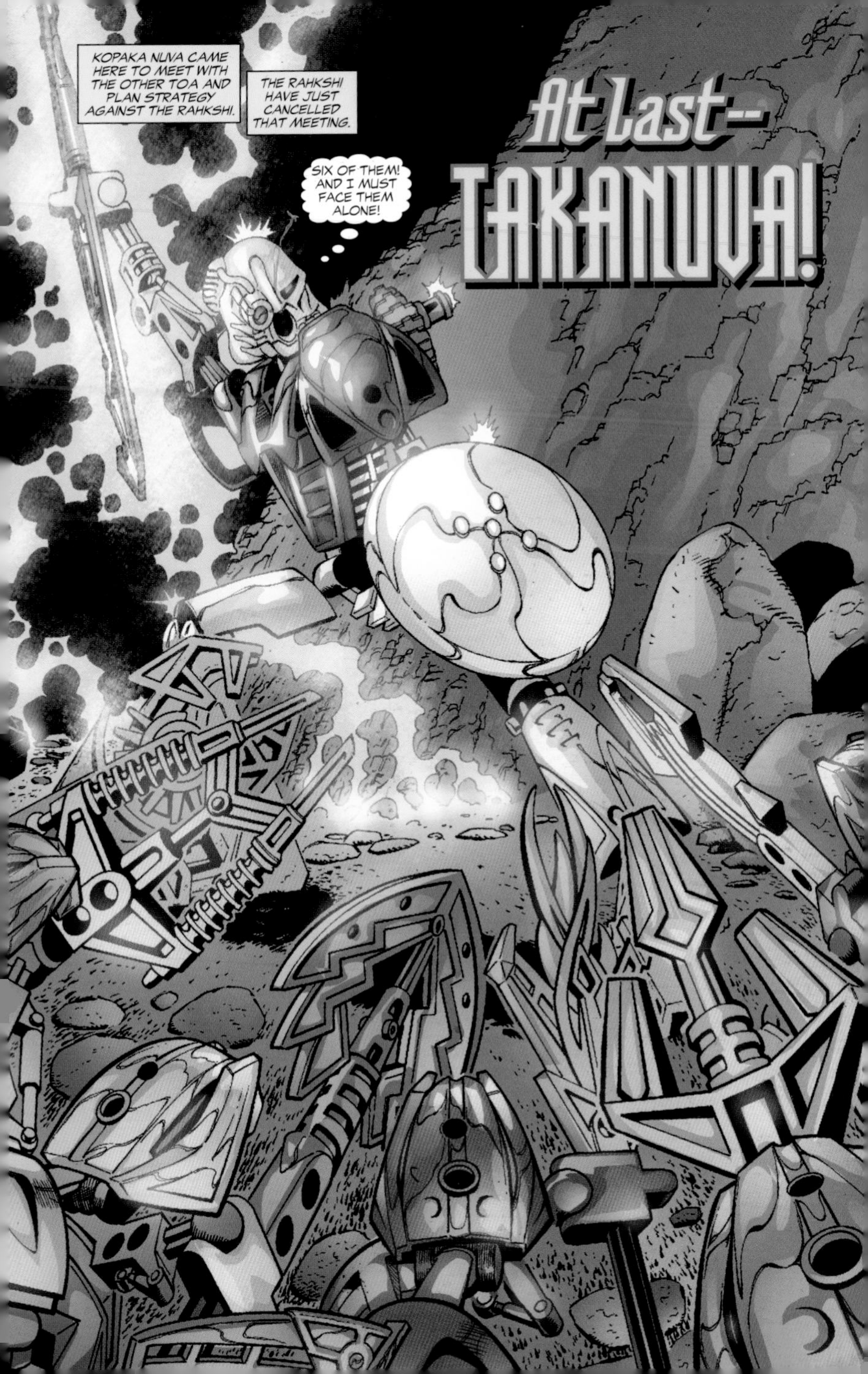

KOPAKA NUVA CAME HERE TO MEET WITH THE OTHER TOA AND PLAN STRATEGY AGAINST THE RAHKSHI.
THE RAHKSHI HAVE JUST CANCELLED THAT MEETING.
SIX OF THEM! AND I MUST FACE THEM ALONE!
At Last--
TAKANUVA!

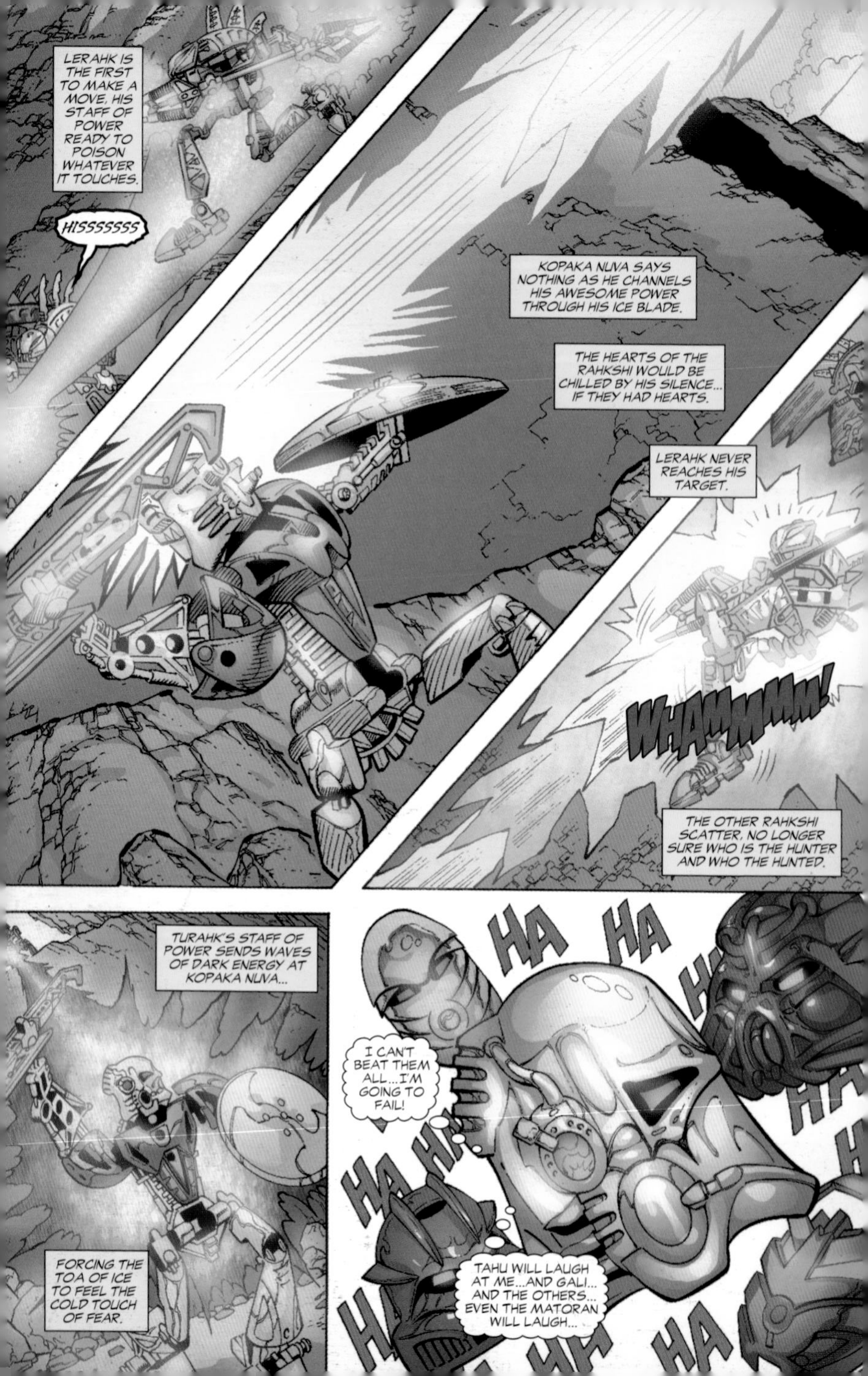
LERAHK IS THE FIRST TO MAKE A MOVE, HIS STAFF OF POWER READY TO POISON WHATEVER IT TOUCHES.
HISSSSSSS
KOPAKA NUVA SAYS NOTHING AS HE CHANNELS HIS AWESOME POWER THROUGH HIS ICE BLADE.
THE HEARTS OF THE RAHKSHI WOULD BE CHILLED BY HIS SILENCE... IF THEY HAD HEARTS.
LERAHK NEVER REACHES HIS TARGET.
WHAMMMMM!
THE OTHER RAHKSHI SCATTER, NO LONGER SURE WHO IS THE HUNTER AND WHO THE HUNTED.
TURAHK'S STAFF OF POWER SENDS WAVES OF DARK ENERGY AT KOPAKA NUVA...
FORCING THE TOA OF ICE TO FEEL THE COLD TOUCH OF FEAR.
HA HA
I CAN'T BEAT THEM ALL... I'M GOING TO FAIL!
TAHU WILL LAUGH AT ME... AND GALI... AND THE OTHERS... EVEN THE MATORAN WILL LAUGH...
HA

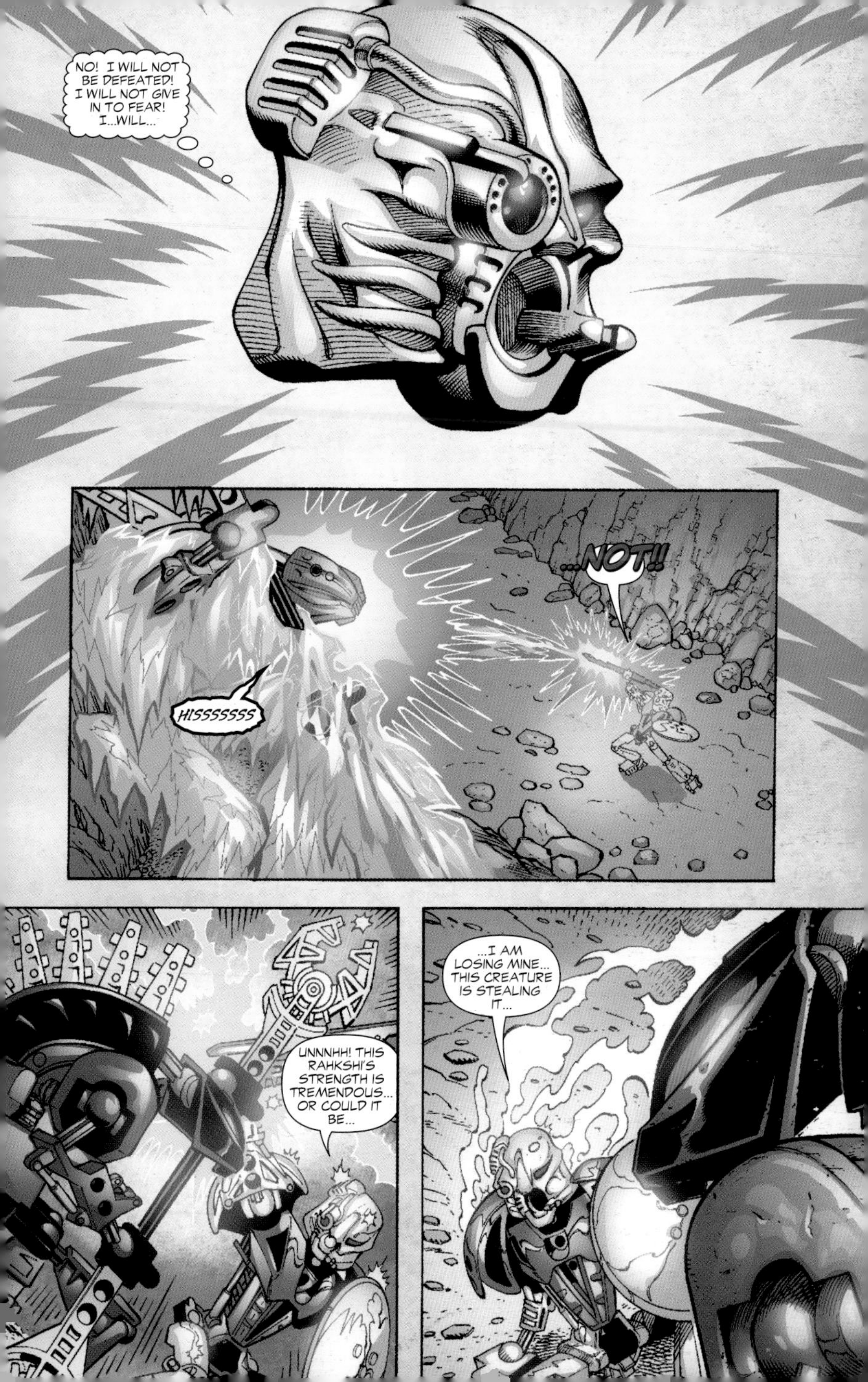
NO! I WILL NOT BE DEFEATED! I WILL NOT GIVE IN TO FEAR! I...WILL...
...NOT!!
HISSSSSSS
UNNNHH! THIS RAHKSHI'S STRENGTH IS TREMENDOUS... OR COULD IT BE...
...I AM LOSING MINE... THIS CREATURE IS STEALING IT...

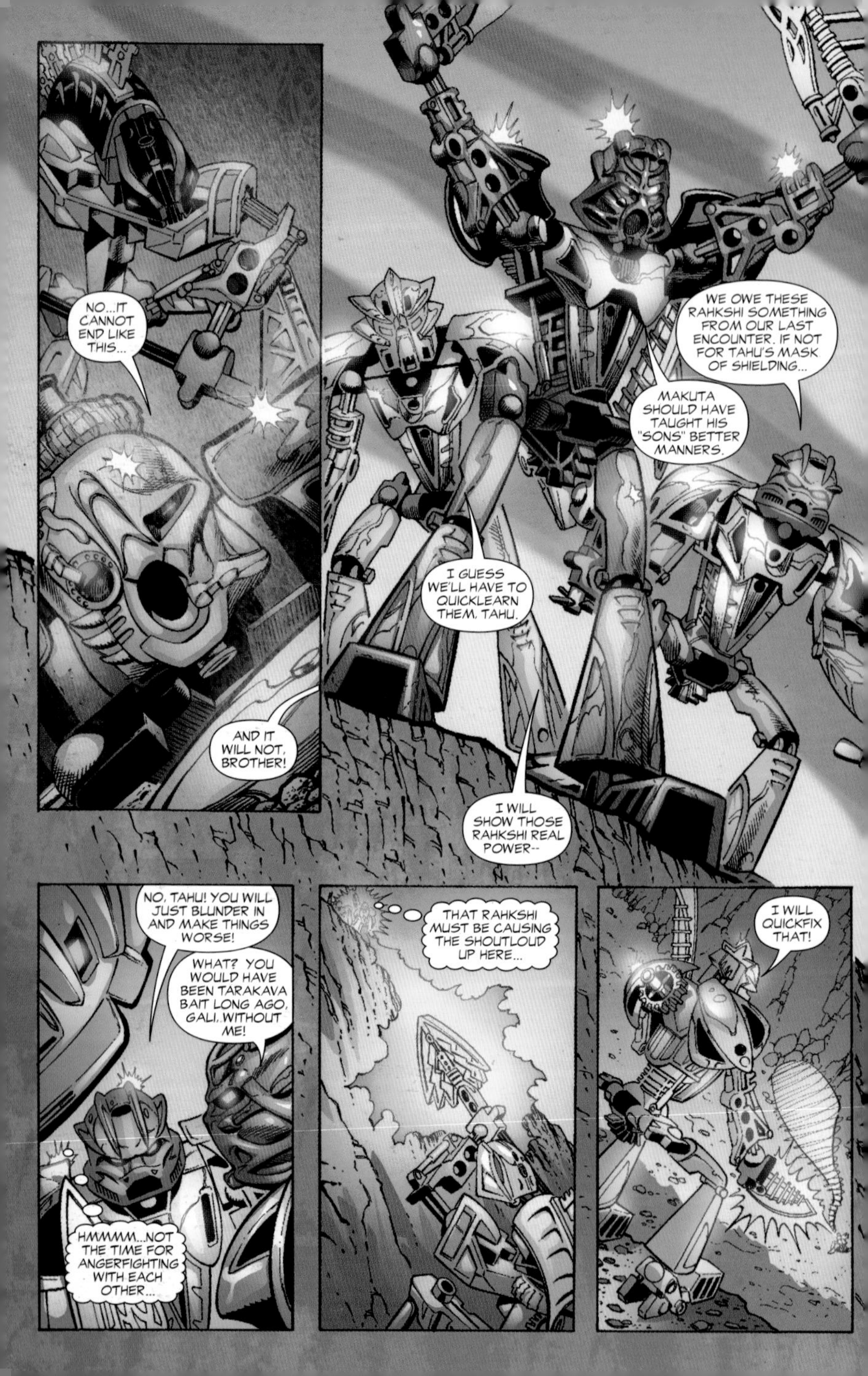
NO...IT CANNOT END LIKE THIS...
AND IT WILL NOT, BROTHER!
WE OWE THESE RAHKSHI SOMETHING FROM OUR LAST ENCOUNTER. IF NOT FOR TAHU'S MASK OF SHIELDING...
MAKUTA SHOULD HAVE TAUGHT HIS "SONS" BETTER MANNERS.
I GUESS WE'LL HAVE TO QUICKLEARN THEM, TAHU.
I WILL SHOW THOSE RAHKSHI REAL POWER--
NO, TAHU! YOU WILL JUST BLUNDER IN AND MAKE THINGS WORSE!
WHAT? YOU WOULD HAVE BEEN TARAKAVA BAIT LONG AGO, GALI, WITHOUT ME!
HMMMMM...NOT THE TIME FOR ANGERFIGHTING WITH EACH OTHER...
THAT RAHKSHI MUST BE CAUSING THE SHOUTLOUD UP HERE...
I WILL QUICKFIX THAT!

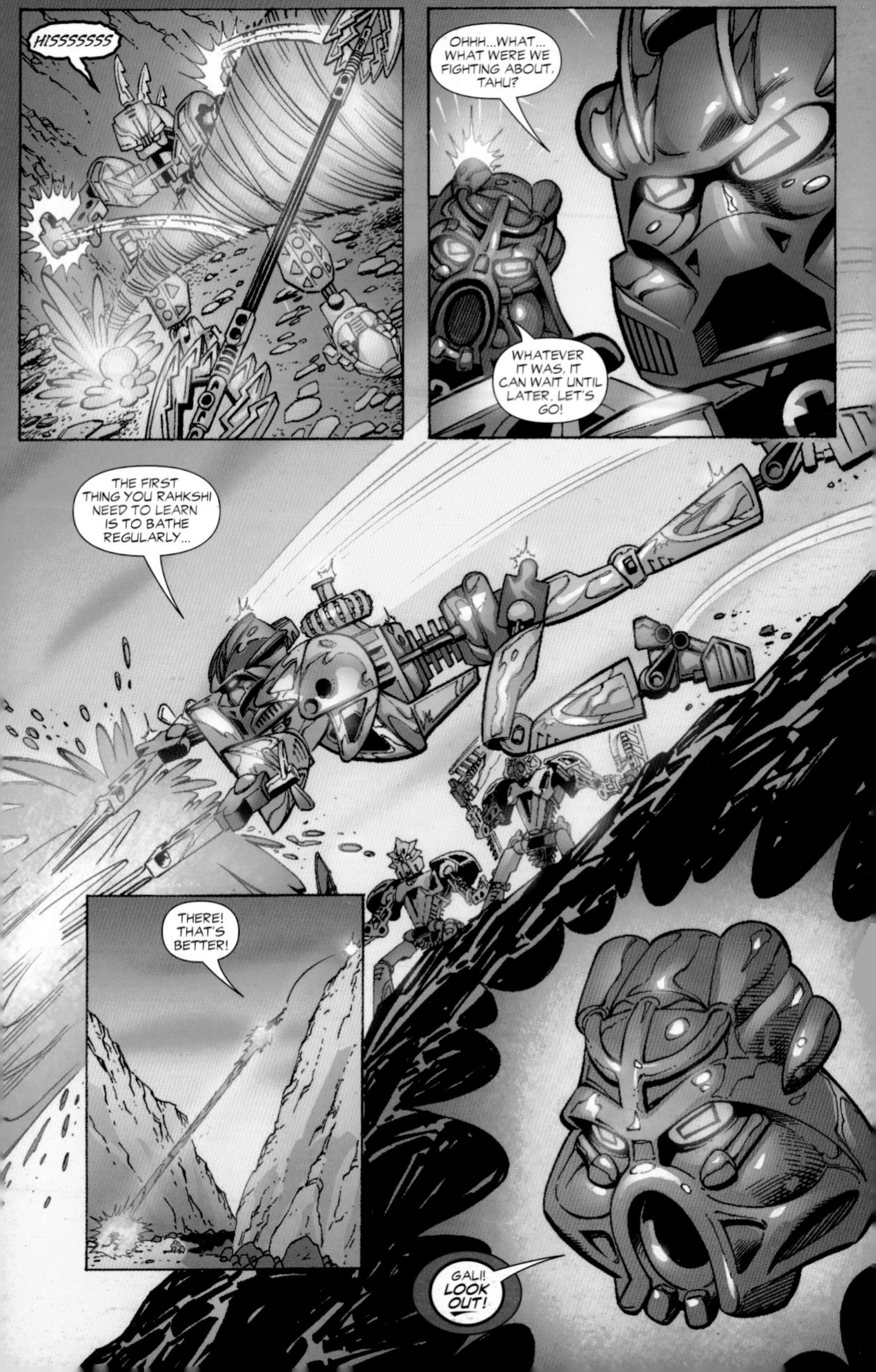
HISSSSSSS
OHHH...WHAT... WHAT WERE WE FIGHTING ABOUT, TAHU?
WHATEVER IT WAS, IT CAN WAIT UNTIL LATER. LET'S GO!
THE FIRST THING YOU RAHKSHI NEED TO LEARN IS TO BATHE REGULARLY...
THERE! THAT'S BETTER!
GALI! LOOK OUT!

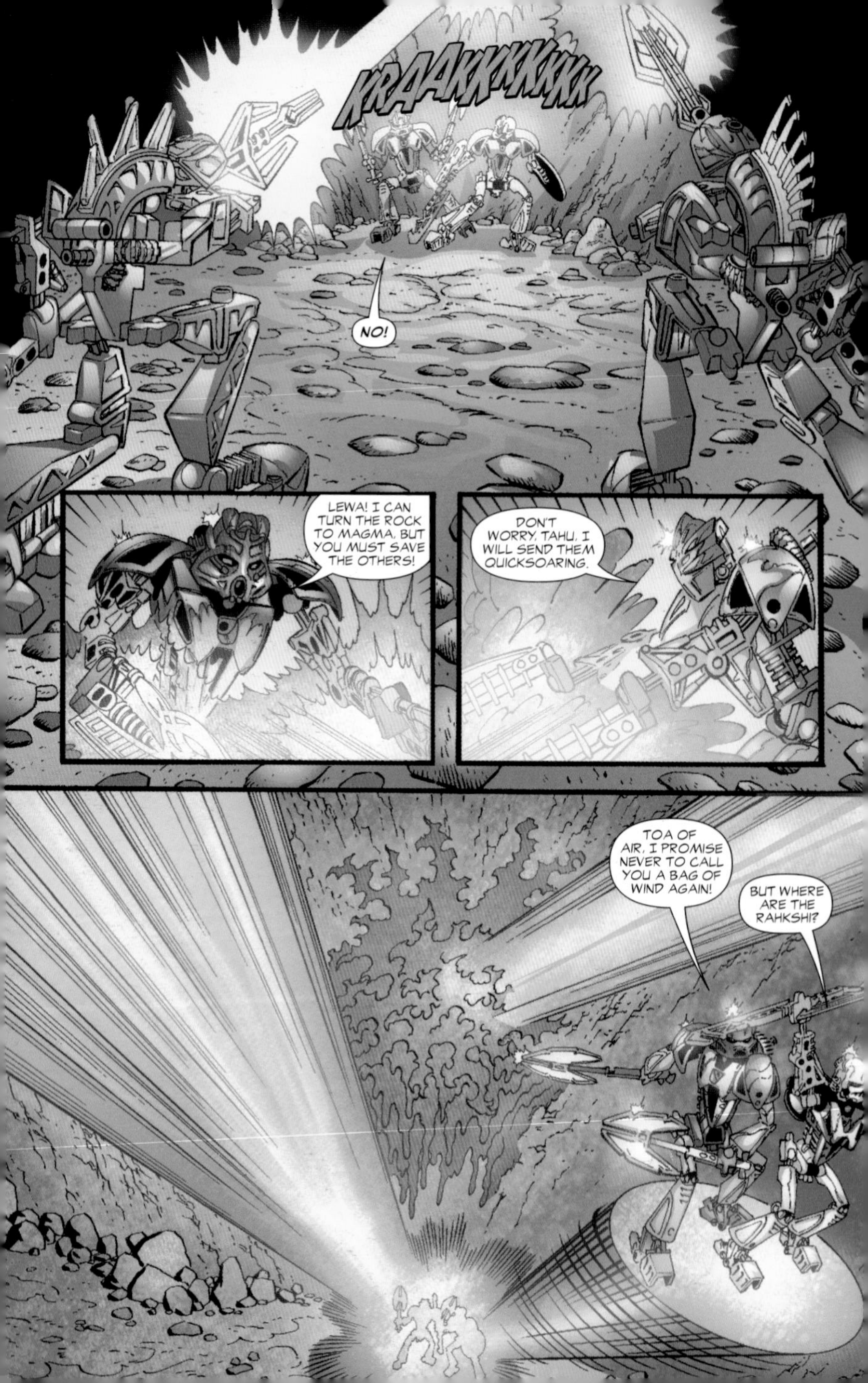
KRAAKKKKKKK
NO!
LEWA! I CAN TURN THE ROCK TO MAGMA, BUT YOU MUST SAVE THE OTHERS!
DON'T WORRY, TAHU, I WILL SEND THEM QUICKSOARING.
TOA OF AIR, I PROMISE NEVER TO CALL YOU A BAG OF WIND AGAIN!
BUT WHERE ARE THE RAHKSHI?

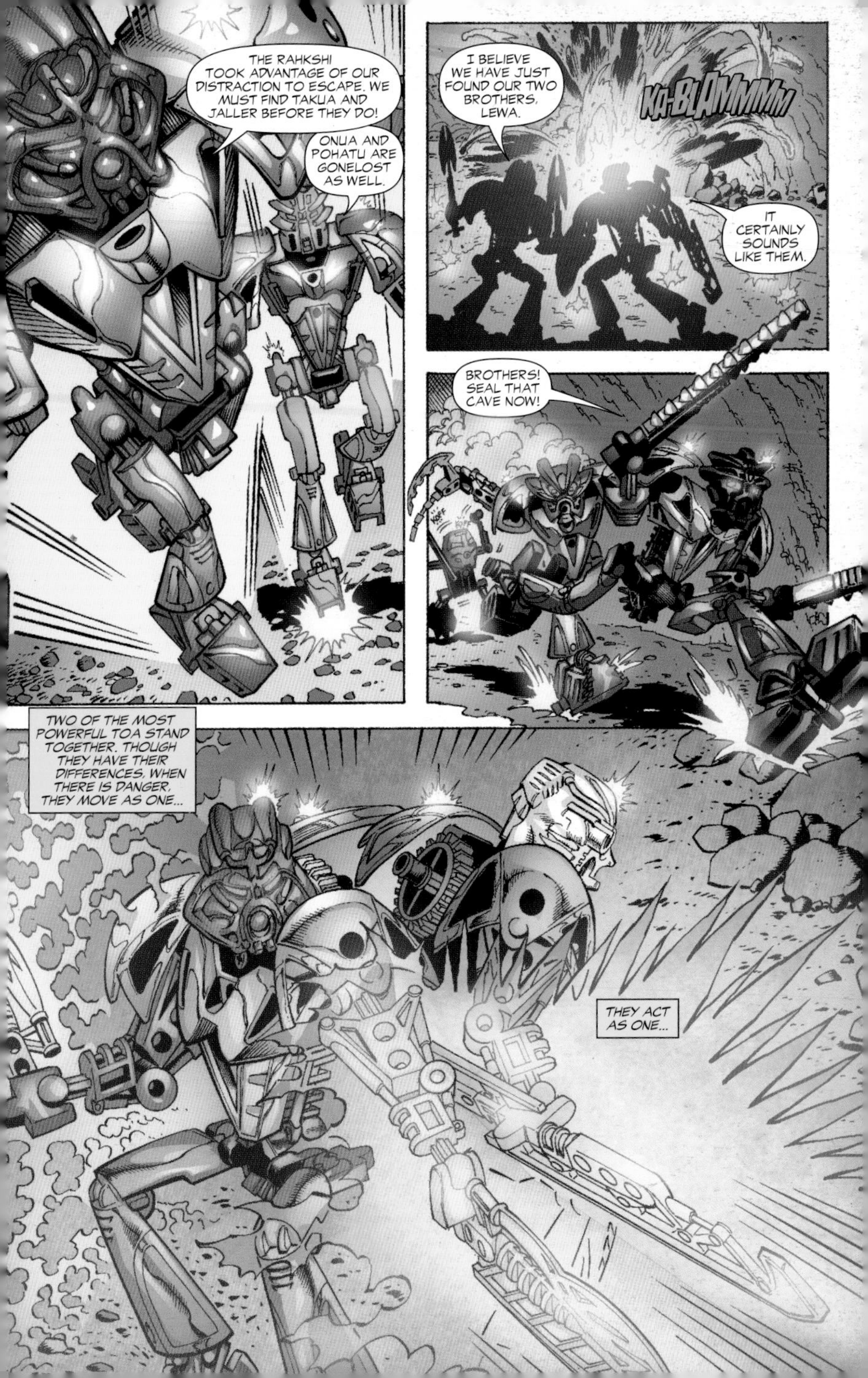
THE RAHKSHI TOOK ADVANTAGE OF OUR DISTRACTION TO ESCAPE. WE MUST FIND TAKUA AND JALLER BEFORE THEY DO!
ONUA AND POHATU ARE GONELOST AS WELL.
I BELIEVE WE HAVE JUST FOUND OUR TWO BROTHERS, LEWA.
KA-BLAMMMM
IT CERTAINLY SOUNDS LIKE THEM.
BROTHERS! SEAL THAT CAVE NOW!
TWO OF THE MOST POWERFUL TOA STAND TOGETHER. THOUGH THEY HAVE THEIR DIFFERENCES, WHEN THERE IS DANGER, THEY MOVE AS ONE...
THEY ACT AS ONE...

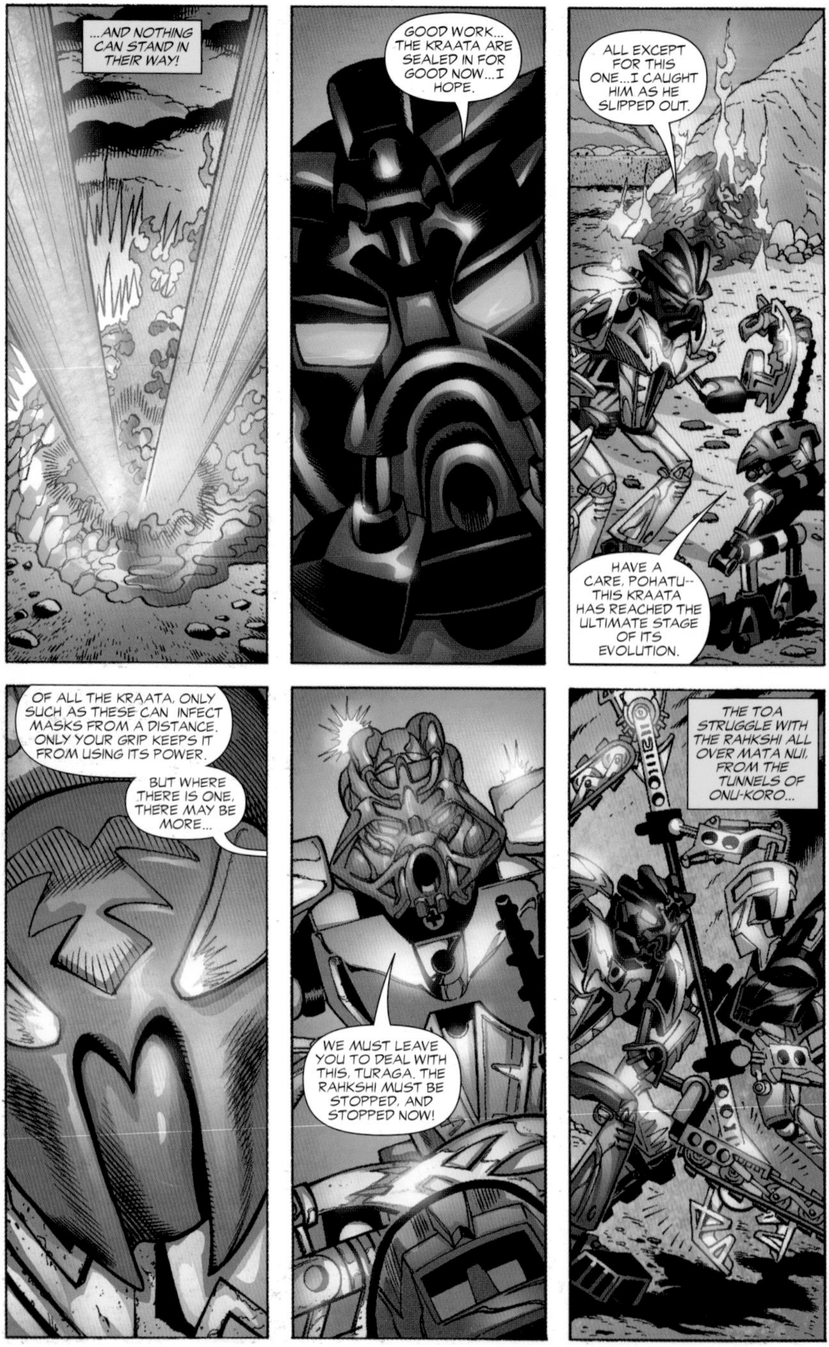
...AND NOTHING CAN STAND IN THEIR WAY!
GOOD WORK... THE KRAATA ARE SEALED IN FOR GOOD NOW... I HOPE.
ALL EXCEPT FOR THIS ONE... I CAUGHT HIM AS HE SLIPPED OUT.
HAVE A CARE, POHATU-- THIS KRAATA HAS REACHED THE ULTIMATE STAGE OF ITS EVOLUTION.
OF ALL THE KRAATA, ONLY SUCH AS THESE CAN INFECT MASKS FROM A DISTANCE. ONLY YOUR GRIP KEEPS IT FROM USING ITS POWER.
BUT WHERE THERE IS ONE, THERE MAY BE MORE...
WE MUST LEAVE YOU TO DEAL WITH THIS, TURAGA. THE RAHKSHI MUST BE STOPPED, AND STOPPED NOW!
THE TOA STRUGGLE WITH THE RAHKSHI ALL OVER MATA NUI, FROM THE TUNNELS OF ONU-KORO...

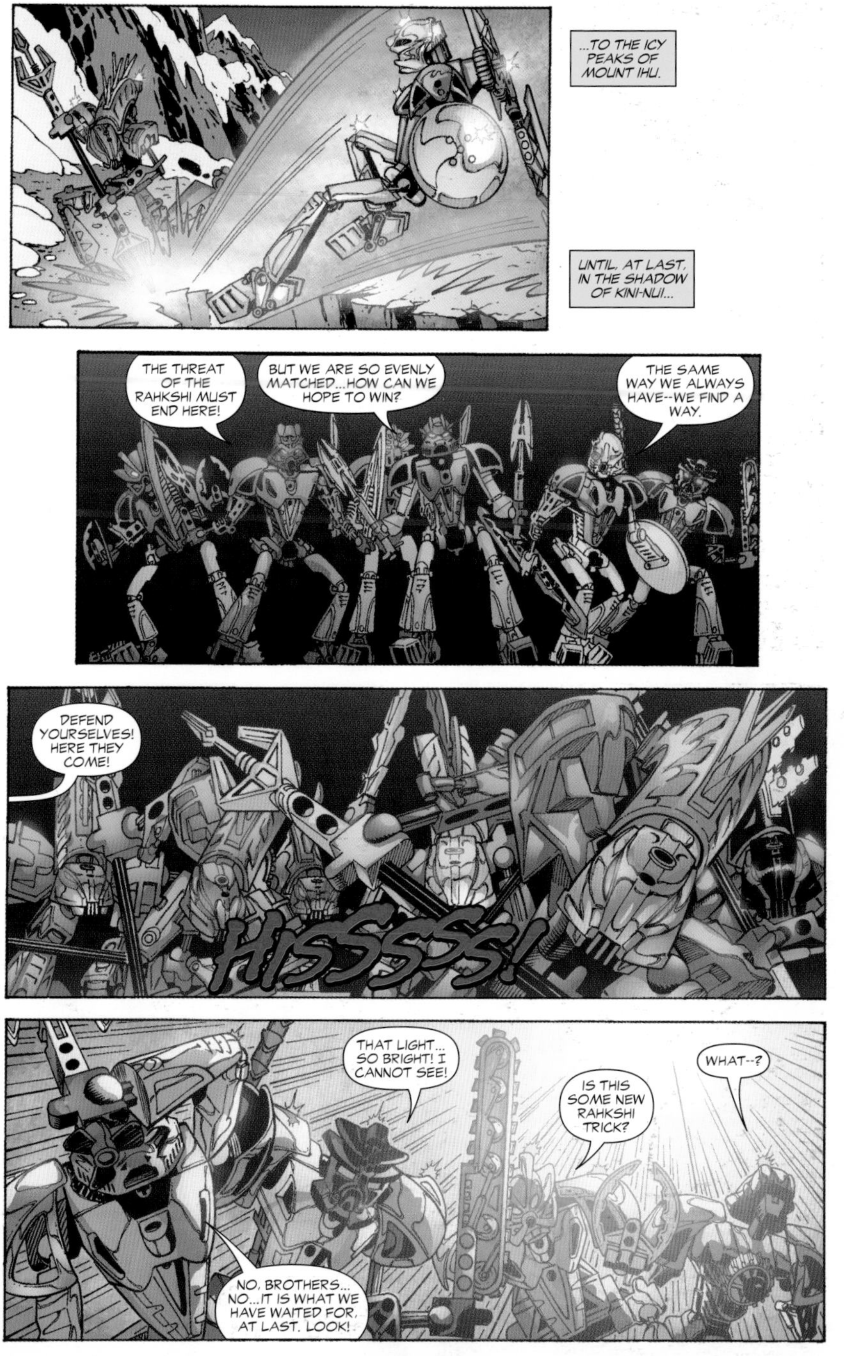
...TO THE ICY PEAKS OF MOUNT IHU.
UNTIL, AT LAST, IN THE SHADOW OF KINI-NUI...
THE THREAT OF THE RAHKSHI MUST END HERE!
BUT WE ARE SO EVENLY MATCHED...HOW CAN WE HOPE TO WIN?
THE SAME WAY WE ALWAYS HAVE--WE FIND A WAY.
DEFEND YOURSELVES! HERE THEY COME!
HISSSSS!
THAT LIGHT... SO BRIGHT! I CANNOT SEE!
IS THIS SOME NEW RAHKSHI TRICK?
WHAT--?
NO, BROTHERS... NO...IT IS WHAT WE HAVE WAITED FOR, AT LAST. LOOK!

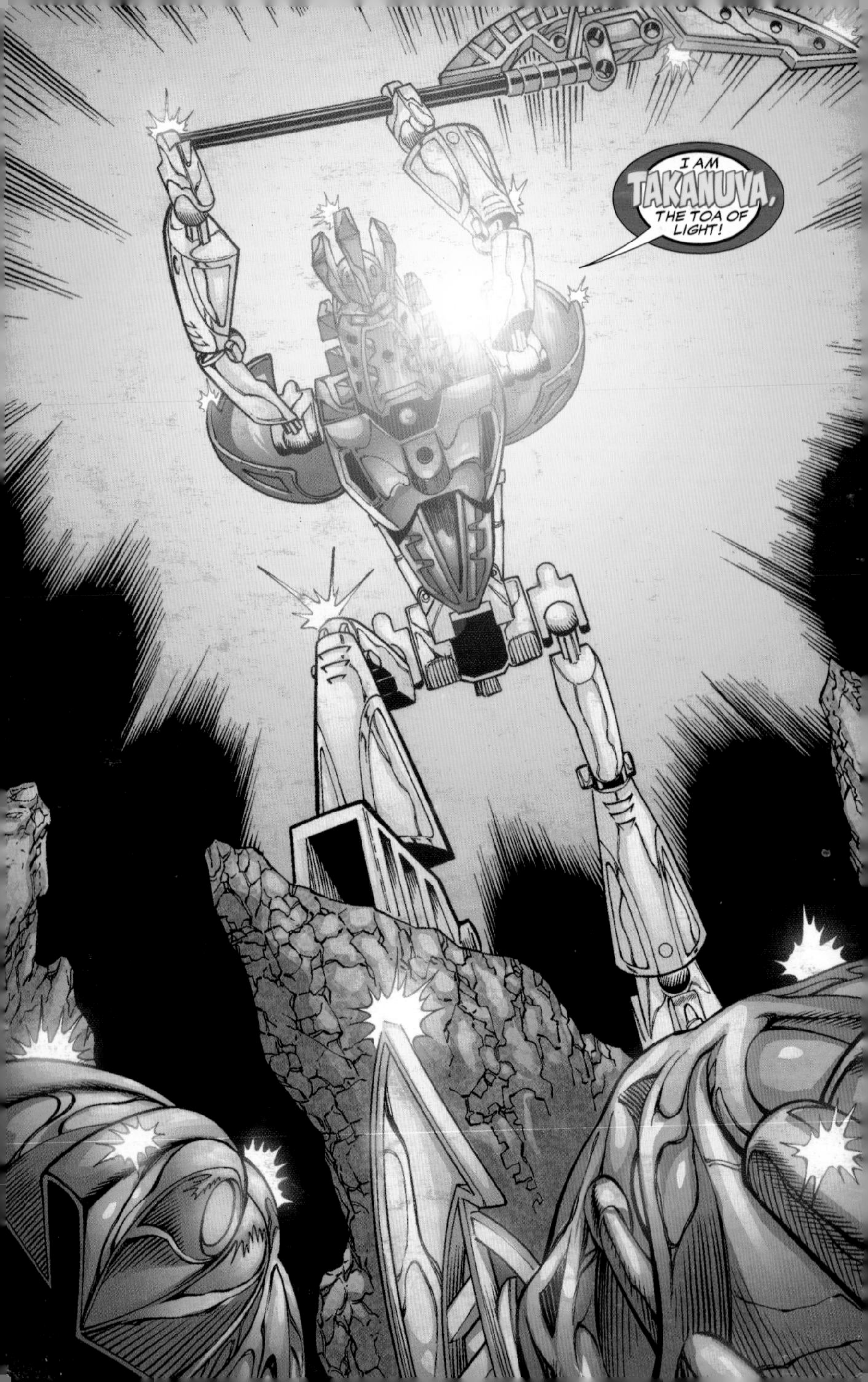
I AM TAKANUVA, THE TOA OF LIGHT!

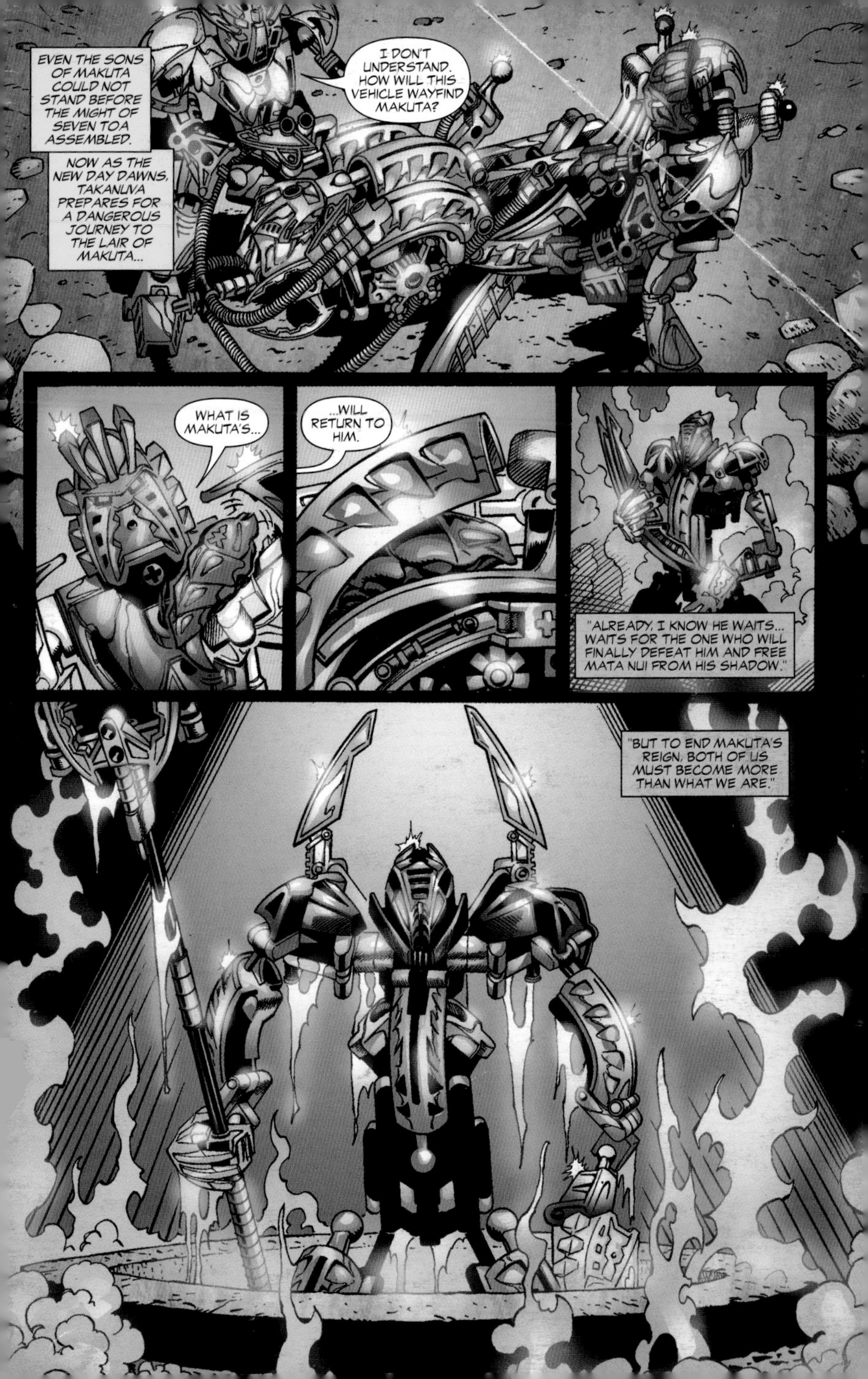
EVEN THE SONS OF MAKUTA COULD NOT STAND BEFORE THE MIGHT OF SEVEN TOA ASSEMBLED.
NOW AS THE NEW DAY DAWNS, TAKANUVA PREPARES FOR A DANGEROUS JOURNEY TO THE LAIR OF MAKUTA...
I DON'T UNDERSTAND. HOW WILL THIS VEHICLE WAYFIND MAKUTA?
WHAT IS MAKUTA'S...
...WILL RETURN TO HIM.
"ALREADY, I KNOW HE WAITS... WAITS FOR THE ONE WHO WILL FINALLY DEFEAT HIM AND FREE MATA NUI FROM HIS SHADOW."
"BUT TO END MAKUTA'S REIGN, BOTH OF US MUST BECOME MORE THAN WHAT WE ARE."

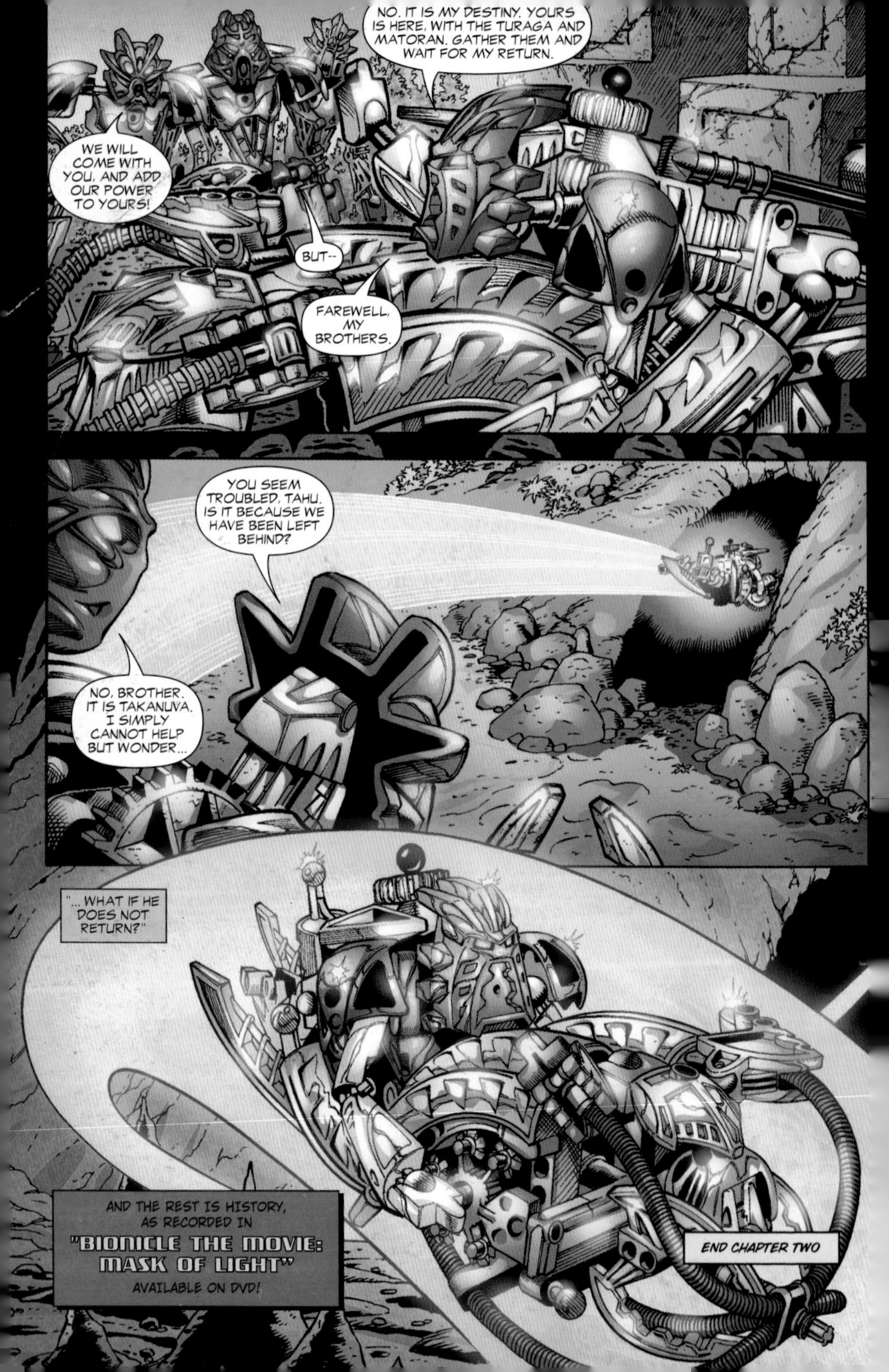
WE WILL COME WITH YOU, AND ADD OUR POWER TO YOURS!
NO. IT IS MY DESTINY. YOURS IS HERE, WITH THE TURAGA AND MATORAN. GATHER THEM AND WAIT FOR MY RETURN.
BUT--
FAREWELL, MY BROTHERS.
YOU SEEM TROUBLED, TAHU. IS IT BECAUSE WE HAVE BEEN LEFT BEHIND?
NO, BROTHER. IT IS TAKANUVA. I SIMPLY CANNOT HELP BUT WONDER...
"...WHAT IF HE DOES NOT RETURN?"
AND THE REST IS HISTORY, AS RECORDED IN
"BIONICLE THE MOVIE: MASK OF LIGHT"
AVAILABLE ON DVD!
END CHAPTER TWO

EPILOGUE

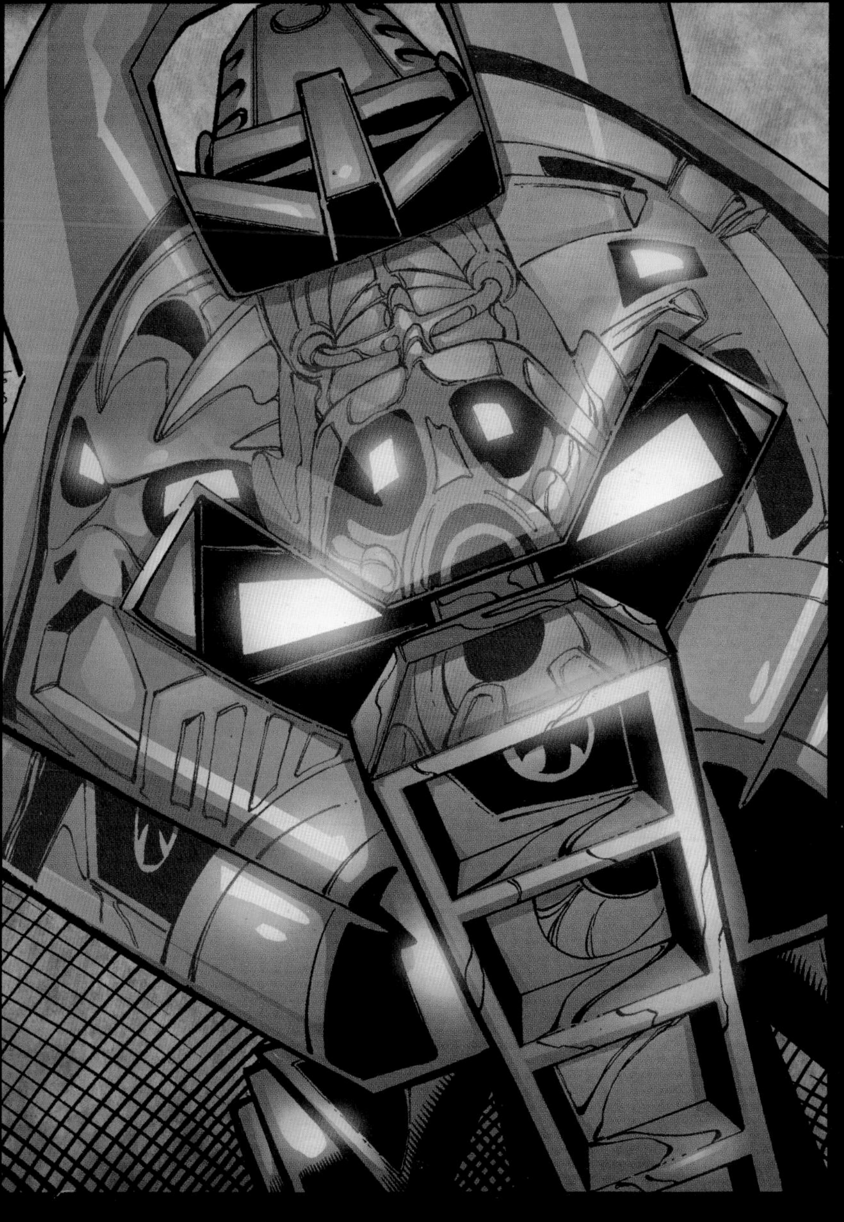

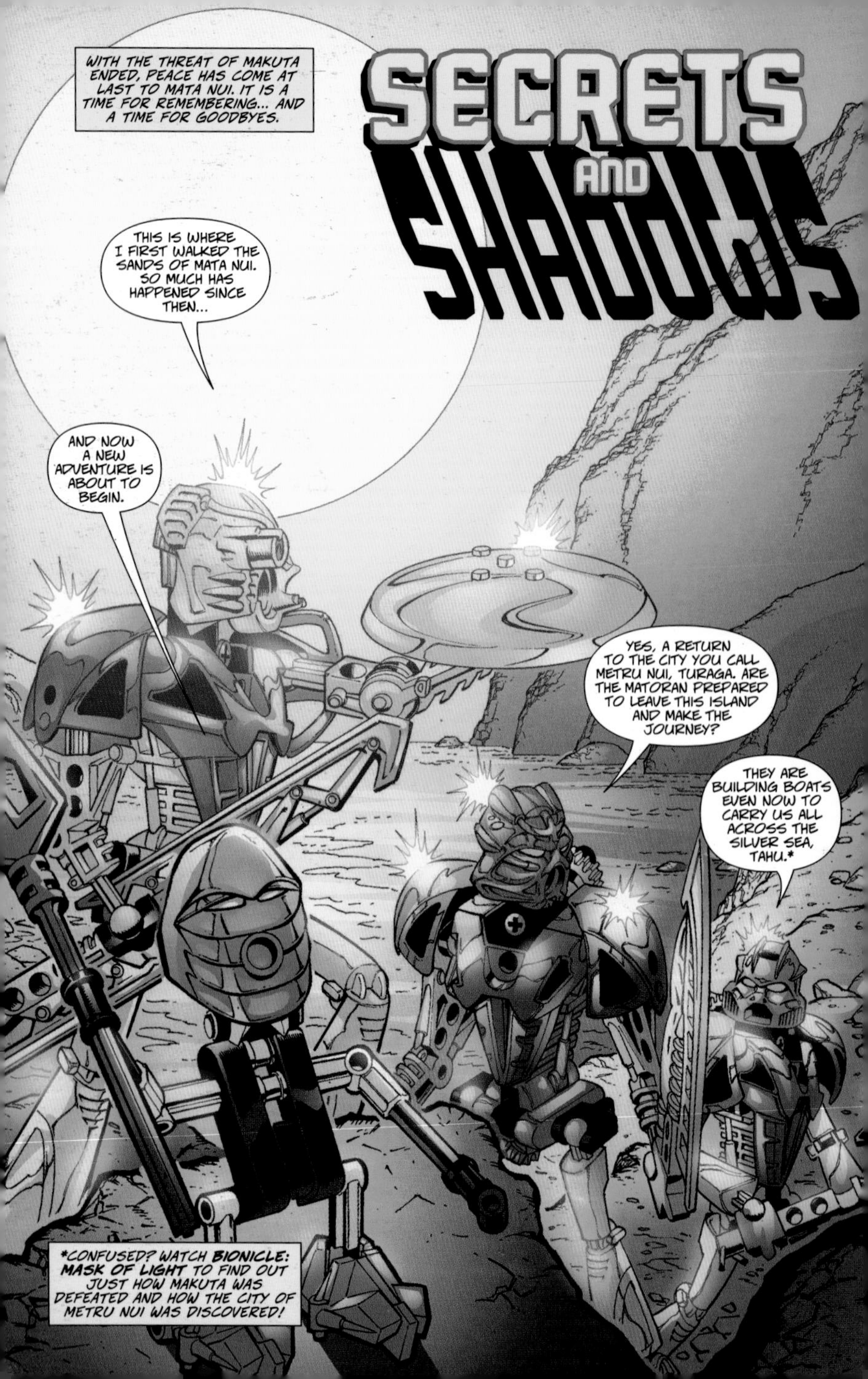
WITH THE THREAT OF MAKUTA ENDED, PEACE HAS COME AT LAST TO MATA NUI. IT IS A TIME FOR REMEMBERING... AND A TIME FOR GOODBYES.
SECRETS AND SHADOWS
THIS IS WHERE I FIRST WALKED THE SANDS OF MATA NUI. SO MUCH HAS HAPPENED SINCE THEN...
AND NOW A NEW ADVENTURE IS ABOUT TO BEGIN.
YES, A RETURN TO THE CITY YOU CALL METRU NUI, TURAGA. ARE THE MATORAN PREPARED TO LEAVE THIS ISLAND AND MAKE THE JOURNEY?
THEY ARE BUILDING BOATS EVEN NOW TO CARRY US ALL ACROSS THE SILVER SEA, TAHU.*
*CONFUSED? WATCH BIONICLE: MASK OF LIGHT TO FIND OUT JUST HOW MAKUTA WAS DEFEATED AND HOW THE CITY OF METRU NUI WAS DISCOVERED!

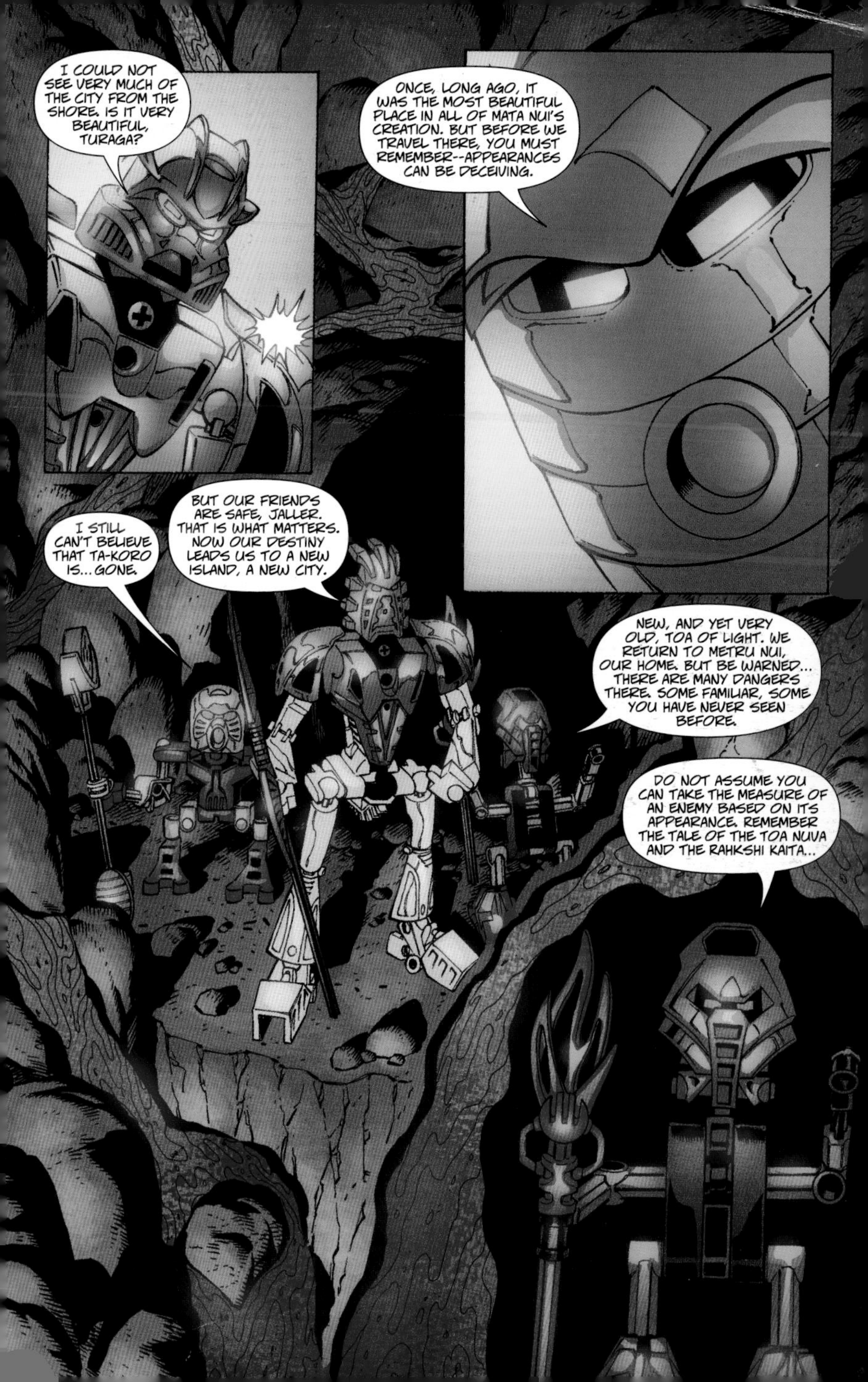

I COULD NOT SEE VERY MUCH OF THE CITY FROM THE SHORE. IS IT VERY BEAUTIFUL, TURAGA?
ONCE, LONG AGO, IT WAS THE MOST BEAUTIFUL PLACE IN ALL OF MATA NUI'S CREATION. BUT BEFORE WE TRAVEL THERE, YOU MUST REMEMBER--APPEARANCES CAN BE DECEIVING.
I STILL CAN'T BELIEVE THAT TA-KORO IS... GONE.
BUT OUR FRIENDS ARE SAFE, JALLER. THAT IS WHAT MATTERS. NOW OUR DESTINY LEADS US TO A NEW ISLAND, A NEW CITY.
NEW, AND YET VERY OLD, TOA OF LIGHT. WE RETURN TO METRU NUI, OUR HOME. BUT BE WARNED... THERE ARE MANY DANGERS THERE. SOME FAMILIAR, SOME YOU HAVE NEVER SEEN BEFORE.
DO NOT ASSUME YOU CAN TAKE THE MEASURE OF AN ENEMY BASED ON ITS APPEARANCE. REMEMBER THE TALE OF THE TOA NUVA AND THE RAHKSHI KAITA...

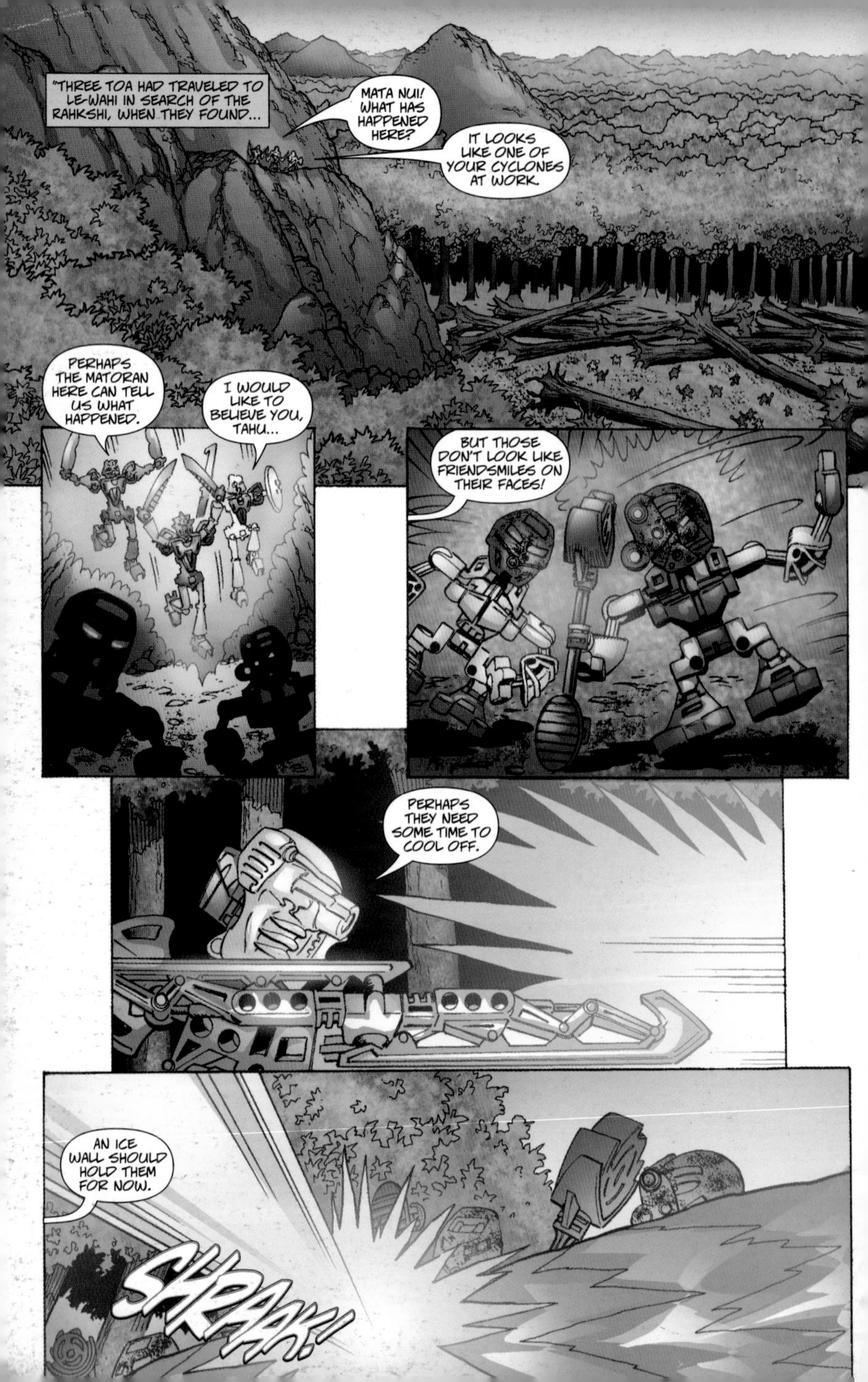

"THREE TOA HAD TRAVELED TO LE-WAHI IN SEARCH OF THE RAHKSHI, WHEN THEY FOUND...
MATA NUI! WHAT HAS HAPPENED HERE?
IT LOOKS LIKE ONE OF YOUR CYCLONES AT WORK.
PERHAPS THE MATORAN HERE CAN TELL US WHAT HAPPENED.
I WOULD LIKE TO BELIEVE YOU, TAHU...
BUT THOSE DON'T LOOK LIKE FRIENDSMILES ON THEIR FACES!
PERHAPS THEY NEED SOME TIME TO COOL OFF.
AN ICE WALL SHOULD HOLD THEM FOR NOW.
SKRAAK!

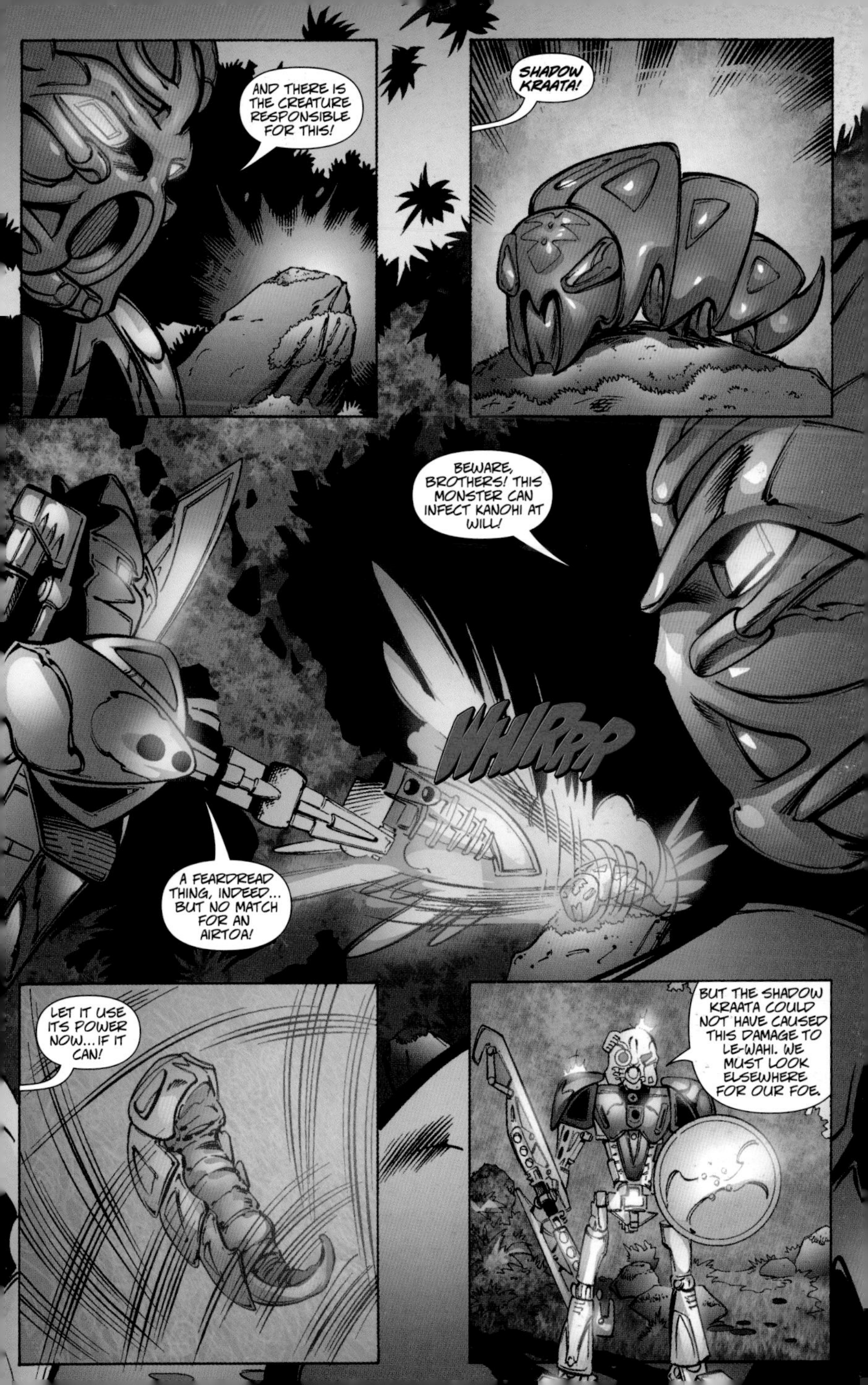
AND THERE IS THE CREATURE RESPONSIBLE FOR THIS!
SHADOW KRAATA!
BEWARE, BROTHERS! THIS MONSTER CAN INFECT KANOHI AT WILL!
WHIRRR
A FEARDREAD THING, INDEED... BUT NO MATCH FOR AN AIRTOA!
LET IT USE ITS POWER NOW... IF IT CAN!
BUT THE SHADOW KRAATA COULD NOT HAVE CAUSED THIS DAMAGE TO LE-WAHI. WE MUST LOOK ELSEWHERE FOR OUR FOE.

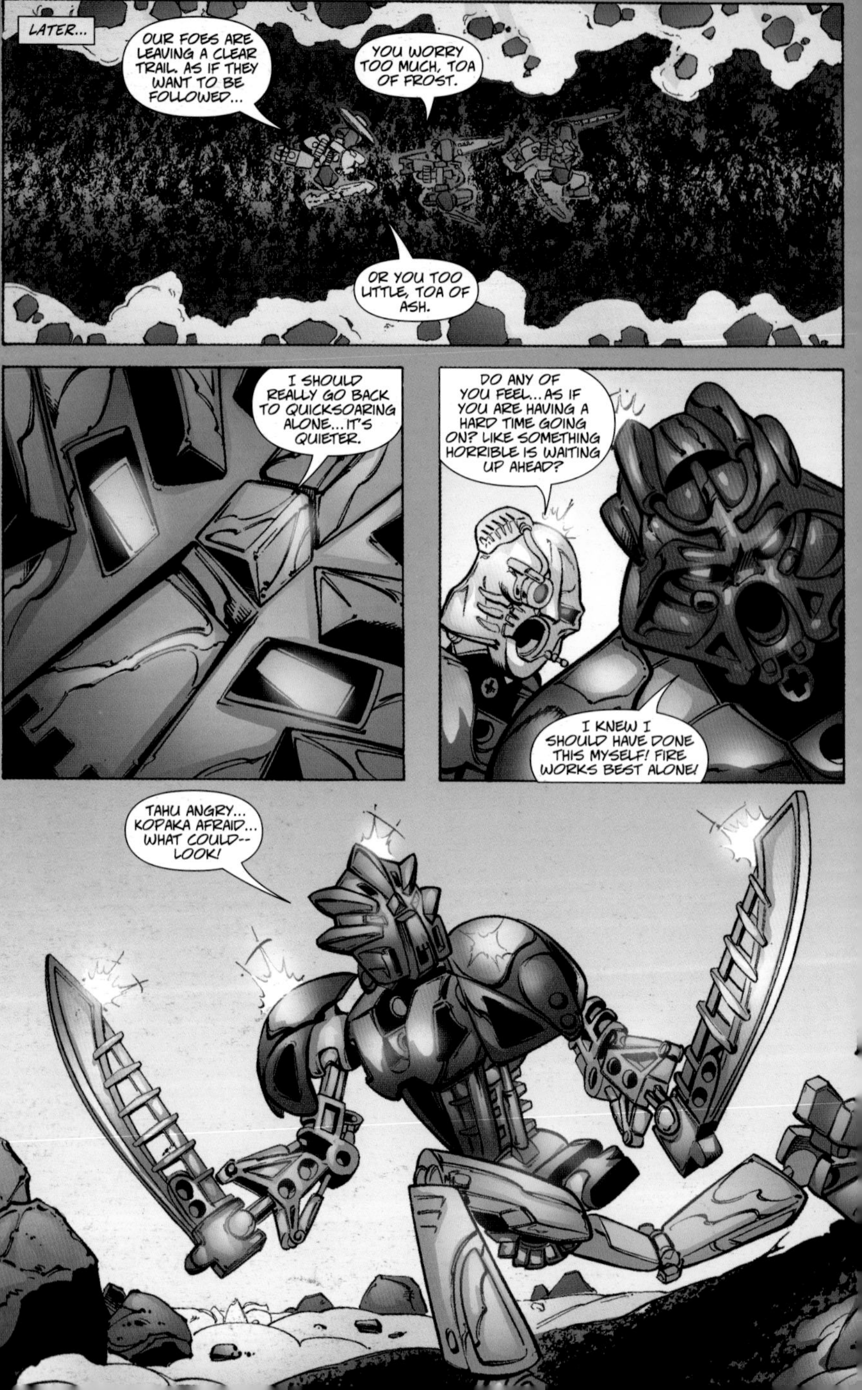

LATER...
OUR FOES ARE LEAVING A CLEAR TRAIL. AS IF THEY WANT TO BE FOLLOWED...
YOU WORRY TOO MUCH, TOA OF FROST.
OR YOU TOO LITTLE, TOA OF ASH.
I SHOULD REALLY GO BACK TO QUICKSOARING ALONE... IT'S QUIETER.
DO ANY OF YOU FEEL... AS IF YOU ARE HAVING A HARD TIME GOING ON? LIKE SOMETHING HORRIBLE IS WAITING UP AHEAD?
I KNEW I SHOULD HAVE DONE THIS MYSELF! FIRE WORKS BEST ALONE!
TAHU ANGRY... KOPAKA AFRAID... WHAT COULD-- LOOK!

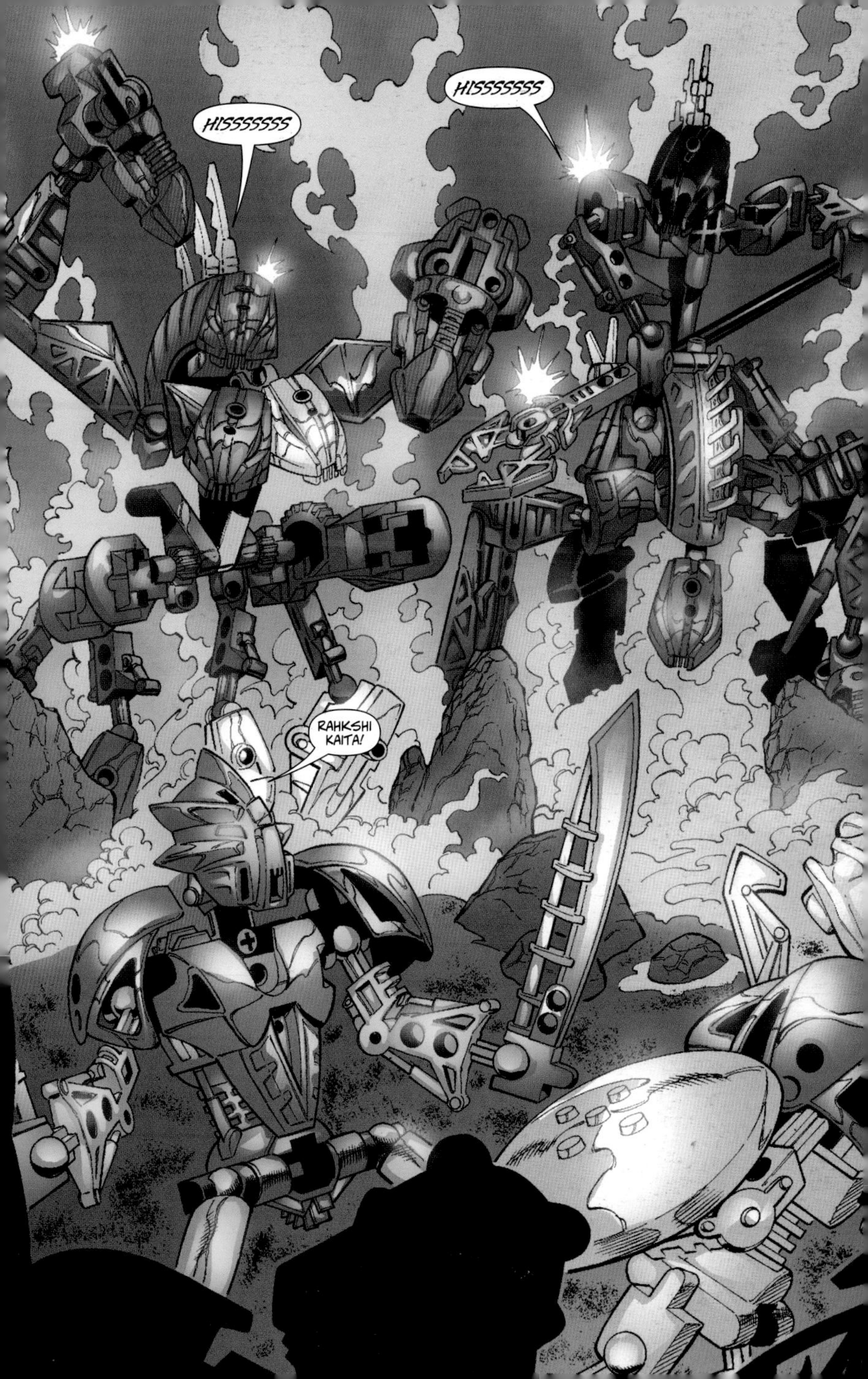
HISSSSSSS
HISSSSSSS
RAHKSHI KAITA!

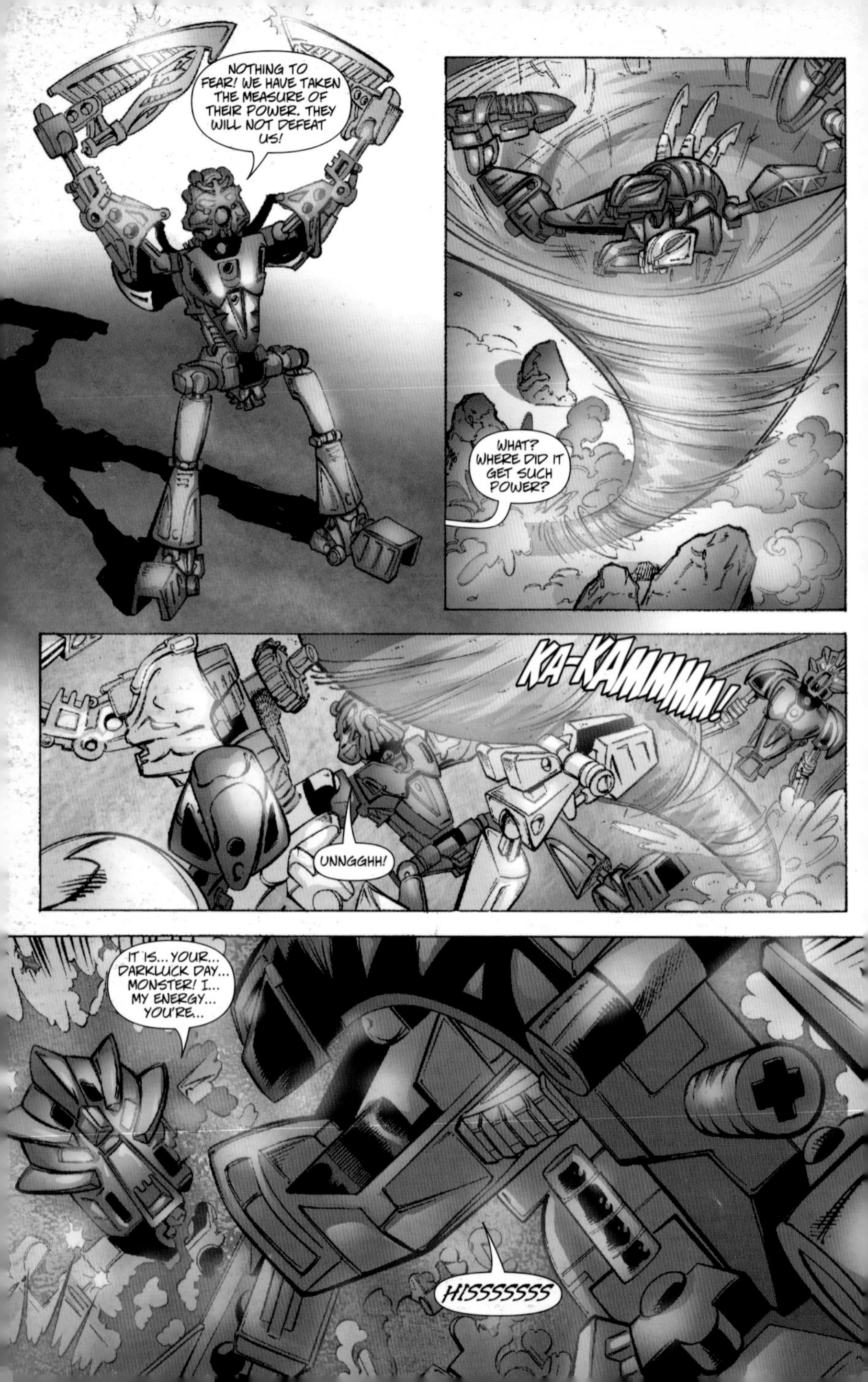
NOTHING TO FEAR! WE HAVE TAKEN THE MEASURE OF THEIR POWER. THEY WILL NOT DEFEAT US!
WHAT? WHERE DID IT GET SUCH POWER?
KA-KAMMMM!
UNNGGHH!
IT IS... YOUR... DARKLUCK DAY... MONSTER! I... MY ENERGY... YOU'RE...
HISSSSSSS

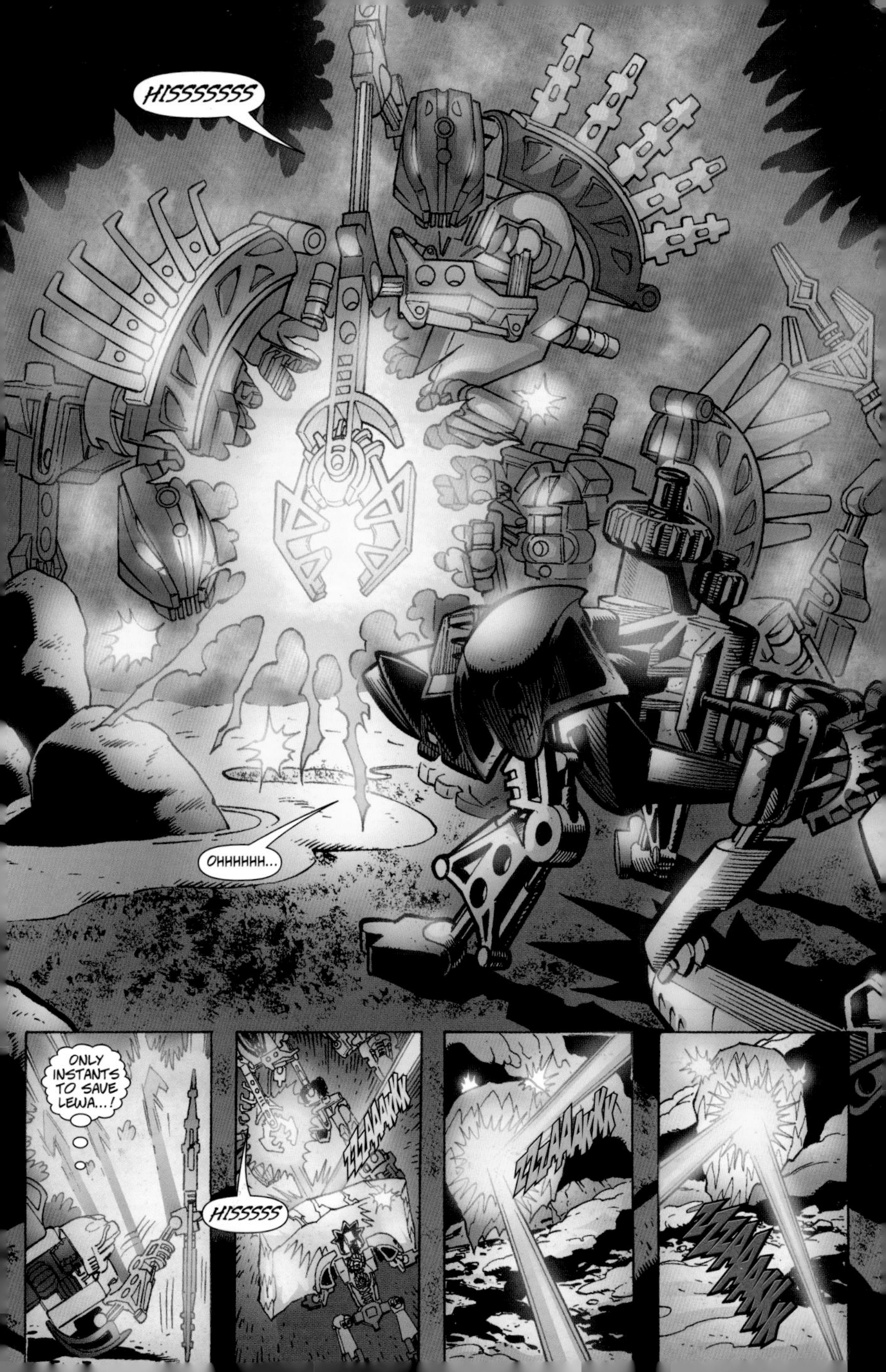
HISSSSSSS
OHHHHHH...
ONLY INSTANTS TO SAVE LEWA...!
HISSSSS
ZZZAAAKKK
ZZZAAAKKK
ZZZAAAKKK

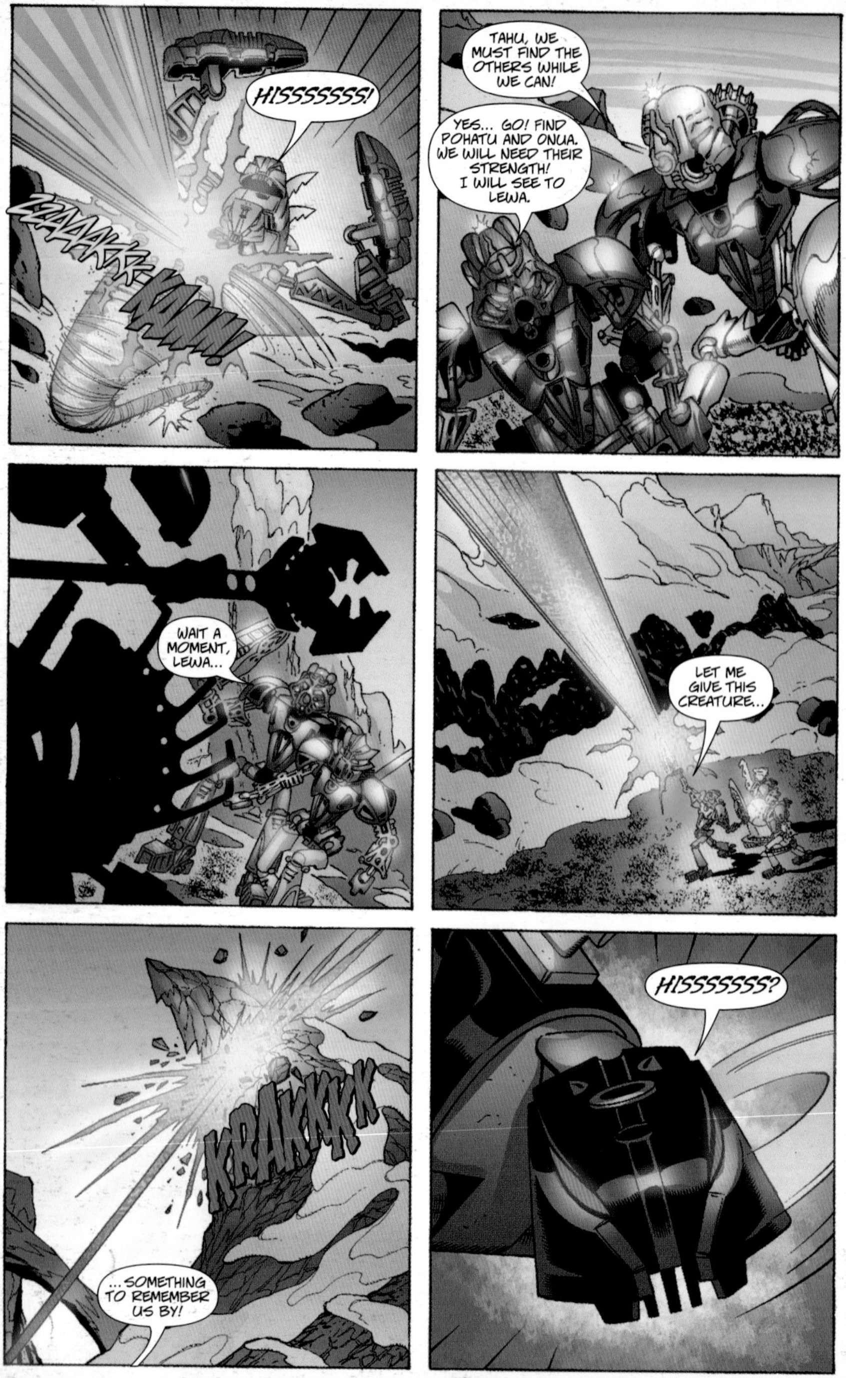
HISSSSSSS!
ZZZAAAAKKK
KAWW!
TAHU, WE MUST FIND THE OTHERS WHILE WE CAN!
YES... GO! FIND POHATU AND ONUA. WE WILL NEED THEIR STRENGTH! I WILL SEE TO LEWA.
WAIT A MOMENT, LEWA...
LET ME GIVE THIS CREATURE...
KRAKKKK
...SOMETHING TO REMEMBER US BY!
HISSSSSSS?

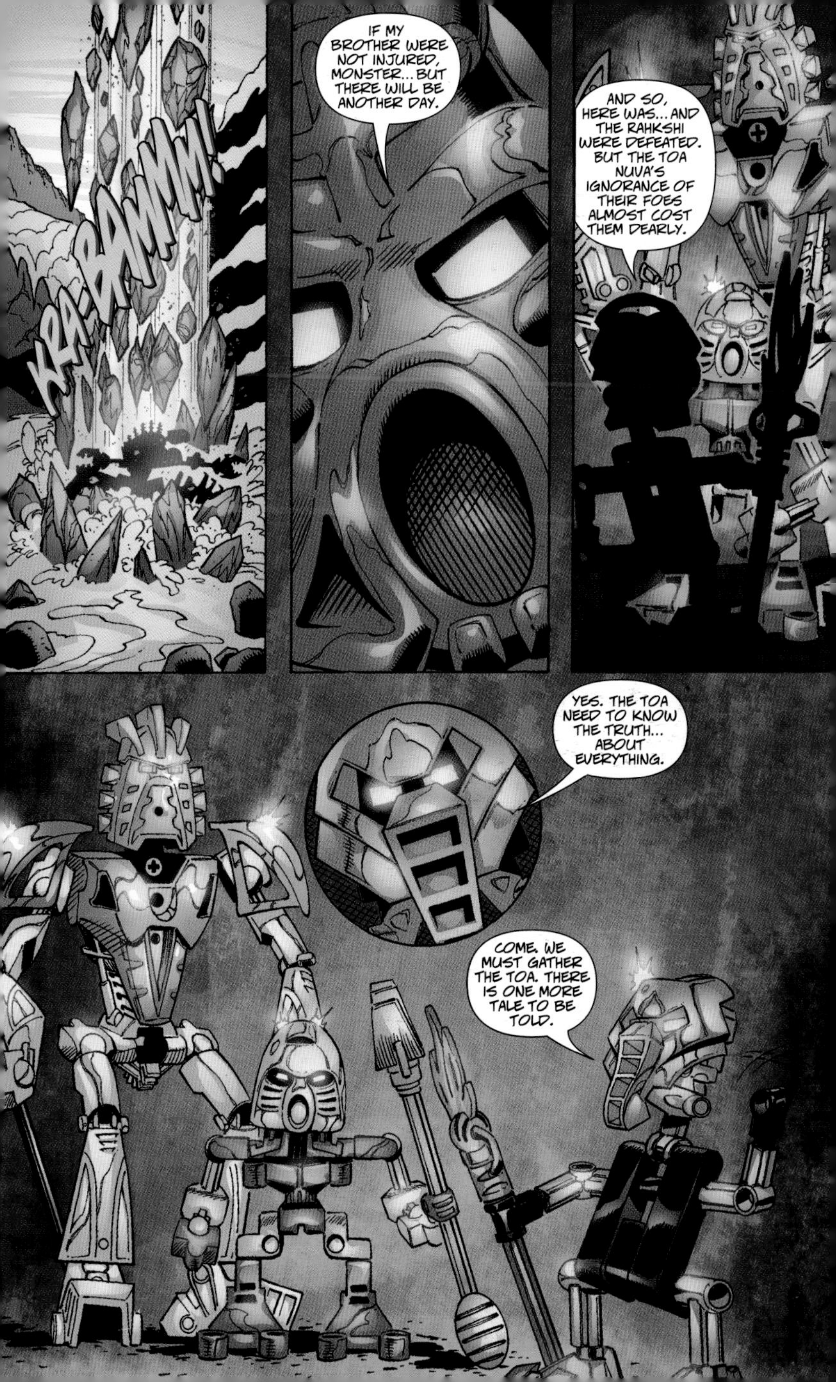
KRA-BAMMM!
IF MY BROTHER WERE NOT INJURED, MONSTER... BUT THERE WILL BE ANOTHER DAY.
AND SO, HERE WAS... AND THE RAHKSHI WERE DEFEATED. BUT THE TOA NUVA'S IGNORANCE OF THEIR FOES ALMOST COST THEM DEARLY.
YES. THE TOA NEED TO KNOW THE TRUTH... ABOUT EVERYTHING.
COME. WE MUST GATHER THE TOA. THERE IS ONE MORE TALE TO BE TOLD.

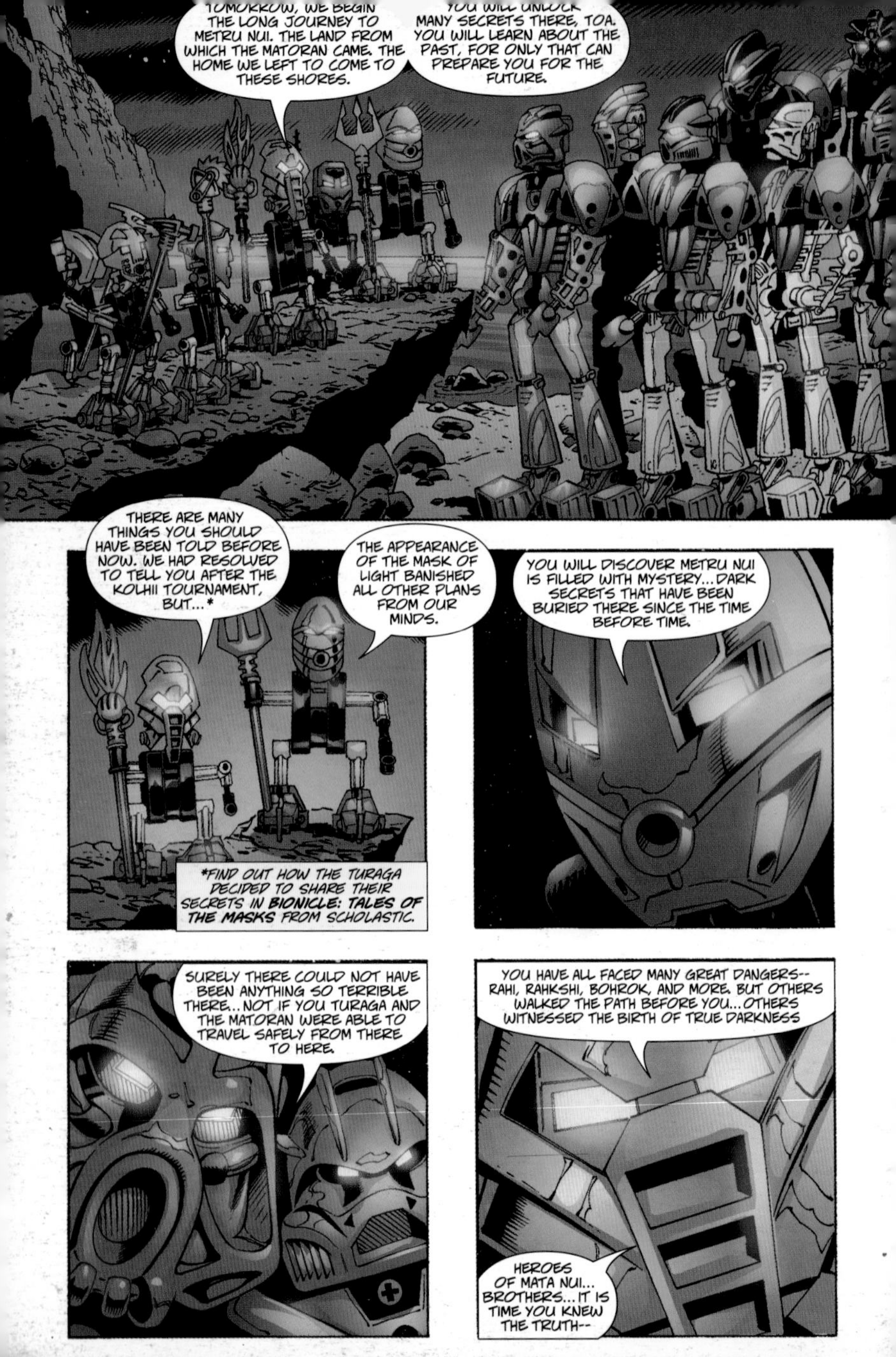
TOMORROW, WE BEGIN THE LONG JOURNEY TO METRU NUI. THE LAND FROM WHICH THE MATORAN CAME. THE HOME WE LEFT TO COME TO THESE SHORES.
YOU WILL UNLOCK MANY SECRETS THERE, TOA. YOU WILL LEARN ABOUT THE PAST, FOR ONLY THAT CAN PREPARE YOU FOR THE FUTURE.
THERE ARE MANY THINGS YOU SHOULD HAVE BEEN TOLD BEFORE NOW. WE HAD RESOLVED TO TELL YOU AFTER THE KOLHII TOURNAMENT, BUT...*
THE APPEARANCE OF THE MASK OF LIGHT BANISHED ALL OTHER PLANS FROM OUR MINDS.
*FIND OUT HOW THE TURAGA DECIDED TO SHARE THEIR SECRETS IN BIONICLE: TALES OF THE MASKS FROM SCHOLASTIC.
YOU WILL DISCOVER METRU NUI IS FILLED WITH MYSTERY... DARK SECRETS THAT HAVE BEEN BURIED THERE SINCE THE TIME BEFORE TIME.
SURELY THERE COULD NOT HAVE BEEN ANYTHING SO TERRIBLE THERE... NOT IF YOU TURAGA AND THE MATORAN WERE ABLE TO TRAVEL SAFELY FROM THERE TO HERE.
YOU HAVE ALL FACED MANY GREAT DANGERS-- RAHI, RAHKSHI, BOHROK, AND MORE. BUT OTHERS WALKED THE PATH BEFORE YOU... OTHERS WITNESSED THE BIRTH OF TRUE DARKNESS
HEROES OF MATA NUI... BROTHERS... IT IS TIME YOU KNEW THE TRUTH--

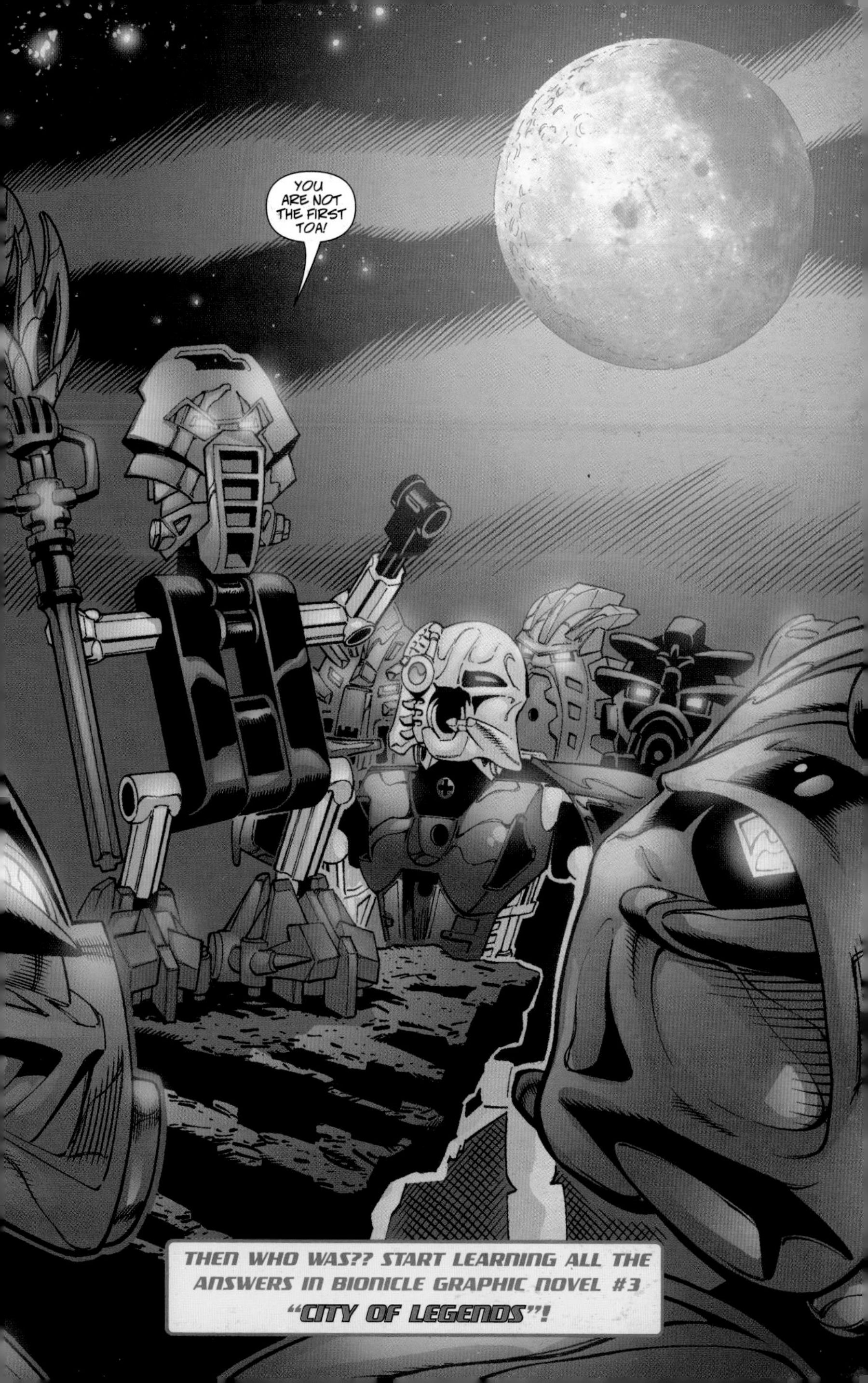
YOU ARE NOT THE FIRST TOA!
THEN WHO WAS?? START LEARNING ALL THE ANSWERS IN BIONICLE GRAPHIC NOVEL #3 "CITY OF LEGENDS"!

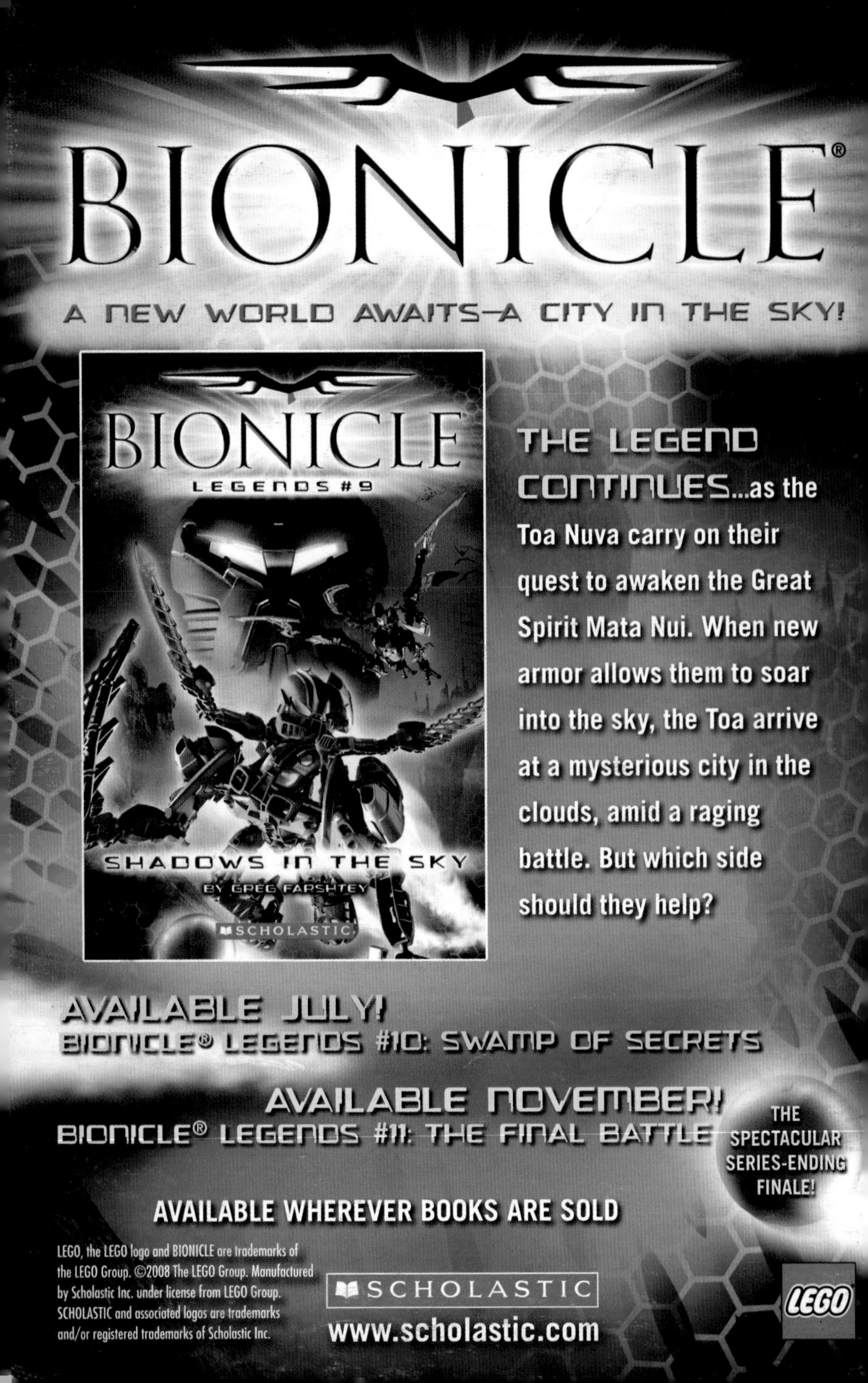
BIONICLE®
A NEW WORLD AWAITS—A CITY IN THE SKY!
BIONICLE
LEGENDS #9
SHADOWS IN THE SKY
BY GREG FARSHTEY
SCHOLASTIC
THE LEGEND CONTINUES...as the Toa Nuva carry on their quest to awaken the Great Spirit Mata Nui. When new armor allows them to soar into the sky, the Toa arrive at a mysterious city in the clouds, amid a raging battle. But which side should they help?
AVAILABLE JULY!
BIONICLE® LEGENDS #10: SWAMP OF SECRETS
AVAILABLE NOVEMBER!
BIONICLE® LEGENDS #11: THE FINAL BATTLE
THE SPECTACULAR SERIES-ENDING FINALE!
AVAILABLE WHEREVER BOOKS ARE SOLD
LEGO, the LEGO logo and BIONICLE are trademarks of the LEGO Group. ©2008 The LEGO Group. Manufactured by Scholastic Inc. under license from LEGO Group. SCHOLASTIC and associated logos are trademarks and/or registered trademarks of Scholastic Inc.
SCHOLASTIC
www.scholastic.com
LEGO

WATCH OUT FOR PAPERCUTZ

If you picked up BIONICLE® Graphic Novel #1: Rise of the Toa Nuva, then you may be wondering who I am and what this section is doing in the back of the second BIONICLE graphic novel. First, allow me to introduce myself, I'm Jim Salicrup the Editor-in-Chief of Papercutz, the publishers of this fine graphic novel that you're now looking at. This little section in the back of the graphic novel is aptly called the Papercutz Backpages, where we try to keep you up-to-date on the exciting goings-on at Papercutz, as well as featuring your feedback. This section would've been included in the first BIONICLE graphic novel, but there just wasn't any room – there were just too many great pages of BIONICLE comics to squeeze in!

This time around, as we present the long-lost prequel comics to the BIONICLE Movie: MASK OF LIGHT (available on DVD) we just managed to have enough room.

In the pages ahead we take a look at a few other Papercutz graphic novels you might find too-amazing to resist. The first one is TALES FROM THE CRYPT, based on the best horror comicbook ever published, the second is CLASSICS ILLUSTRATED DELUXE, and the third is CLASSICS ILLUSTRATED, both also based on a famous comicbook series. Check 'em out!

One last request. Let us know what you thought of this BIONICLE graphic novel. Email me at:

salicrup@papercutz.com

or write me at:

Jim Salicrup,
PAPERCUTZ, 40 Exchange Place, Suite 1308,
New York, NY 10005.

Love us or hate us – be sure to tell us!

Thanks,

THE OLD EDITOR
Caricature by Rick Parker

Greetings, Fiends!

It's your ol' pal the CRYPT-KEEPER here, giving a guided TERRIFYING TOUR through the SCARIEST GRAPHIC NOVEL ever! It's TALES FROM THE CRYPT #4 "CRYPT-KEEPING IT REAL."

You'll not only find page after page of PULSE-POUNDING CHILLS, but me and my fellow GhouLunatics decided to get all COMPUTER AGE-Y on you! Wait till you see the stories we found on the INTERRED-NET site known as YOU-TOOMB! The SHOCKS and SUS-PENSE come at you FAST and FURIOUS!

But that's not all! Just gaze upon the CREEPY COVER on the next page, if you DARE! That poor guy made the UNFORTUNATE MISTAKE of appearing on a REALITY TV SHOW that was perhaps a little TOO REAL! The show is called "JUMPING THE SHARK" and you can see a quick preview starting right after the next PUTRID PAGE!

THE CRYPT-KEEPER

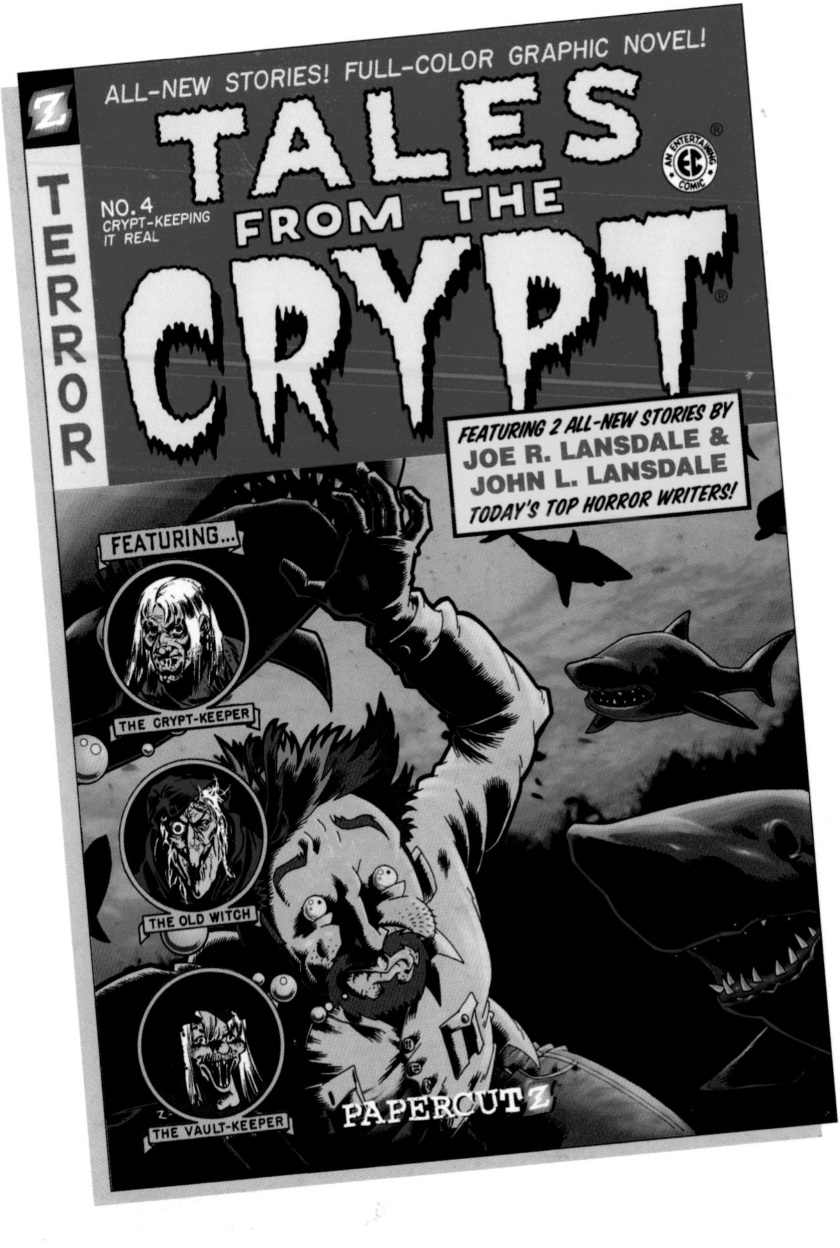
ALL-NEW STORIES! FULL-COLOR GRAPHIC NOVEL!
TERROR
TALES FROM THE CRYPT
AN ENTERTAINING EC COMIC
NO. 4
CRYPT-KEEPING IT REAL
FEATURING 2 ALL-NEW STORIES BY JOE R. LANSDALE & JOHN L. LANSDALE TODAY'S TOP HORROR WRITERS!
FEATURING...
THE CRYPT-KEEPER
THE OLD WITCH
THE VAULT-KEEPER
PAPERCUTZ

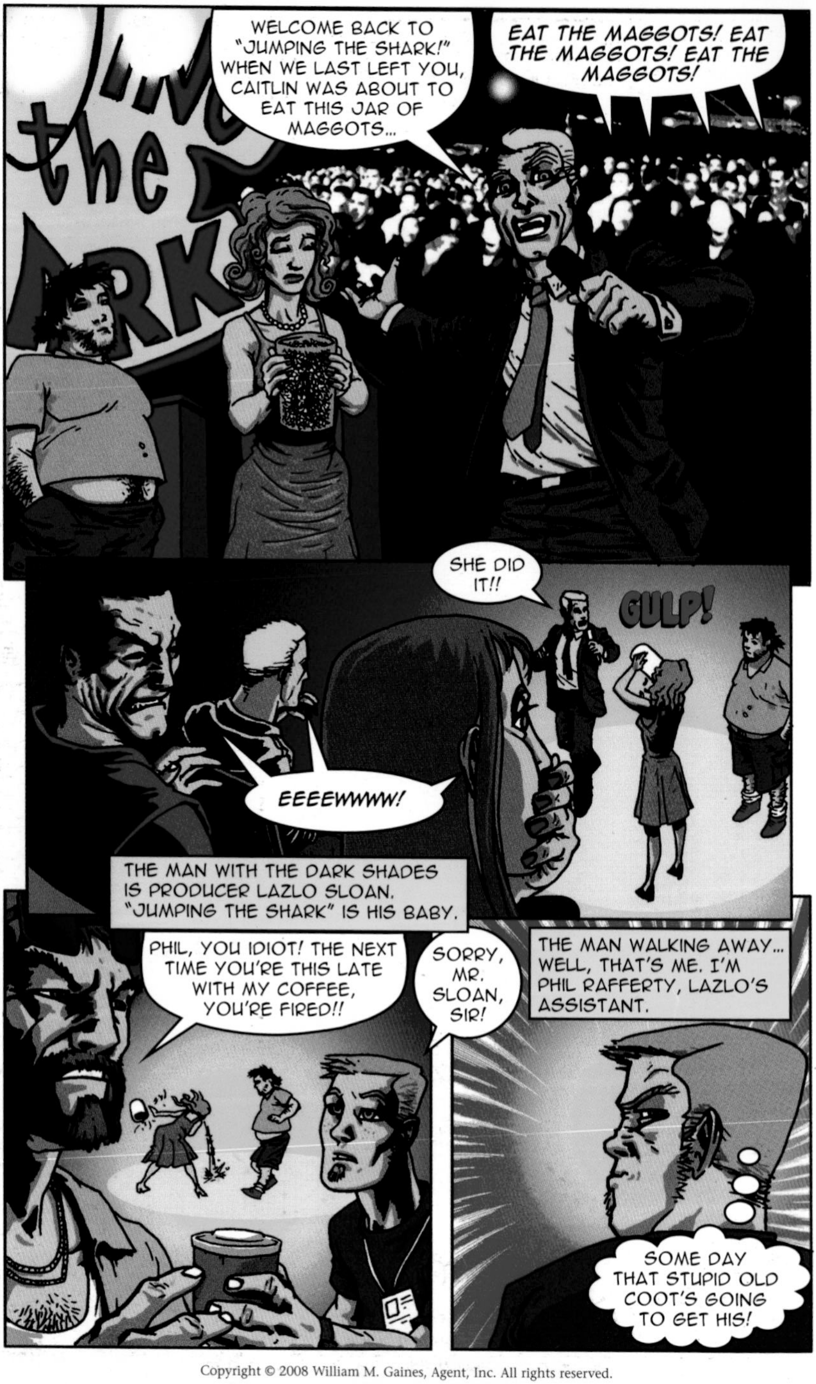
WELCOME BACK TO "JUMPING THE SHARK!" WHEN WE LAST LEFT YOU, CAITLIN WAS ABOUT TO EAT THIS JAR OF MAGGOTS...
EAT THE MAGGOTS! EAT THE MAGGOTS! EAT THE MAGGOTS!
SHE DID IT!!
GULP!
EEEEWWWW!
THE MAN WITH THE DARK SHADES IS PRODUCER LAZLO SLOAN. "JUMPING THE SHARK" IS HIS BABY.
PHIL, YOU IDIOT! THE NEXT TIME YOU'RE THIS LATE WITH MY COFFEE, YOU'RE FIRED!!
SORRY, MR. SLOAN, SIR!
THE MAN WALKING AWAY... WELL, THAT'S ME. I'M PHIL RAFFERTY, LAZLO'S ASSISTANT.
SOME DAY THAT STUPID OLD COOT'S GOING TO GET HIS!

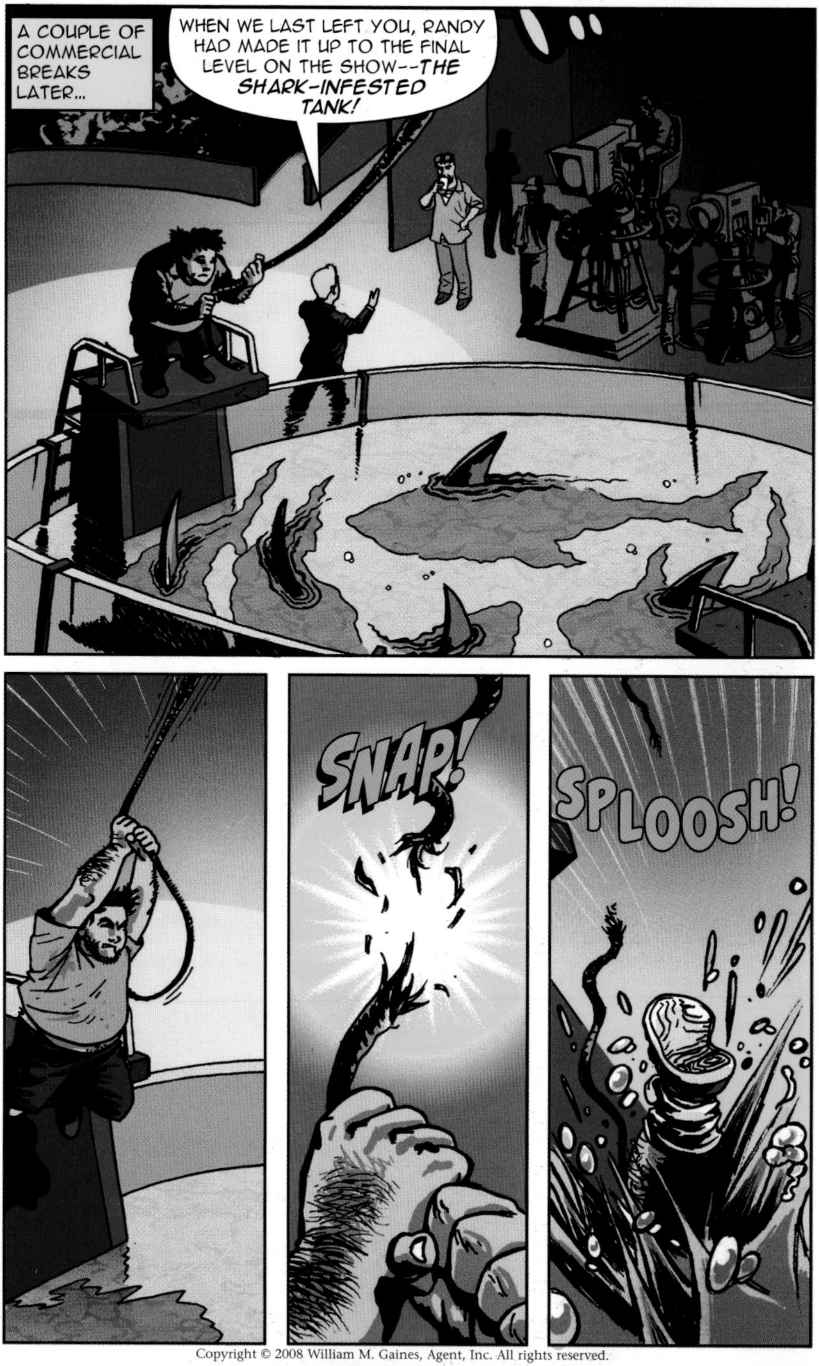
A COUPLE OF COMMERCIAL BREAKS LATER...
WHEN WE LAST LEFT YOU, RANDY HAD MADE IT UP TO THE FINAL LEVEL ON THE SHOW--*THE SHARK-INFESTED TANK!*
SNAP!
SPLOOSH!

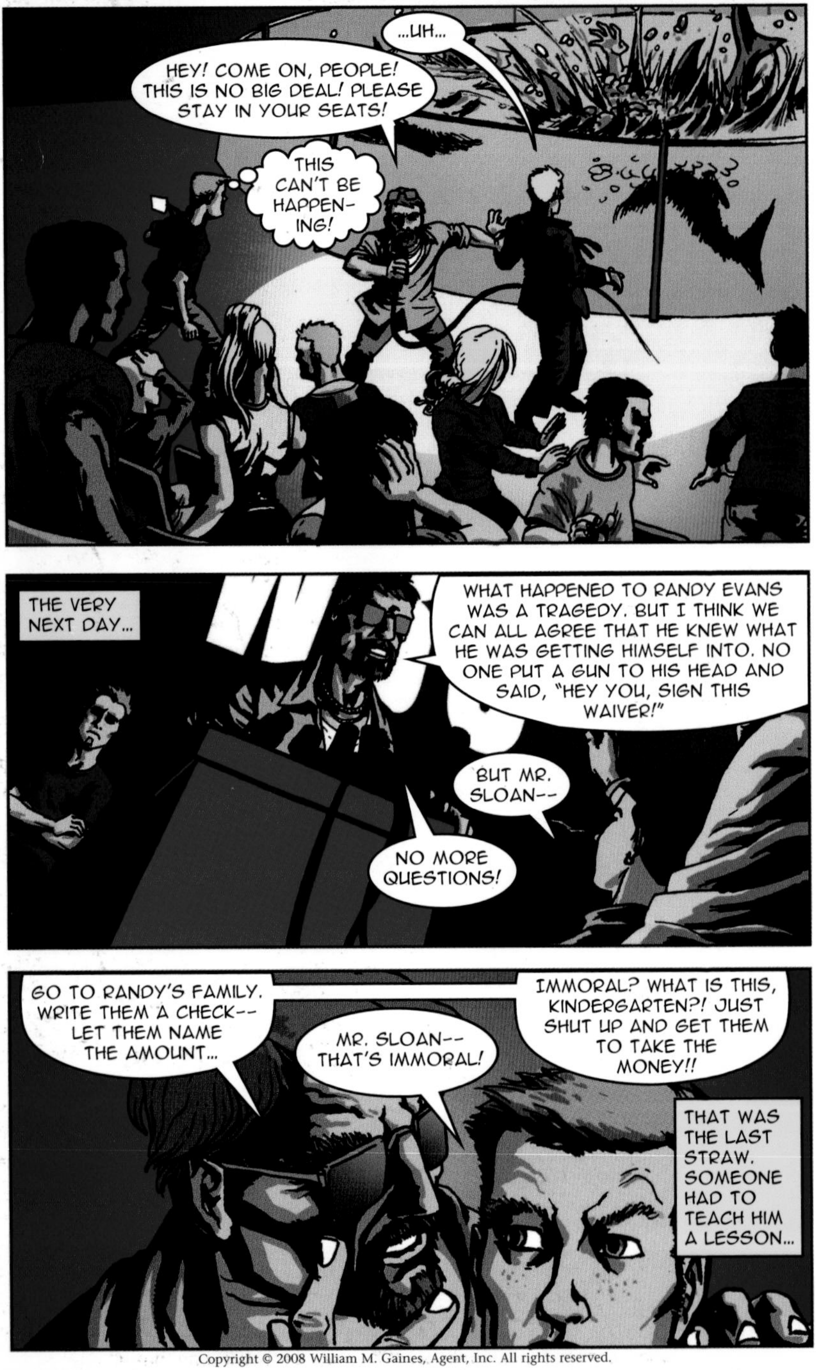
HEY! COME ON, PEOPLE! THIS IS NO BIG DEAL! PLEASE STAY IN YOUR SEATS!
...UH...
THIS CAN'T BE HAPPEN-ING!
THE VERY NEXT DAY...
WHAT HAPPENED TO RANDY EVANS WAS A TRAGEDY. BUT I THINK WE CAN ALL AGREE THAT HE KNEW WHAT HE WAS GETTING HIMSELF INTO. NO ONE PUT A GUN TO HIS HEAD AND SAID, "HEY YOU, SIGN THIS WAIVER!"
BUT MR. SLOAN--
NO MORE QUESTIONS!
GO TO RANDY'S FAMILY. WRITE THEM A CHECK-- LET THEM NAME THE AMOUNT...
MR. SLOAN-- THAT'S IMMORAL!
IMMORAL? WHAT IS THIS, KINDERGARTEN?! JUST SHUT UP AND GET THEM TO TAKE THE MONEY!!
THAT WAS THE LAST STRAW. SOMEONE HAD TO TEACH HIM A LESSON...

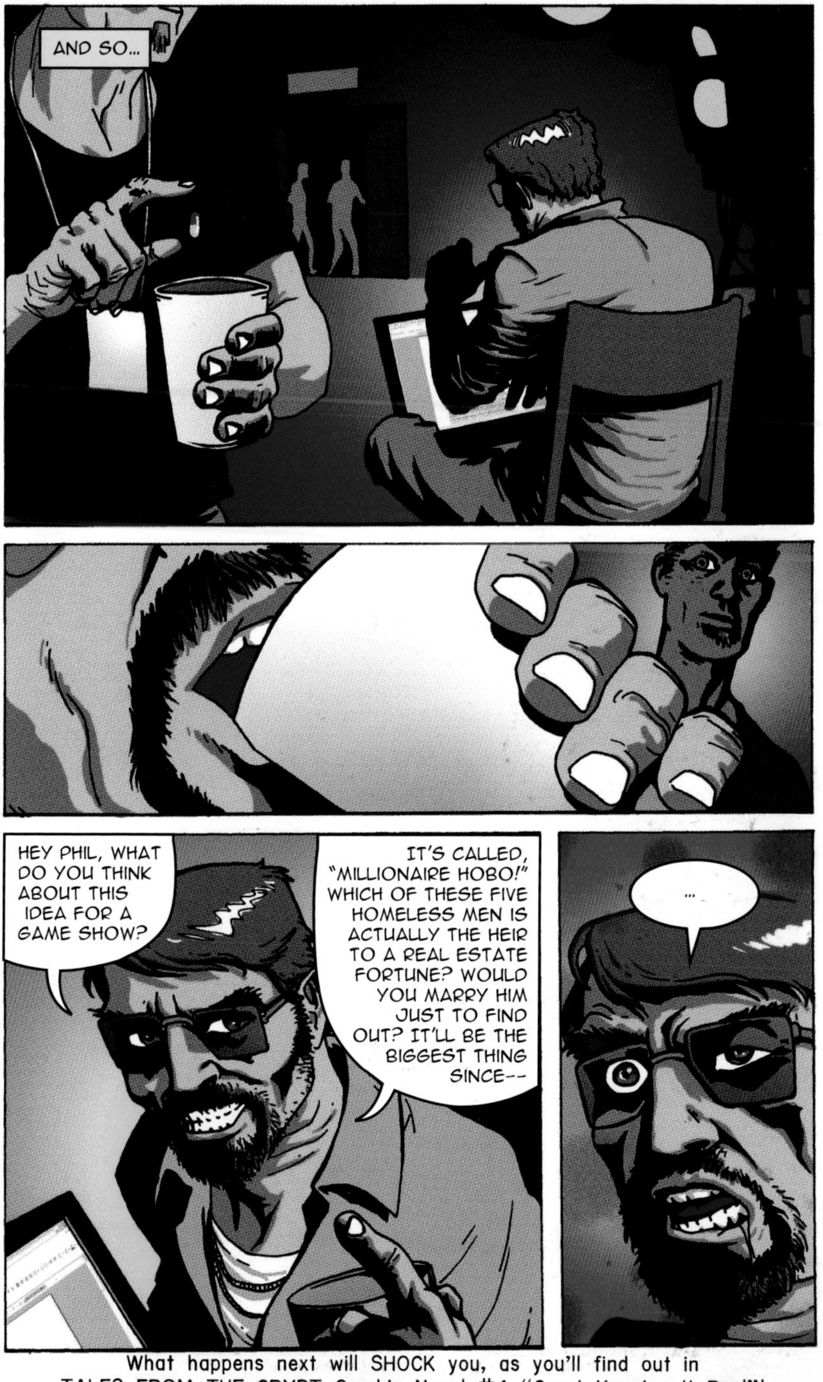
AND SO...
HEY PHIL, WHAT DO YOU THINK ABOUT THIS IDEA FOR A GAME SHOW?
IT'S CALLED, "MILLIONAIRE HOBO!" WHICH OF THESE FIVE HOMELESS MEN IS ACTUALLY THE HEIR TO A REAL ESTATE FORTUNE? WOULD YOU MARRY HIM JUST TO FIND OUT? IT'LL BE THE BIGGEST THING SINCE--
...

What happens next will SHOCK you, as you'll find out in TALES FROM THE CRYPT Graphic Novel #4 "Crypt-Keeping It Real"!

But in the meantime here's a quick peek at "MOONLIGHT SONATA" also in CRYPT #4...

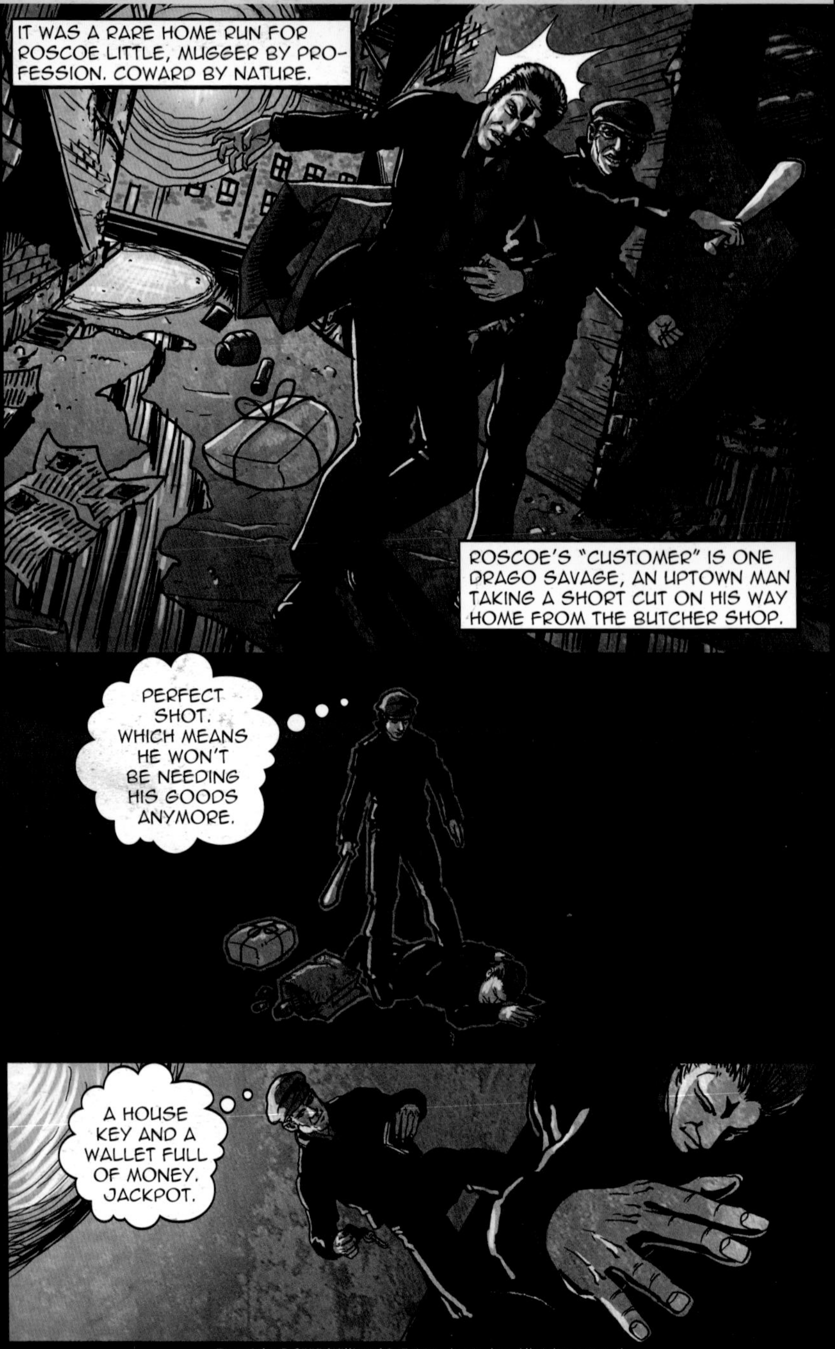
IT WAS A RARE HOME RUN FOR ROSCOE LITTLE, MUGGER BY PROFESSION. COWARD BY NATURE.
ROSCOE'S "CUSTOMER" IS ONE DRAGO SAVAGE, AN UPTOWN MAN TAKING A SHORT CUT ON HIS WAY HOME FROM THE BUTCHER SHOP.
PERFECT SHOT. WHICH MEANS HE WON'T BE NEEDING HIS GOODS ANYMORE.
A HOUSE KEY AND A WALLET FULL OF MONEY. JACKPOT.

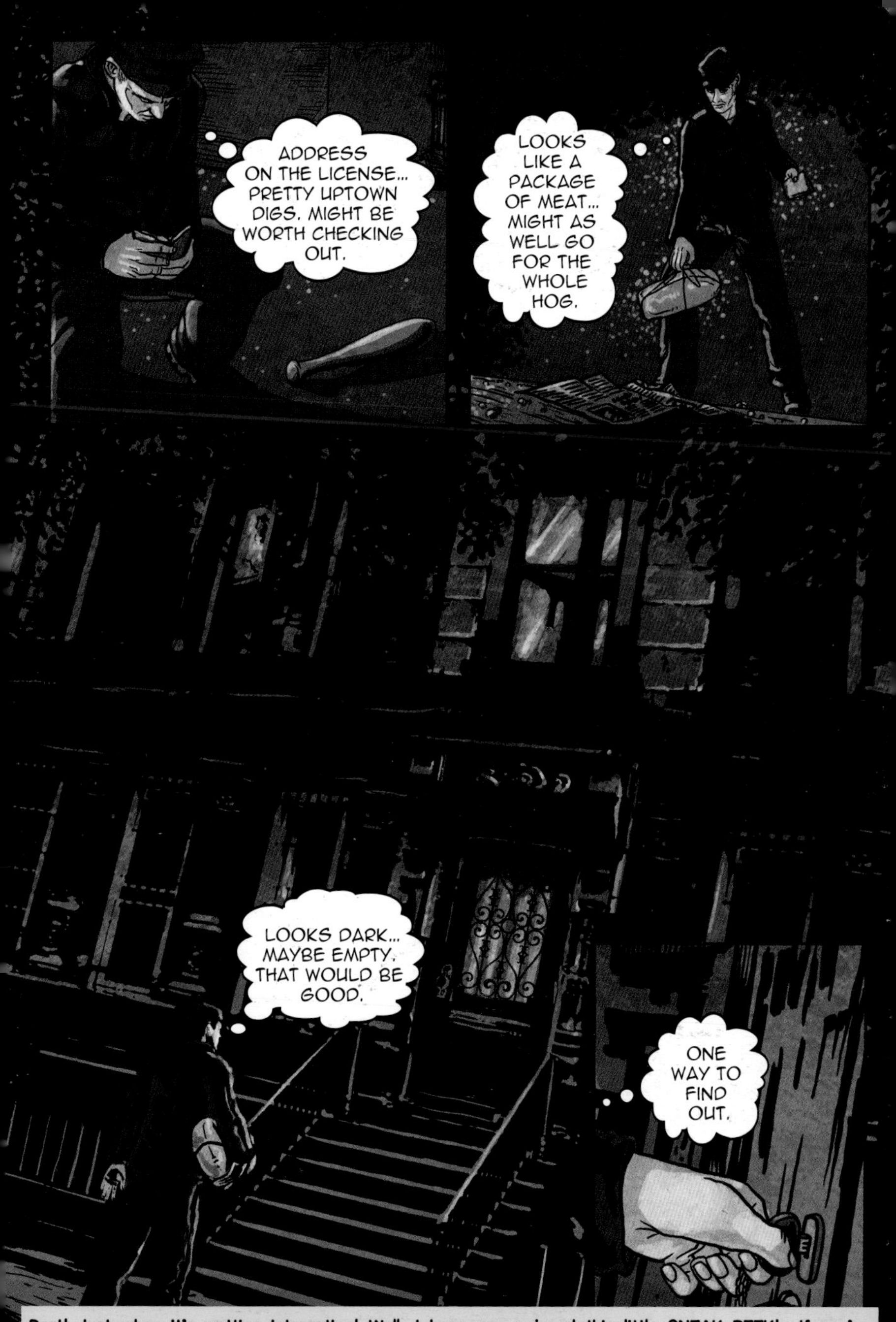
ADDRESS ON THE LICENSE... PRETTY UPTOWN DIGS. MIGHT BE WORTH CHECKING OUT.
LOOKS LIKE A PACKAGE OF MEAT... MIGHT AS WELL GO FOR THE WHOLE HOG.
LOOKS DARK... MAYBE EMPTY. THAT WOULD BE GOOD.
ONE WAY TO FIND OUT.

CLASSICS Illustrated

Featuring Stories by the World's Greatest Authors

Returns in two new series from Papercutz!

The original, best-selling series of comics adaptations of the world's greatest literature, CLASSICS ILLUSTRATED, returns in two new formats--the original, featuring abridged adaptations of classic novels, and CLASSICS ILLUSTRATED DELUXE, featuring longer, more expansive adaptations-from graphic novel publisher Papercutz. "We're very proud to say that Papercutz has received such an enthusiastic reception from librarians and school teachers for its NANCY DREW and HARDY BOYS graphic novels as well as THE LIFE OF POPE JOHN PAUL II...*IN COMICS!*, that it only seemed logical for us to bring back the original CLASSICS ILLUSTRATED comicbook series beloved by parents, educators, and librarians," explained Papercutz Publisher, Terry Nantier. "We can't thank the enlightened librarians and teachers who have supported Papercutz enough. And we're thrilled that they're so excited about CLASSICS ILLUSTRATED."

Upcoming titles include The Invisible Man, Tales from the Brothers Grimm, and Robinson Crusoe.

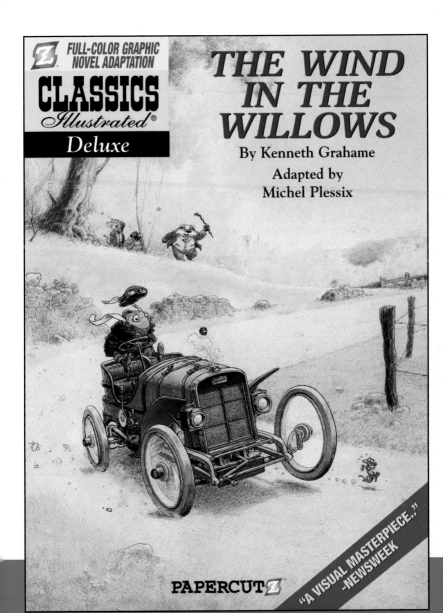

FULL-COLOR GRAPHIC
NOVEL ADAPTATION

CLASSICS
Illustrated®
Deluxe

THE WIND
IN THE
WILLOWS
By Kenneth Grahame

Adapted by
Michel Plessix

PAPERCUTZ

"A VISUAL MASTERPIECE."
-NEWSWEEK

CLASSICS Illustrated
THE THREE MUSKETEERS

CLASSICS Illustrated
Ivanhoe

CLASSICS Illustrated
THE LAST OF THE MOHICANS

CLASSICS Illustrated
Robin Hood

CLASSICS Illustrated
ARABIAN NIGHTS

CLASSICS Illustrated
LES MISERABLE

CLASSICS Illustrated
THE HOUSE OF THE SEVEN GABLES

A Short History of CLASSICS ILLUSTRATED...

CLASSICS Illustrated
THE MAN IN THE IRON MASK

William B. Jones Jr. is the author of Classics Illustrated: A Cultural History, which offers a comprehensive overview of the original comic-book series and the writers, artists, editors, and publishers behind-the-scenes. With Mr. Jones Jr.'s kind permission, here's a very short overview of the history of CLASSICS ILLUSTRATED adapted from his 2005 essay on Albert Kanter.

CLASSICS Illustrated
THE TOILERS OF THE SEA

CLASSICS ILLUSTRATED was the creation of Albert Lewis Kanter, a visionary publisher, who from 1941 to 1971, introduced young readers worldwide to the realms of literature, history, folklore, mythology, and science in over 200 titles in such comicbook series as CLASSICS ILLUSTRATED and CLASSICS ILLUSTRATED JUNIOR. Kanter, inspired by the success of the first comicbooks published in the early 30s and late 40s, believed he

CLASSICS Illustrated
The Song of Hiawatha

CLASSICS Illustrated
Two Years before The Mast

CLASSICS Illustrated
FRANKENSTEIN

CLASSICS Illustrated
The PRINCE and the PAUPER

CLASSICS Illustrated

CLASSICS Illustrated
THE BLACK ARROW

CLASSICS Illustrated

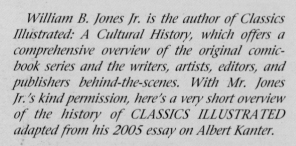

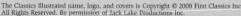

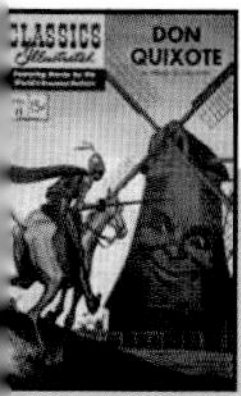
CLASSICS
DON QUIXOTE
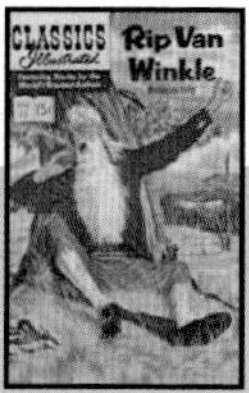
CLASSICS Illustrated
Rip Van Winkle
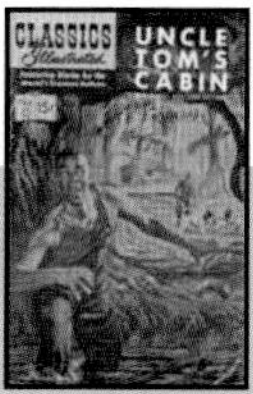
CLASSICS Illustrated
UNCLE TOM'S CABIN
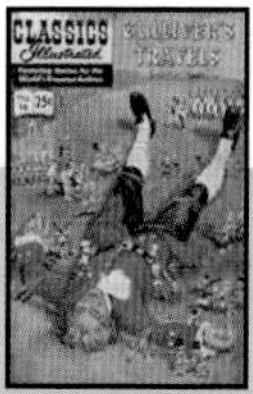
CLASSICS Illustrated
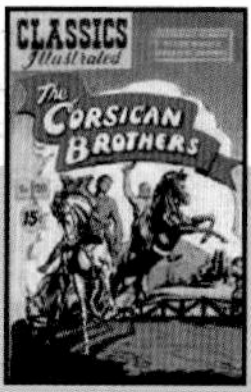
CLASSICS Illustrated
The Corsican Brothers
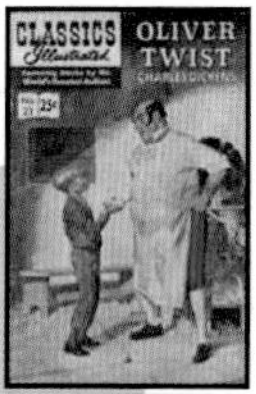
CLASSICS Illustrated
OLIVER TWIST

could use the same medium to introduce young readers to the world of great literature. CLASSIC COMICS (later changed to CLASSICS ILLUSTRATED in 1947) was launched in 1941, and soon the comicbook adaptations of Shakespeare, Stevenson, Twain, Verne, and other authors, were being used in schools and endorsed by educators.

CLASSICS ILLUSTRATED was translated and distributed in countries such as Canada, Great Britain, the Netherlands, Greece, Brazil, Mexico, and Australia. The genial publisher was hailed abroad as "Papa Klassiker." By the beginning of the 1960s, CLASSICS ILLUSTRATED was the largest childrens publication in the world. The original CLASSICS ILLUSTRATED series adapted into comics 169 titles; among these were Frankenstein, 20,000 Leagues Under the Sea, Treasure Island, Julius Caesar, and Faust.

Albert L. Kanter died, March 17, 1973, leaving behind a rich legacy for the millions of readers whose imaginations were awakened by CLASSICS ILLUSTRATED.

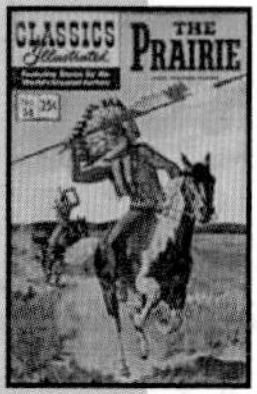
CLASSICS Illustrated
THE PRAIRIE
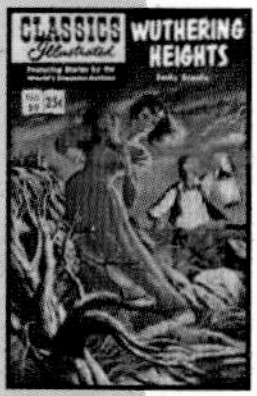
CLASSICS Illustrated
WUTHERING HEIGHTS
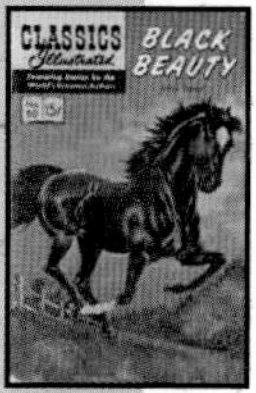
CLASSICS Illustrated
BLACK BEAUTY
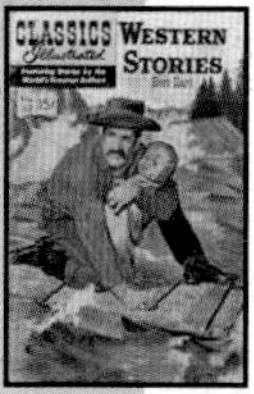
CLASSICS Illustrated
WESTERN STORIES
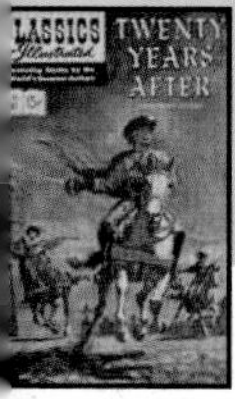
CLASSICS
TWENTY YEARS AFTER
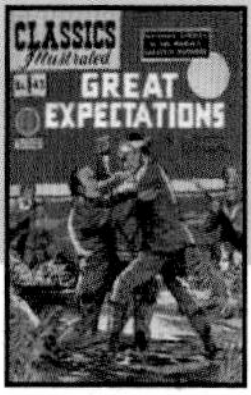
CLASSICS Illustrated
GREAT EXPECTATIONS
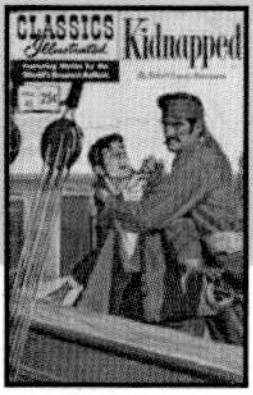
CLASSICS Illustrated
Kidnapped
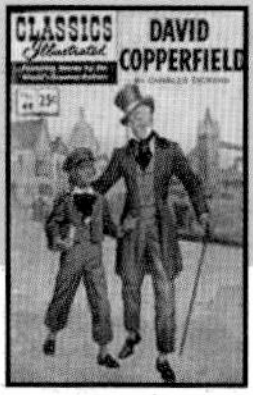
CLASSICS Illustrated
DAVID COPPERFIELD
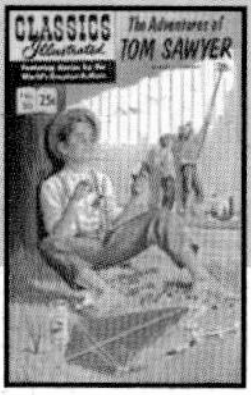
CLASSICS Illustrated
TOM SAWYER
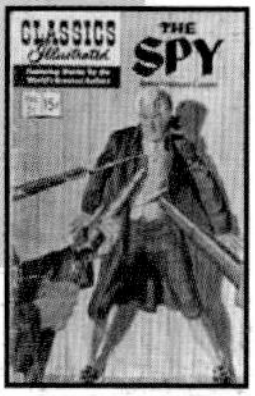
CLASSICS Illustrated
THE SPY

I'M AFRAID THERE'S NO FOOD FOR THE YOUNG MAN YOU SPOKE OF. I CAME UPON HIM JUST NOW... I THOUGHT HE WAS YOU!
WHERE, BOY, WHERE?!
ON A HILL YONDER, BUT HE RAN OFF.
HE TOOK THE FILE, AND I LEFT HIM MUTTERING, AS HE SET TO WORK ON THE LEG-IRON
CURSE THE RAT... I'LL GET HIM... I'LL PULL HIM DOWN LIKE A BLOODHOUND!

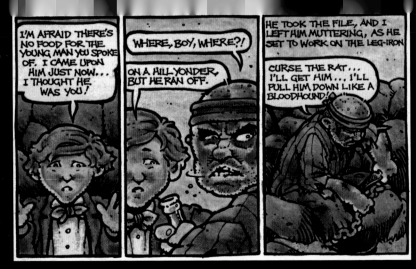

CLASSICS ILLUSTRATED was re-launched in 1990 in graphic novel/book form by the Berkley Publishing Group and First Publishing, Inc. featuring all-new adaptations by such top graphic novelists as Rick Geary, Bill Sienkiewicz, Kyle Baker, Gahan Wilson, and others. "First had the right idea, they just came out about 15 years too soon. Now bookstores are ready for graphic novels such as these," Jim explains. Many of these excellent adaptations have been acquired by Papercutz and will make up the new series of CLASSICS ILLUSTRATED titles.

The first volume of the new CLASSICS ILLUSTRATED series presents graphic novelist Rick Geary's adaptation of "Great Expectations" by Charles Dickens. The bittersweet tale of one boy's adolescence, and of the choices he makes to shape his destiny. Into an engrossing mystery, Dickens weaves a heartfelt inquiry into morals and virtues-as the orphan Pip, the convict Magwitch, the beautiful Estella, the bitter Miss Havisham, the goodhearted Biddy, the kind Joe and other memorable characters entwine in a battle of human nature. Rick Geary's delightful illustrations capture the newfound awe and frustrations of young Pip as he comes of age, and begins to understand the opportunities that life presents.

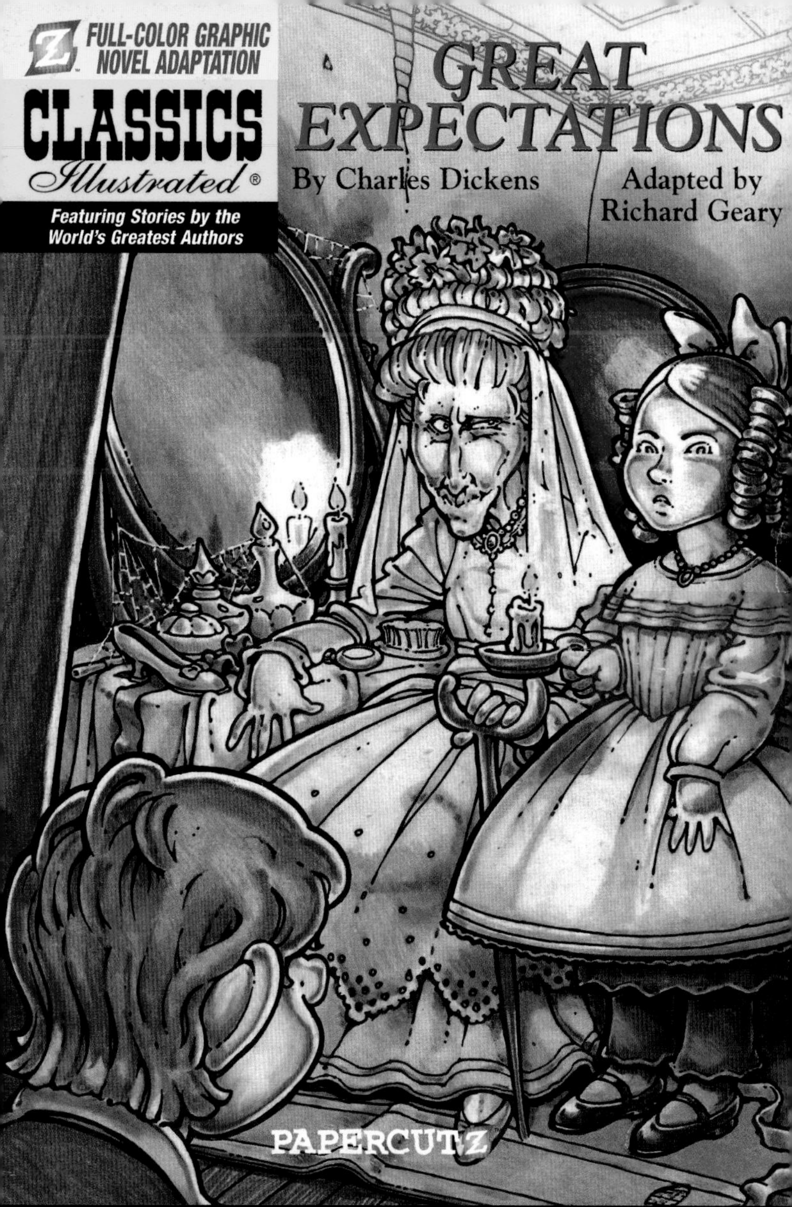
FULL-COLOR GRAPHIC NOVEL ADAPTATION
CLASSICS Illustrated®
Featuring Stories by the World's Greatest Authors
GREAT EXPECTATIONS
By Charles Dickens
Adapted by Richard Geary
PAPERCUTZ

Here is a page of CLASSICS ILLUSTRATED #1 "Great Expectations" by Charles Dickens, as adapted by Rick Geary.

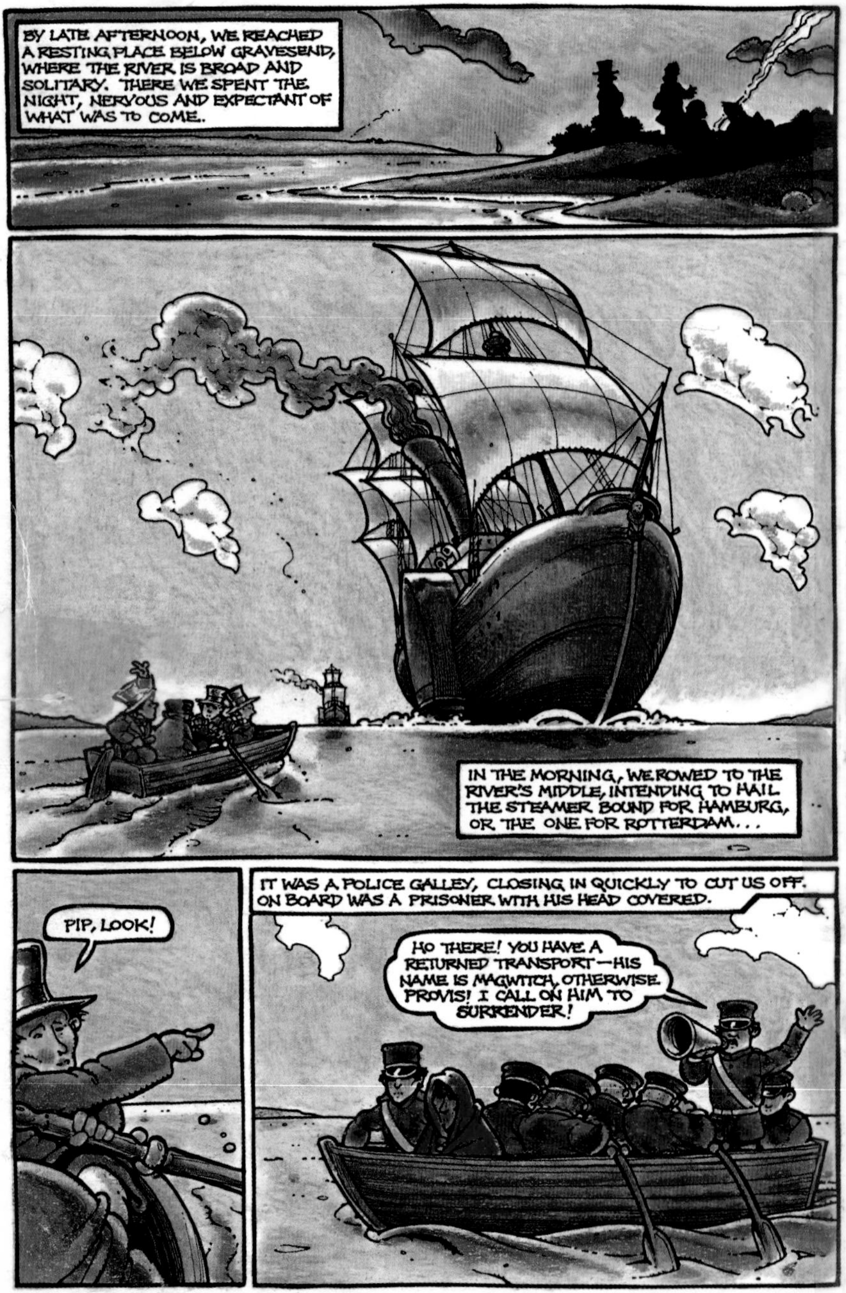
BY LATE AFTERNOON, WE REACHED A RESTING PLACE BELOW GRAVESEND, WHERE THE RIVER IS BROAD AND SOLITARY. THERE WE SPENT THE NIGHT, NERVOUS AND EXPECTANT OF WHAT WAS TO COME.
IN THE MORNING, WE ROWED TO THE RIVER'S MIDDLE, INTENDING TO HAIL THE STEAMER BOUND FOR HAMBURG, OR THE ONE FOR ROTTERDAM...
PIP, LOOK!
IT WAS A POLICE GALLEY, CLOSING IN QUICKLY TO CUT US OFF. ON BOARD WAS A PRISONER WITH HIS HEAD COVERED.
HO THERE! YOU HAVE A RETURNED TRANSPORT—HIS NAME IS MAGWITCH, OTHERWISE PROVIS! I CALL ON HIM TO SURRENDER!